Praise for *The Death of a Dancing Fool*...

"Berry's portrayal of New York City nightlife—with plenty of sex, drugs and rock & roll—and an exciting final twist make for a fast paced read."
—*Time Out New York*

"Carole Berry's tight plot and witty style make *The Death of a Dancing Fool* appealing."
—*Ft. Lauderdale, FL Sun Sentinel*

"Bonnie is amusing, feisty, and fun to be around. This enjoyable, fast-moving mystery should please fans of the series and delight those meeting Bonnie for the first time."
—*I Love a Mystery*

"Lively, amusing and very clever, with Carole Berry's usual array of characters that jump off the page and run around the room . . . Lots of action, lots of fun for the reader."
—*Mystery News*

"The Manhattan settings and Bonnie's sense of humor still shine."
—*Booked & Printed*

"Bonnie cha-chas in and out of trouble and still finds time to go shopping for her wedding dress—very impressive!"
—*Murder Ink*

DEATH
OF A
DIMPLED
DARLING

MORE MYSTERIES FROM THE
BERKLEY PUBLISHING GROUP ...

CHINA BAYLES MYSTERIES: She left the big city to run an herb shop in Pecan Springs, Texas. But murder can happen anywhere... "A wonderful character!" *–Mostly Murder*

by Susan Wittig Albert

THYME OF DEATH	WITCHES' BANE
HANGMAN'S ROOT	ROSEMARY REMEMBERED
RUEFUL DEATH	

KATE JASPER MYSTERIES: Even in sunny California, there are cold-blooded killers... "This series is a treasure!"*–Carolyn G. Hart*

by Jaqueline Girdner

ADJUSTED TO DEATH	MURDER MOST MELLOW
THE LAST RESORT	FAT-FREE AND FATAL
TEA-TOTALLY DEAD	A STIFF CRITIQUE
MOST LIKELY TO DIE	A CRY FOR SELF-HELP

BONNIE INDERMILL MYSTERIES: Temp work can be murder, but solving crime is a full-time job... "One of detective fiction's most appealing protagonists!" *–Publishers Weekly*

by Carole Berry

THE DEATH OF A DIFFICULT WOMAN	GOOD NIGHT, SWEET PRINCE
THE LETTER OF THE LAW	THE DEATH OF A DANCING FOOL
THE YEAR OF THE MONKEY	DEATH OF A DIMPLED DARLING

MARGO SIMON MYSTERIES: She's a reporter for San Diego's public radio station. But her penchant for crime solving means she has to dig up the most private of secrets... "Well-researched and highly readable." *–The Purloined Letter*

by Janice Steinberg

DEATH OF A POSTMODERNIST	DEATH CROSSES THE BORDER
DEATH-FIRES DANCE	THE DEAD MAN AND THE SEA

EMMA RHODES MYSTERIES: She's a "Private Resolver", a person the rich and famous can turn to when a problem needs to be solved quickly and quietly. All it takes is $20,000 and two weeks for Emma to prove her worth... "Fast...clever ...charming."*–Publishers Weekly*

by Cynthia Smith

NOBLESSE OBLIGE	IMPOLITE SOCIETY

DEATH
OF A
DIMPLED
DARLING

CAROLE BERRY

BERKLEY PRIME CRIME, NEW YORK

DEATH OF A DIMPLED DARLING

A Berkley Prime Crime Book/published by arrangement with
the author

PRINTING HISTORY
Berkley Prime Crime edition/November 1997

The Putnam Berkley World Wide Web site address is
http://www.berkley.com

ISBN: 0-425-16097-1

Berkley Prime Crime Books are published
by The Berkley Publishing Group,
a member of Penguin Putnam Inc.
200 Madison Avenue, New York, NY 10016.
The name BERKLEY PRIME CRIME and the BERKLEY PRIME
CRIME design are trademarks belonging to
Berkley Publishing Corporation.

PRINTED IN THE UNITED STATES OF AMERICA

10 9 8 7 6 5 4 3 2 1

For Elizabeth Wehner and Peter Hurley:
Congratulations and thanks for the rehearsal dinner.

IN THE FEW MINUTES THAT I WAS IN THE kitchen starting the coffee, the women developed a blood lust.

Those who have not gone through childbirth gasp and shiver, yet hang on every word, titillated, while those who have given birth seem determined to bring the thrills and chills of the delivery room right into my apartment. Every grisly detail brings a clamoring for another. Contractions, spinals, forceps. They can't seem to get enough of them.

My best friend, Amanda LaMarca, is on the sofa, fondling a crib-size quilt appliquéd with pink, blue, and yellow balloons and listening, spellbound, to a description of an episiotomy.

Episiotomy. Having just learned what the word means, I can hardly hear it spoken without curling up into a fetal position. You'd think that Amanda, who is generally even more squeamish than I am, would be in a dead faint by now, but she's taken to this pregnancy business with a zest that amazes me.

When she walked in a couple of hours ago Amanda surely had some notion that she was in for a high-cholesterol lunch followed by a few hours of carrying on over bibs and one-zies and tales of broken water. Still, she put on a terrific act when we all shouted "Surprise!" clasping her hands to her cheeks and squealing, "Oh, no! Are you responsible for this, Bonnie? You shouldn't have!" as if a baby shower, and especially one arranged by me, was the last thing on earth she ever expected.

Forewarned or not, it didn't take Amanda long to get into the giddy spirit of the occasion, tuck away a hearty lunch—Amanda is eating for two now, you know—and get to the presents. Little Emily—yes, it's a girl—will come into the world without a stitch on but she won't remain in that condition long. She'll start life with a set of wheels, too, in the form of a top-of-the-line stroller that converts to a carrier and a car seat and, for all I know, may metamorphose into a three-wheeler when the kid's old enough for one.

By now the gift opening is almost done. Ribbons and bows are all over the place, to the delight of my cat, Moses. He likes parties anyway, and today's activities, which began with me preparing shrimp salad, must approach his idea of a day in cat heaven. As I watch, he plucks at a yellow bow with his paw, then bats it away and chases it into a heap of discarded wrapping paper. It's not my imagination that once done with this maneuver, he glances around the room to be sure it's been appreciated. A comic, Moses loves the attention his antics receive.

I'm sitting cross-legged on the living room floor but I won't be able to stay here much longer. Apart from the fact that a good hostess doesn't remain still for long, my knees are starting to hurt. I turned forty earlier this year and came through it just fine, but now and then a twinge reminds me that my career as a chorus-line dancer, such as it was, is over.

My name is Bonnie Indermill. I'm five-four, with reddish-blond hair and a body that's good as long as I do my crunches and watch the bonbons. I live in a rent-stabilized apartment that comes with a view of the Hudson River, an occasional roach, and plenty of street life, some of which I actually enjoy.

The apartment's in Washington Heights, one of Manhattan's seedier neighborhoods, but I doubt if it was my neighborhood that kept the various Dunn women I invited from showing up today. If that was the case, they could have had a limo drop them at my door and wait, however long it took, to whisk them back to their more fashionable part of town. No. I suspect that I might have been the deterrent. They mailed their presents, and their regrets.

That's okay. I'm having a hard enough time dealing with this afternoon's festivities without having to deal with the Dunns. I'm the hostess, sure, but it's not the carrot cake waiting on the kitchen counter, or the coffee dripping into the urn, that's distracting me. My thoughts keep traveling back to the last shower I attended.

It was for Courtney Dunn, a bride-to-be, and so breech deliveries and umbilical cords didn't enter into the conversation. But a blood lust? Yes, there was that. It was less obvious than what's going on here, but also less innocent. Not long after Courtney's shower, things turned very lethal.

Amanda was at that bridal shower too, but she doesn't appear to be reliving it the way that I am. That's not surprising. Her pregnancy kept her at a distance. Amanda never had to wipe a dead woman's blood from her hands.

I remember the day it began for me.

The Herald
New York City (May 9, 1996)

Last night in the South Bronx, fire destroyed the top floor of a partly renovated apartment building. A firefighter suffering from smoke inhalation was taken to Lincoln Hospital, and was released a short time later. The fire is believed to have been set accidentally by squatters who have been illegally occupying the building, which is part of a renovation project funded by the City of New York. A spokesman for the city said that Dunn Construction Company, a contractor on the project, was supposed to have installed firewalls on the affected floor. When questioned by a reporter, Herbert Dunn, company president, said that firewalls had been ordered but that a shipping problem had delayed their installation. "Dunn Construction has an excellent record of quality control,'' Dunn said. ''If you're looking to put the blame somewhere, try the security service hired by the city. It's their responsibility to keep transients off the property.''

When I'd finished reading the article, I pointed it out to Amanda, who was sitting next to me on the Madison Avenue bus. ''That's the guy you're 'lookin' to' impress.''

''I can't imagine why you're showing me this,'' she said after giving the story a cursory glance. ''My business has nothing to do with the South Bronx and squatters. My business is elegance. The Dunns are the crème de la crème.''

''Crème de la crème? These are not the Astors, Amanda. Herbert Dunn's a nouveau riche builder.''

''He may have started as a builder, but he definitely married up. When I spoke with his wife, she was so . . . cultured, so . . .'' Amanda shook her head. ''Oh, you'll see.''

Mere words clearly were inadequate to describe the experience of speaking with Kitty Dunn.

The bus continued on its poky way up Madison Avenue, Manhattan's epicenter of business elegance. When it reached Seventy-sixth Street, Amanda and I got off. It was a beautiful spring day, and our destination was only two blocks farther, one block west to Fifth Avenue, and one block north to Seventy-seventh Street. Nevertheless, Amanda put her hand up and flagged a cab.

''Why are we doing this?'' I asked, climbing into the cab after her.

''We don't want to just come trudging up the street like we took the bus or something.''

Personally I've never found yellow cabs all that impressive, but Amanda knew whereof she spoke. At the Dunns' apartment building, one of several doormen hurried to the curb and opened the cab door for us.

''Amanda LaMarca,'' Amanda told him while I paid the fare. ''The Dunns are expecting us.''

I'd never heard her sound so imperious, or, for that matter, look quite so queenly. Appearances can be so deceiving, can't they? Once we were in the elevator out of anyone else's hearing, Amanda collapsed against a wall, shut her eyes and said, "I've never been so nervous in my life. I feel like throwing up."

The bride-to-be had graduated from college the previous February, but hadn't quite decided what it was she would do when and if she entered the working world. "Maybe advertising," Courtney Dunn said one moment, but "communications," seemed likely the next. To me, her uncertainty made her seem even younger than her young age. She was trying to be emphatic, to put power behind her words and gestures, but her voice was girlish and her hands waved tentatively through the air.

Tentative or not, though, this young woman was going to be a perfect bride-magazine-type bride. Her face was heart-shaped, and her thick light brown hair fell in shining waves to her shoulders. When she smiled, dimples flickered in her cheeks. Her coloring was peaches-and-cream, and her complexion smooth as that of a month-old baby. Studying her, I wondered if she'd ever been bothered by a pimple.

The bride's mother was perfection too—a mature but well-kept version of her daughter. She didn't smile as often, but when she did, there were those dimples in her cheeks. Thanks, I'm certain, to the wonders of chemistry, Kitty Dunn's hair was a shade lighter than her daughter's, but equally shiny. Like her daughter, she was slender and flawlessly, expensively groomed. Unlike her daughter, she seemed supremely sure of herself, and spoke with an easy eloquence I associate with people born with one of those silver spoons in their mouths. Merely being in her presence made me straighten my spine and round my vowels.

The father of the bride-to-be was a handsome man: strong features, full, rather sensuous lips, a head of graying hair and a middle as flat, and perhaps as hard, as the slab of marble covering the floor of the apartment's entrance-way.

"I was down at our place in Boca earlier this month," he had said, explaining how he came to have such a deep tan in May.

Herbert Dunn was rougher around the edges than his

wife and daughter, his diction more Bronx than Fifth Avenue. He had an appraising stare that I imagined could unnerve anyone trying to get the best of him in a business deal. He was newly rich, a developer of prime New York City commercial property these days. In the not-too-distant past, he'd been a slumlord, something he wasn't ashamed of. "Started with one tenement," he'd announced only a few minutes after we'd met.

Amanda, either genuinely awed or doing her usual nice job of acting, had responded, "Ooh."

"And now I've got dozens of them," he'd added disarmingly.

If Herbert Dunn wasn't as easy to dislike as I'd anticipated, the Dunns' penthouse apartment—a vast expanse of muted colors that doubtless had come about at a vast expenditure of green—wasn't the tasteless monstrosity I'd expected, either. The beige carpeting was of a natural fiber that picked up the gold of the late afternoon sun. Over the endless taupe sofa hung a massive modern oil painting, the subject of which, I believe, was a woman with some extra anatomical appendages, and a sculpture—the lean contorted outline of a woman occupied a place of honor between the living and dining areas. Otherwise, decorations were minimal. The sweeping view of Central Park beyond the sizable terrace more than sufficed.

Two fawn-colored Siamese cats lounged on an ottoman in front of a floor-to-ceiling window. They were thin and haughty right down to their cynical gazes. Like everything else in the place, they had to be worth a bundle. Moses probably could have taken both of them with one of his paws wrapped in a cast, but where attitude was concerned these cats had it all over him.

I figured that the decor, including the designer cats, was Kitty Dunn's doing. Herbert Dunn, though nicely packaged by Giorgio Armani these days, had clearly started out in the land of plastic slipcovers and Formica-topped end tables. Like me.

My presence in the midst of all this elegant good taste was Amanda's doing. I'm an unlikely wedding planner, and had gone along only to boost her courage. "Think about how much this will help you put together your own wedding,'' she had coaxed, as if choosing a dress and a caterer was all that was keeping me from my second march down the aisle.

Yes, I was engaged then, as the diamond glittering on my left hand kept reminding me. My fiancé, Sam Finkelstein, a widower, had a house on Long Island where I'd been spending most of my time. His nineteen-year-old son, Billy, lived there too, and so, occasionally, did the ghost of Sam's dead wife.

But more about that later. It's Courtney Dunn's engagement and wedding that's at the center of this story.

The plan had been that I would be introduced as exactly what I was, Amanda's engaged friend, but then, intimidated by the Dunns and trying hard to impress them, Amanda had wimped out and introduced me as her ''secretary,'' who would ''take notes.'' This didn't make me especially happy, but for the sake of Amanda's new business I'd taken a pen from my bag and started writing on the note pad she handed me.

''Amanda LaMarca, For The Elegant Wedding,'' her ad in *New York* magazine had read. That wording had evolved after considerable debate. Trying to compete with wedding consultants who advertised themselves as Rent-a-Yenta and Saved By The Bell, Amanda's ideas had turned toward the sugary: ''From 'Will You?' to 'I do,' Amanda will see you through.'' My suggestions had been more in the line of ''From pre-nup agreement to divorce court, Amanda's your cohort.'' In the end, simplicity won out, and that simplicity had attracted Courtney Dunn and her parents.

Not that simplicity had much to do with the wedding they were asking Amanda to plan.

''It must be tasteful,'' Kitty Dunn said. ''That is the most important thing.''

''I want it to be traditional,'' her daughter added, ''and very beautiful and romantic. But you understand that, I'm sure.''

As she spoke, Courtney gazed wide-eyed at Amanda.

Both Courtney and her mother had taken one glance at Amanda's cream-colored silk suit and assumed she knew what she was doing when it came to getting someone married in style. Clothes may not make the woman, but the right ones don't hurt her, either. So what if Amanda's elegant suit was a relic from the days when a married businessman had contributed heavily to her clothing allowance? My friend looked stunning. Miffed as I was about this secretary business, I had to give her credit for that.

Like me, Amanda lacks the antecedents for high society, and she lacks the money, too. Nevertheless, unlike me, she has the instincts. Her dark hair had been pulled back into a sophisticated twist and her makeup was subdued. As for her outfit—as I've said, she's got the instincts. Otherwise, how would she have known that everyone in the room, with one unfortunate exception, would be wearing silk or linen in varying non-colors: cream, beige, taupe.

And the exception to the natural fiber, no-color scheme? Me. Nestled into that taupe sofa, I must have been an eyeful in my red polyester dress.

"It's got to be big," Herbert Dunn was saying. "Bigger than Trump's. There's a lot of important people we have to invite: business contacts, political types."

"About how many guests will you have?" asked Amanda.

"Three hundred, maybe four . . ."

Kitty interrupted her husband. "We would like to keep the guest list at around two hundred and fifty, and no more than three hundred. We don't want a crush. I've asked Justin to get his list together by this weekend."

Justin Harwood III, was Courtney's fiancé. There were to be five bridesmaids. One was the bride's older sister, Maryann, a lawyer, who would be maid of honor. Three were friends of the bride-to-be who, like Courtney, had unisex names: Stacey, Taylor, and Alex.

"And don't forget Tiffany," Herbert said. "We've got to have Tiffany."

As names go, Tiffany is poles apart from Stacey or Taylor. Apparently this Tiffany was poles apart in other ways, too. Courtney developed a slight pout when her father said the name, and Kitty frowned and gave the slightest shake of her head.

"I know we must," she said.

I added the name to the others in my notebook.

"And of course Pookey will play a large part."

I glanced toward the cats, the only likely Pookeys I'd seen in the apartment. Noticing, Kitty smiled.

"Pookey's our son."

"Purchasing director for the company," Herbert Dunn put in.

"Pookey was christened Paul Kenneth," Kitty continued, "but when I brought him home from the hospital, Maryann couldn't pronounce . . ."

The rich may be different, but some of their too-cute stories are almost identical to ones repeated in trailer parks across the country. Of course, any trailer park kid worth his K-Mart sneakers would have put a stop to this "Pookey" business damned fast.

Kitty explained that since Courtney's fiancé's widowed father was coming from out of town, Pookey and his wife would be hosting the rehearsal dinner. Not at their Long Island beach house, she added, but at their Sutton Place duplex.

I jotted "Pookey Dunn—Rehearsal Dinner," in my notebook.

As the meeting progressed I made other notes: the Dunns wanted the wedding held at a well-known church on Fifth Avenue, St. Bonaventure's. The reception following the ceremony would be held in the ballroom of the Ambassador, a once-grand old East Side hotel owned, and currently being renovated, by Herbert's company.

"So half your problems are already taken care of," Herbert said to Amanda. "We've picked the church, and you don't have to look for a place for the reception. I got you one that isn't going to cost me a penny."

"But, Daddy—" Courtney began.

"The Ambassador's ballroom will be fine," he assured his daughter. "The place is a class act. Just wait until you see that fireplace. Amazing," he added. "We got that hotel for a song."

"And when will the wedding be?" Amanda asked Courtney.

"The second Saturday in June."

This was early May. Assuming Courtney meant a year and a month from now, I jotted that down.

"Oh, then we have lots of time. . . ." Amanda began.

"No we don't," Kitty said sharply. "We mean this June. We—you—have four and a half weeks, if you take the job."

A few minutes earlier Courtney had mentioned that she'd known Justin for several years. Hadn't they had a clue that they might want to get married and have a big wedding? So why the sudden rush? My glance went, almost unconsciously, to the prospective bride's middle. Not a bulge showed under her linen slacks. Nevertheless, I figured she was pregnant. I glanced at Amanda to see if her thoughts were running along the same path as mine. Often they don't. She has a gullibility—maybe it's an innocence—that I lack.

Amanda had gone so pale that Kitty Dunn might have stuck a siphon into her carotid artery. "But you have to reserve St. Bonaventure's at least a year in advance."

"We've got the church."

The way Herbert said that left no room for doubt.

"Are you still interested?" Kitty asked.

"Of course," said Amanda quickly. "It's just that everything will have to be . . . accelerated."

I know Amanda well, and from the way her words tumbled out and the way her hands were clenched, I knew that she was fighting off an anxiety attack.

"So accelerate," Herbert said impatiently. Raising his right hand, he rubbed his thumb and forefinger together. "You'd be surprised what you can do with money. It's a great expediter. Just don't do anything foolish with mine. How much is this going to cost me, anyway?" he asked. "I mean for your services. And your secretary's."

He didn't even look at me when he said that. Perhaps my red dress was too jarring a sight in this neutral wonderland. Or maybe it was my hair. I can do any number of things with my hair, but none of them are terribly sophisticated.

Amanda bit into her lower lip. She does that when she's

distressed. Since deciding to start this business, she had debated endlessly over what to charge. The figure she'd finally come up with had sounded adequate to me at the time, in view of her almost total lack of experience. However, in view of the show the Dunns expected to put on in less than five weeks, the amount now struck me as ludicrously small. Amanda opened her mouth. I could see the trivial figure forming on her lips.

"Seventy dollars an hour and all travel expenses," I blurted, my voice ringing out like a clarion.

Amanda looked sick. Herbert Dunn shifted in his chair so that he faced me, and his eyes, shrewd to begin with, narrowed. To that point I'd been the almost-silent secretary, the poorly dressed, badly coiffed handmaiden who knew her place. Suddenly I was outspoken, maybe even as loud as my dress.

They were all staring at me. Amanda looked as surprised as the Dunns. Shrugging, I said, "I handle the finances."

Herbert Dunn appraised me with new interest. "I may have money, but I don't throw it around. That seems a bit steep."

"Under normal circumstances, possibly, but considering the accelerated timetable, it's reasonable," I said firmly.

He glanced at the gold watch gleaming on his wrist, and then at Amanda. "Fine. As far as I'm concerned, you can be Courtney's temporary mom for this affair." Standing, he said to his wife, "I have an appointment, so the planning's up to you ladies. I'll eat dinner out."

Kitty's eyes followed him as he walked from the room.

"Mom and I have studied dresses in magazines. . . ."

Courtney started describing what she wanted in a wedding gown. She used the word "simple" several times, but at the same time kept embellishing things with words that didn't sound simple at all, like "hand-beaded" and "re-embroidered lace."

As Courtney described to Amanda a cathedral train she had admired, I glanced at her mother. Kitty Dunn's attention had wandered away from the upcoming wedding. It was only after the apartment's front door had opened and closed that she refocused on the silk-faced satin that her daughter was now talking about.

"There's no point in going on too much about the gown," she said to Courtney. "You'll know the perfect one when you see it. Just remember that you're going to have to choose one that's in stock. There's no time to be silly about a dress."

That made sense to me, as not much else in this silly affair did. Don't misunderstand. I'm all for weddings, at least in theory, and if someone wants an elaborate one and can afford it, why not? Given the right circumstances, I might be able to get into billowing silk-faced satin myself. To me, though, the circumstances surrounding Courtney's wedding weren't right. Sure, the money for a traditional, elaborate wedding was there, but for a bride who might well be pregnant, a good old shotgun wedding in front of a justice of the peace seemed more appropriate.

The bridal party planned to shop for their outfits at a Madison Avenue bridal boutique the very name of which intimidated me. I'd walked by Zoe's Bridal Salon many times. It was so refined, so utterly restrained, that merchandise wasn't shown in its windows. Instead, the windows displayed open drawing pads in which fragments of gowns and renderings of details had been sketched. I would no more have considered shopping for a wedding dress at Zoe's than I would have considered popping into Chanel for a new suit. It was the kind of place I could imagine might actually refuse my bourgeois business.

Amanda and I have different talents. Dickering over money had sent her into panic, but she took to this stuff about dresses like a duck to water. I don't know how Amanda knew the workings of that bridal shop, but she knew them, and even called the owner by her first name—Zoe.

While she, Kitty, and Courtney exchanged a silly piece of gossip about a fitting-room glitch, I stared at the view over Central Park. Treetops had filled with the pale green leaves of late spring. The lowering sun glinted off the windows of the Plaza Hotel to the south, and by turning slightly north I could see the ornate domed roof of the Museum of

Natural History on the other side of the park.

I leaned back into the sofa's inviting cushions and, for those few moments, lost track of much of the conversation and forgot my note-taking altogether. I enjoyed experiencing the way the Dunns lived, sitting on their sofa, drinking in their view, exchanging glares with their snotty cats. There was no pretending on my part. I did not imagine myself, even briefly, as a pampered Manhattan society woman. For me, sitting in the Dunns' penthouse apartment on Manhattan's Upper East Side was in some ways as strange and exotic an experience as sitting in a yurt on a mountainside in Mongolia would have been.

I was listening, but not giving it my all, when Kitty said, "Courtney? Would you and Bonnie get us some coffee and maybe a couple of those cookies from . . . ?"

Forcing my gaze away from the treetops, I rose.

Amanda was bending over the coffee table toward Kitty, talking about engraved invitations.

"Ecru, of course," she was saying. "Forty-pound bond with a vellum finish and beveled . . ."

From moral support to coffee server is a steep drop, but Amanda didn't notice the pained look I gave her as I followed Courtney from the living room.

In my experience there are few things in the civilized world less pleasing than a Manhattan kitchen. Ancient, cramped, rusty, roachy. It's not the availability of great restaurants that brings Manhattanites out at night in search of dinner. It's their disgusting kitchens. Face it: when the choice is another blip on the credit card or another night in the roach hole, a lot of otherwise reasonable people will flash the plastic yet again.

The Dunns' kitchen, however, wasn't one of the horrors that chases good women and manly men out into the streets. My mother—even my sister-in-law, New Jersey's answer to Martha Stewart—would have been proud to call this tile-and-chrome wonderland her own.

Courtney poured fresh coffee beans into a grinder and flipped a switch. The machine hummed, filling the spacious room with the wonderful aroma of high-quality coffee.

"Weeknights the cook doesn't get here until five-thirty, and the maid's off today," she said.

Pity.

Nodding toward a pitcher, Courtney asked hesitantly, "Do you think you could fill that with water?"

She seemed actually to think that I might say no.

I filled the pitcher and then relaxed against the counter. Courtney had put some cookies from a bakery carton on a plate. Taking one, she passed the plate to me.

"The peanut butter chips are my favorites."

I shook my head. "I'm trying to lose weight."

"Oh. I probably should, but all this is making me so nervous. Justin doesn't eat sweets at all. Or fats either, for that matter," she added. "He's in great shape. He runs five miles on the treadmill every morning before he goes to work, and lifts free weights three times a week."

"Em," was my reaction to that.

"I've been going to Justin's personal trainer for a couple of months," Courtney said. "He's helping me work on my upper-body strength. I've been taking tennis lessons forever but"—she shrugged helplessly—"Justin still beats me most of the time."

This Justin was sounding like as much fun as a bad day at the office. "What does Justin do for a living?" I asked.

"He's an investment banker."

Even more fun. I've never been sure what it is that investment bankers fill their work days with, but I nodded as if my social circle included dozens of them.

"Where did you two meet?"

Courtney blinked at me, then switched her gaze to the coffee carafe which was filling up.

"We met at a club dance."

"A disco?"

"Oh, no. Our country club. In Westchester. You're engaged, too," she added with a glance at my ring.

"Yes."

"When . . . ?"

"We haven't set a date."

A brief but uncomfortable silence followed. I was relieved when Courtney announced that the coffee was fin-

ished and that we could proceed with our waitressing
duties.

"We can pour out there." She took a crystal bowl of
sugar from the counter. "Oh," she said, "I'm so hopeless
in the kitchen. I forgot the cream. Could you get some from
the refrigerator? There's a creamer on the shelf. . . ."

Looking into the cabinet Courtney nodded at on her way
out, I found myself with a couple of choices. Did I want
the cream served in almost translucent Rosenthal porcelain,
or a more robust and colorful Villeroy & Boch? Choosing
strength over delicacy—I've been known to drop things—I
took the brightly patterned creamer.

A phone in a room near the kitchen began ringing, and
as I opened the refrigerator, Kitty Dunn answered it. The
room's door was partly open, and I heard her clearly.

"Hello? Oh, hello, sweetheart."

Was I about to overhear Kitty Dunn speaking to a lover?
No. She killed off that tantalizing notion with her next
words.

"Can I call you right back? I'm meeting with your sister's wedding consultant."

There was a pause, and then Kitty said, in a tone not so
genteel as it had been, "You know how your father feels
about that. What in the world do you need it for?"

"Well, I'm sorry," she said after a second pause, "but
I don't have that much on hand. I can loan you a thousand
or so, and if you can wait . . . Well, in that case you're
going to have to sell some stock. . . . Yes, I know the market's down, but . . ."

Poor "sweetheart"—either Maryann or Pookey—had to
sell in a down market.

I returned to the living room, cookie plate and creamer
in hand, just ahead of Kitty. I had hardly set the tray on
the coffee table before Amanda dictated an address to me.

"That's where we're going to order the invitations. I'll
do that this afternoon," she added as I hurriedly jotted the
address down.

"Who's going to address them?" Courtney asked
Amanda.

"Do you know a calligrapher who is available on such short notice?" Kitty asked.

Amanda shook her head. To my knowledge she didn't even know an unavailable calligrapher.

Kitty Dunn, who was impressing me as a practical woman, though not necessarily as my future friend, came to Amanda's rescue.

"That's something a secretary with decent handwriting can do."

It wasn't my imagination that, as she spoke, Kitty was regarding me with a thin smile.

Amanda—and some friend she was turning out to be— glanced my way and raised an eyebrow. "Bonnie? Do you suppose . . . ?"

This was getting out of hand. "My handwriting's awful. Illegible."

"Then we'll get one of the secretaries at the office to do it. Violet has nice handwriting."

"Who's going to ask her?" Courtney said.

Kitty looked at her daughter. "We don't *ask* Violet. We *tell* her."

"Does that mean we have to invite her?"

"No one will notice Violet at the church," said Kitty, "and at the reception there will be an inconspicuous table for office staff."

Turning back to Amanda, Kitty asked her about her contacts at *The Times*.

"It might be too short notice for the engagement, but the wedding shouldn't be a problem."

Kitty wanted her daughter's wedding not only to make *The Times*, but to be the spotlighted wedding in *The Sunday Times*.

Amanda didn't miss a beat. "Unfortunately, my society page contact at *The Times* is on maternity leave."

If that was intended to soften Kitty up, it didn't work. "Surely you know someone else."

Amanda's eyes shifted uneasily, and it occurred to me that although Herbert had okayed employing Amanda as wedding consultant, Kitty hadn't given her final blessing.

"Well, there is someone," Amanda said. "She's more a friend of Bonnie's, but . . ."

Oh my! Amanda *was* desperate for this job. A couple of months earlier I had had several run-ins with a woman—I would hardly call Elsie Scott a friend—who was fast becoming well known as a celebrity gossip columnist. Frankly, I didn't think the kind of exposés Elsie Scott dealt in were what Kitty Dunn had in mind.

When Kitty looked at me I quickly shook my head. "My contact is also on"—saying the word "maternity" with Elsie in mind was sure to bring down a curse on my head—"leave. Book leave. She's writing a book." I added that in any event my contact was at another paper, and not at *The Times*.

Kitty sighed, and the slight frown lines in her forehead deepened. "Well, then, it looks as if I'll have to take care of the papers. I know some people, mostly through Herbert's business. But I'm a very busy woman," she cautioned Amanda. "I expect you to take care of everything else. Everything, start to finish. You have complete control of this wedding."

And so Amanda LaMarca, a cop's wife from Queens, became temporary "mom" to the darling dimpled daughter of one of Manhattan's nouveau riche.

With so little time to work with, the plan started falling into place immediately. Amanda agreed to meet Courtney the next day at the Ambassador, where the reception was to take place. Her father would take care of showing them around, Courtney said.

After they looked the hotel over, Courtney and Amanda would go on to Bloomingdale's, where they'd be joined by Courtney's fiancé, Justin. There, with Amanda's help, the couple would choose gifts at the bridal registry.

"Actually," Amanda said, smiling at Courtney in a most mom-like way, "this is Wedding Spectacular Week at Bloomingdale's. There are exhibits, hors d'oeuvres, a fashion show . . ."

Courtney glanced at her mother, almost as if asking for approval. Kitty shrugged. "It doesn't sound like something I'd enjoy." She turned to Amanda and asked, "Do you think it would be worthwhile for Courtney to spend some time there?''

She looked so serious, she might have been wondering about attending a session of the UN Security Council rather than a Wedding Spectacular.

Looking equally serious, Amanda nodded. "It could be. We might get some ideas.''

"Well, better you than me,'' Kitty said.

My sentiments exactly.

A few minutes later, when Amanda and I were about to leave, Courtney's older sister arrived at the door. Without waiting for introductions, or even appearing curious, she pushed past us and into the foyer.

Kitty Dunn introduced Maryann to us, explaining, as she did, what we were doing there. From that, and from Maryann's reaction, it seemed that she was not the sweetheart who had called and asked Kitty for money earlier. In any case, referring to Maryann as "sweetheart" might have been a stretch for even her mother.

"How do you do?'' she said brusquely, then immediately walked away, making it clear that she didn't care in the least how either of us did.

Considering what Kitty and Courtney looked like, Maryann was a surprise. She was slender, but hardly sylphlike. Haggard is the better description. Her dark brown hair was lank, and her complexion, untouched by makeup, sallow. The navy blue suit she wore was a little baggy and a lot too long. I figured her for the product of recessive genes. She had nothing of her mother's beauty and polish, and had missed out on her father's rougher good looks, too.

We'd been told earlier that Maryann was a lawyer, and the leather briefcase she had left by the apartment door looked suitably lawyer-like: stuffed to the point of bursting.

On our way out, wanting to say goodbye to Courtney, I peered into the living room. Maryann was sitting on the sofa, her open briefcase beside her. As I watched, she released a small Dictaphone from a leather strap that secured it in the case, and began speaking into the device.

Courtney was nowhere in sight.

*   *   *

"That Maryann seems kind of brusque," Amanda said.

"At least she has a normal name. I think there's more going on with this wedding than meets the eye," I added.

"What do you mean?"

"For one thing, don't you think that Courtney's pregnant?"

Amanda looked at me as if I'd suggested the girl worked in a bordello.

"Of course not. She has a darling figure."

"Then why does she have to get married in such a rush? She better order the dress a little big."

"You're such a cynic."

Amanda walked to a bus shelter with me. She still had to go order the wedding invitations, so I expected her to say goodbye there. Instead, she propped herself against the shelter's wall and pressed her hand against her temple. "I hope I'm able to do it. Four weeks isn't enough time."

I rubbed my thumb and forefinger together. "As Herbert said, 'It's a great expediter.' "

A green-and-white city bus lumbered to the curb and its door swung open. As I waited for the woman in front of me to climb the steps, I turned to say goodbye. Amanda hadn't moved, but seeing me watching her, she straightened.

"Are you okay?"

She nodded. "I'm just so nervous about this job that I'm feeling sick. What if the Dunns find out I'm a complete amateur?"

"You didn't seem like an amateur to me," I said. "How do you know all that stuff, anyway? About Zoe, and forty-pound vellum and beveled edges and everything?"

Standing taller, Amanda said, "I was born knowing that kind of thing."

Amazing. She should have married a diplomat instead of a cop from Queens.

I spent that night with Sam at his house in Huntington.

Sam and I had known each other since the previous August, and by November Moses and I had sort of "moved in."

Sam was the perfect man for me. That's what Amanda, my parents, assorted other relatives, and, it seemed, everyone else in the New York/New Jersey area thought. Attractive, considerate, hard-working, financially comfortable, he was, in my mother's words, "a very good catch."

And so what was my problem, anyway? Why was I dragging my feet about setting a wedding date? My exasperated mother had suggested that I was "living in sin" to embarrass her, but that was hardly the case. As I'd told Mom, if embarrassing her had been my goal, there were more effective ways of doing it than living quietly on Long Island with a widower.

The truth was, there was no major problem in my relationship with Sam. There was simply a miasma of small, swirling difficulties that increasingly seemed to be lumping together as if they were magnetically attracted particles.

I hate to think of myself as adding up faults the way a high-school hall monitor adds up demerits, but that night as we were finishing dinner, another particle attached itself to the lump. I'd just mentioned a Broadway show that I wanted to see. It had gotten great reviews, and all sorts of awards. . . .

"*Bring in 'Da Noise*?"

Sam's jaw didn't drop, but his face lengthened enough so that it was noticeable.

"That doesn't sound like my kind of thing."

The problem here was that even when the show was Sam's kind of thing—say *Showboat*—our chances of seeing it together were nonexistent. Driving into Manhattan for pleasure? Ridiculous, he thought. And parking? Impossible. As for taking the train—forget that!

"You might try it," I said.

Surely my meatloaf didn't need as much chewing as it received then. "Why don't you go with one of your girlfriends?" Sam finally said as he pushed his chair back and began clearing the kitchen table. "That's what Eileen used to do."

There she was again. Eileen. While Sam rinsed the dishes I stared at his back. As forty-seven-year-old men go, he looked awfully good, with a headful of salt-and-pepper hair and the kind of build that comes from years of manual labor, but his looks were the furthest thing from my thoughts. I was thinking, But I'm not Eileen.

2

THERE'S NO PIECE OF KITCHEN PARA-
phernalia I love more than a dishwasher.
Those of you who have lived for years
with these wonderful inventions may not
understand my infatuation, but in my
Manhattan apartment building you stand
a better chance of finding a carrier pigeon
than a dishwasher.

The following morning the phone rang
as I was putting the breakfast dishes into
the rack, something I did meticulously, as
if I were being graded on neatness.

I grabbed the receiver. "Hello?"

"Bonnie. It's Amanda. I'm sick. I can't meet the Dunns
at the hotel this morning."

"Sick? You're not sick, Amanda. You're anxious. You
can't stay home from work just because you're anxious."

"But Bonnie, my stomach is actually churning. I'm not
going to be able to make a decent impression when I feel
this queasy. I just can't be . . . dynamic."

Unbelievable! If I had backed out of every job that made

me queasy, had called in sick every time I couldn't be dynamic, my work record would be a full-blown disaster.

At that point I didn't have the remotest suspicion that Amanda might be pregnant, and from the pep talk I proceeded to deliver you would have thought I was Dale Carnegie or somebody. It just seemed to make Amanda sicker. Come to think of it, it probably would have had the same effect on me if our situations had been reversed.

"Can't you handle the Dunns for me?" she pleaded. "Just for today? Meet them at the hotel, then go to Bloomie's bridal registry with Courtney? You seemed to hit it off all right with her."

"Right. And I hit it off all right with her mother, too, when I refused to address the invitations. What am I supposed to tell them you're doing while your secretary handles the wedding plans?"

"Tell them I had another appointment. In Connecticut. There are lots of society weddings in Connecticut. Please, Bonnie?"

This was followed by a pathetic combination whimper-groan that all but quavered through the phone line. Sliding the last dish into the rack, I surveyed my handiwork and then shut the dishwasher door, twisted the knob, and was rewarded with that wonderful humming sound.

It was a little before nine o'clock, and Sam and Billy were long gone. I had planned to spend the morning working on the books for Finkelstein Boys Moving Company, Sam's business. Bookkeeping, like loading dishwashers, is one of my areas of expertise. During the afternoon, I would work at whatever sort of housewifery I could rouse myself to tackle.

"We'll compromise," I finally said. "I'll meet them at the hotel while you pull yourself together. Then you meet us at the bridal registry. I have no intention of helping this kid choose dishes."

Amanda promised she'd be there. Two o'clock on the dot. "And Bonnie," she said. "You be sure to take complete notes at the hotel. Bring a camera, too, and take lots of pictures. Try to capture the atmosphere on the street outside, and in the lobby. And I want to know exactly what that ballroom looks like. And the dimensions. You better bring a measuring tape. And, Bonnie?''

"Yes?''

"Maybe you could wear something . . . subdued? Your red dress is nice, but if you have something quieter, and maybe in a natural fabric . . .''

Amanda certainly didn't have any problem being dynamic now that I'd agreed to do half her work!

I promised to do everything she wanted, and nothing to embarrass her. After we hung up, I went upstairs to do something about my hair and to scout my part of the closet for something in beige or taupe.

The old Ambassador Hotel, soon to be the new Dunn Ambassador Hotel, had been on a downhill slide for decades. As I understand it, years of neglect by a number of owners had brought about a state of near-dilapidation. It was a smallish hotel, with only ten floors, built around the turn of the century. I knew, from something I'd read, that its elevator had been among Manhattan's first, and that its rooms once had been considered among the most elegant in the city.

The Ambassador had initially been a luxury resting spot for the aristocratic traveler. Ultimately the aristocrats had given way to rich business travelers and Hollywood types. By the late sixties and early seventies, the only rich and famous types staying at the Ambassador were rock stars. After a few years, and more than a few trashed rooms, the rock stars had moved on, and for a decade or so the hotel had survived by putting up tourists who were trying to do New York City on eighty dollars a day. Ultimately they too had found the Ambassador's charms too shabby.

However, the East Side location, not far off Fifth Avenue, was one of the best in town. Though the "song" Herbert Dunn had paid for the hotel was far from the full-blown aria he would have paid for a better-kept property in the same area, it had amounted to considerably more than a quick little jingle. Its zip was 10021. The monarch of Manhattan zip codes.

I was directly across the street from the old hotel when

I first raised my camera, focused, and snapped a picture. I caught yellow cabs rolling past, and two well-dressed older women walking along the sidewalk beneath the scaffolding that spanned the front of the building. A young boy in a private school jacket and tie approached from the other direction. Was this what Amanda had meant by atmosphere on the street? Probably, though her idea of atmosphere wouldn't have included the construction workers going in and out of the hotel.

The Ambassador's design was unusual. I don't possess the knowledge, or the language, of architecture, but with its tiny window panes and dark bricks and stonework, cut through by an occasional band of stucco, the building had a Tudor look to it. There was a Moorish touch, too, in the minaretlike tower at the building's top. Whatever the design, the building's spirit was decidedly brooding. It made me think of old black-and-white Dracula movies. The tower cast a creepy shadow on the bland white brick building immediately behind me. Even on this almost cloudless day it was possible to imagine that tower silhouetted in the night, and not too much of a stretch to picture cracks of lightning slashing the dark sky behind it.

Mounted above the scaffolding that crisscrossed the bottom floors of the hotel was a sign that was becoming more and more familiar in Manhattan—"Another Dunn Property." Several floors above this, huge nets had been extended, winglike, on long poles jutting from the windows. These nets no doubt were there to stop falling debris from the top floors from hitting the street below. Noticing them, though, something tweaked at the edge of my memory. Years before hadn't there been a murder here? Yes. An actor had been pushed from a window, but when I searched my memory for his name, all that came back to me was a black-and-white photo of the shrouded shape on the sidewalk. There had been an incident after that one, too. This I remembered. A rock star who had been staying at the hotel for several days had killed himself in his room.

The spring day was warm but with the tower's shadow falling over me, I was chilled. On top of that, I suddenly got the odd feeling that someone was watching me. The impression was so strong that I glanced up and down the street, and behind me, too.

Though the sidewalks weren't crowded, they were far from deserted. A corner coffee shop seemed to be doing a good business. Yellow cabs and cars moved slowly down the one-way street in front of me, and behind was nothing more than that bland building. Its bottom floor appeared to be filled with dentists' offices, and through a set of partly opened blinds I glimpsed one of those white-jacketed sadists, instrument of torture in hand, approaching his victim. Reacting on its own, one of my teeth gave a sympathetic twinge.

A glance at my watch showed me that Courtney would be arriving at any minute. In any event, Herbert Dunn was probably already inside surveying this new addition to his kingdom. Focusing my camera once again, I took a quick shot of the hotel's façade and then, at a break in traffic, crossed the street.

Keeping Amanda's instructions in mind, I stayed in the light of day long enough to snap a few shots of the hotel's street-level entrance. From the far side of the street the scaffolding had blocked my view of the entrance. Up close, it was hard to miss the grotesque gargoyle over the double doors. Its head looked like that of a starving rat, and its body a hunch-shouldered buzzard. In its day the gargoyle may have been someone's idea of something magnificent, but its day had passed. I found it creepy.

Both sets of doors at the building's entrance had been propped open. From inside, above the scream of an electric drill, a man shouted instructions. The floor had been covered with sheets of plywood which bounced as I made my way over them.

"We're closed," a worker in a hardhat called when he spotted me.

I decided to wait outside for the others, and was heading back toward the entrance when Courtney, again a study in non-colors, arrived.

"Hi, Bonnie. Have you seen my dad yet?" She glanced around the lobby and frowned. "This place is a mess. And where's Amanda?"

"I haven't seen your dad. Amanda . . ."

It wasn't my imagination that when I explained about Amanda's other appointment—that society wedding in Connecticut—the dimpled darling's upper lip curled into a pout.

"I'll take lots of notes and pictures," I assured her. "And Amanda will meet us at Bloomingdale's."

"Are you sure?"

I'd coerced my hair into something approaching a neat, businesswoman's "do." My navy blue suit was—dare I say the word?—rayon, but in the right light it looked enough like silk to pass. Nevertheless, for Courtney I'd been identified as a secretary, and a secretary I would stay.

"Amanda is very reliable," I said.

"I hope so! I'm counting on her."

There may have been a lull in street traffic, for an instant later we both turned at the sound of heels clattering across the plywood planks. Or maybe there was no lull. The heels which made such a racket were about as high as any I've ever seen. So, for that matter, was the hemline of the knit dress at the other end of the new arrival's legs.

They—the legs—weren't awful, but they weren't worth the effort that had gone into displaying them. Bitchy of me to say this, but this young woman's figure was one of those things that would have been better left to the imagination. Her hot-pink dress—and pink doesn't come any hotter—hugged curves that barely escaped being bulges, and her black stockings looked stretched to their limit at her thighs. As for the rest of her, think "too much" and you've got the idea. Too much suntan; too much makeup, especially around the eyes; too much hair, too curly, bleached too blond. In the newcomer's presence I suddenly felt like an arbiter of good taste.

"Your dad can't make it," she said to Courtney. "He sent me to show you around."

Scowling, Courtney looked at me as if to ask, What now?

I realized she wasn't going to introduce me to the other woman, so I introduced myself.

"I'm Tiffany McKinney," the blonde responded. "Courtney's cousin. I work for Dunn Construction."

"You don't have to bother staying with us, Tiffany," said the bride-to-be. "Just show us where the ballroom is. We'll look around ourselves."

Courtney's voice seemed to have risen to an almost desperate level.

"Oh, it's no bother," Tiffany said. "I want to see how a wedding consultant works. One of these days I'm going to get married. All I've got to do is find a decent man. Most of the ones I meet are totally tacky."

I could just imagine!

"Bonnie's not really a bridal consultant," Courtney said.

Poor Courtney wasn't having much of a day, was she? No Amanda, no Daddy. And such shabby stand-ins.

A couple of the workers knew Tiffany. One called out, "Yo, Tiffany. Lookin' good. Where'd you get that tan?"

"Spent a few days in Florida."

Another workman whistled. Tiffany waved in response, and the tiny gold jewels embedded in her crimson nail polish flickered. She was a veritable walking compendium of fashion magazine don'ts.

"Hey, Neil," she yelled to a man at the far end of the room. "Glad to see you finally got out of the South Bronx."

"Yeah. About time. Any word when that oak flooring is coming in? We're going to be ready for it—"

Though he was dressed like the other workers, this man spoke like someone in charge.

"Be right back," Tiffany said to her cousin and me. "I gotta talk to the assistant foreman about some inventory. His name's Neil Howard. He's a serious babe, isn't he?"

This question was aimed at both of us, but if Courtney had an opinion about Neil Howard, she kept it to herself. As for me, without my glasses he was just one more male animal in a hardhat. For the heck of it, I dug my glasses from my tote and slipped them on. Yup! Neil Howard was tall, broad-shouldered, and very seriously a babe, and one with a flair for fashion. His tan workboots had red laces with tassels at their ends.

"The ballroom's up there," Tiffany added, nodding toward a flight of half-a-dozen steps at the west side of the lobby. "But wait for me. I wouldn't want you to bump into anything dangerous."

"You can't let her go to the bridal registry with us, Bonnie," Courtney said the second her cousin was out of earshot. "She is just too . . . awful. I'll die of embarrassment."

I didn't say, Oh, come now!, but might have if Amanda's career hadn't depended on Courtney Dunn.

I turned my attention to the stairs Tiffany had pointed out. They were pink marble, shaped in a gentle half-moon. At their top, beyond a marble landing about five feet wide, stood a pair of wide wooden doors. An ornate pattern was carved into these doors, but decades of varnish had left it almost invisible.

Waiting for Tiffany, I paused at the bottom of the stairs and took a picture. In spite of my ambivalence about weddings in general, I began slipping a little into the spirit of things. The old Ambassador Hotel may have been a bit on the somber side, but like many aging dowagers, it had "good bones." Once the flooring was down, and perhaps some area rugs—pastel Orientals would be perfect—and the wallpaper replaced, and the light fixtures refurbished . . .

"You ready to take a look at this room?"

As Tiffany passed us, an elevator at the far side of the lobby clanked its way down to the lobby floor. The door opened noisily, but then slammed shut before its passengers could get out. Within seconds, they were shouting and pounding on the inside of the door.

"Is that thing safe?" I asked.

"They're working on it," Tiffany responded.

She waved her hand gracelessly, indicating that we should follow her. At the top of the curving stairs she threw open the two wood doors.

"All this carved wood is going to be stripped and refinished."

"In time for the wedding?" I asked.

Courtney, who had joined me on the landing, said, "Oh, Daddy will make sure of that. Everything will be perfect."

Her voice was filled with confidence, but once she walked into the ballroom itself and took a good look at it, that confidence seemed to fade. "Eeeew," she whined. "It's so . . . gloomy."

Gloomy. I couldn't have said it better myself.

The ballroom, a big octagon, was actually in decent shape. Its oak flooring looked as if all it needed was cleaning, and the light fixtures and the big chandelier appeared to be in good condition. Unfortunately, it wasn't a particularly pretty room. Even in its tender youth, it hadn't been. The dark mahogany paneling gave it such a men's-club quality that I could envision it decorated with maroon leather chairs, oil paintings of hounds chasing terrified hares, and mounted mooseheads. The fireplace—I had pictured something elegant, or at least cozy—was made of that same dark stone that was everywhere else, and looked like the kind of thing Henry VIII might have roasted wild boars in. The mantel was a huge slab of carved marble which may once have looked terrific, in a sort of massive way, but now was cracked and discolored. The windows were small, and even when cleaned would allow little light to penetrate the gloom. Over all this—literally—was a pinkish-yellow stucco ceiling crisscrossed by dark wood beams.

Courtney was looking at me with alarm. "Will Amanda be able to make it beautiful and romantic?"

Given enough money, Amanda might be able to make a coal mine look presentable, but I didn't want to raise Courtney's hopes too high. There was her father's cheap streak to consider. I took my measuring tape from my bag and walked slowly to the fireplace. As I measured the mantel—the monster was ten feet long—I shook my head. "It won't be easy."

Tiffany, who was trying to open one of the windows at the front of the room, called out, "That old mantel's being replaced. Anyway, once everything's cleaned up it will look all right."

"I don't want just 'all right,' " her cousin responded. "I want beautiful. I wanted the Central Park boathouse."

"So what's the big deal? Nobody's going to be paying much attention to the room. All you got to do is bring in a lot of flowers, Courtney. Purple and white orchids would look real nice. And maybe we can have lavender bridesmaids dresses. This girlfriend of mine, her bridesmaids wore lavender gowns with iridescent sequins. They looked gorgeous!''

Courtney didn't think much of those suggestions. ''Iridescent lavender? That's the most hideous thing I've ever heard of. And purple orchids sound revolting! The flowers will be pale blue hyacinth blossoms and darker blue pansies.''

''What about our dresses? Blue sounds boring.''

''I'm hoping we can find bridesmaids dresses in an off-white. Except for the flowers, I want this to be an all-white wedding.''

''All white? That's weird. Is that for all us pure virgins? Like your sister and . . .'' Tiffany scratched her head, sending the jumble of curls into even more disarray. ''Who's that girlfriend of yours with her nose up in the air? Stacey? She's a virgin for sure.''

Her peachy complexion reddening, Courtney took a few steps toward her cousin. Well-bred or not, she wasn't going to put up with that. She was several inches taller than Tiffany, and between her tennis lessons and whatever she did with that personal trainer, probably packed a decent punch.

Tiffany, in contrast, looked as if she had never completed so much as a sit-up. Still, she had a street-fighter quality that seemed to be saying, Just try me.

''My sister and my friends are none of your business,'' Courtney said angrily.

Tiffany cupped her hands so that her nails looked like claws. ''My, aren't we sensitive.''

This was deteriorating fast. Wouldn't Amanda be thrilled if I told her that things had gotten violent, and maybe even showed her a photograph or two.

I stepped quickly between the young women.

''You were trying to open a window and get some air into this place?'' I said to Tiffany.

She still looked ready to go tooth and nail, but after a second she muttered, ''Yeah. Right,'' and went back to struggling with the device that opened the window.

''Amanda *is* a professional,'' I told Courtney. ''She'll be able to make this room everything you've ever hoped for.''

The calming effect this had on the bride-to-be amazed me. From my view of the meeting the day before, the most impressive thing about Amanda had been her suit, but that obviously had been enough for Courtney.

She took a deep breath. "You're right. I can tell Amanda knows exactly what she's doing." The angry glint left her eyes, and a second later she had borrowed my tape measure and was pacing the room.

In the meantime Tiffany had resumed her efforts to open the casement windows. They opened out, or should have, by means of a brass handle that was rotated by hand. In the case of the window Tiffany was standing near, the handle was locked into place by years of rust. A puddle of oil and some rust-colored debris on the sill below indicated that an attempt had been made to free the device.

Moving to a second window, she turned the lever. This one worked, and the window opened enough to let some much needed air into the ballroom.

"These levers were supposed to have been replaced," she said.

Taking a tiny tape recorder from her handbag, she fumbled with it for a moment and then raised it to her mouth.

"Ambassador ballroom. Check on fireplace mantel and window—"

The machine clicked. "Damn!" Tiffany said. "The tape's run out. I have to turn it over. There's something wrong with my machine and it's hard to get the tapes to eject."

She struggled with the recorder for a moment, and finally ended up balancing it on a windowsill to reverse the tape and begin recording on the other side.

"—and window levers," she said into the microphone. "All of them were supposed to be replaced, but the mantel hasn't been touched and the levers have only been oiled."

Clicking off the recorder, she slipped it back into her bag.

"Will this hotel really be finished by the wedding?" I asked, keeping my voice low so that Courtney wouldn't overhear.

"No way," Tiffany responded, "but the entrance and

lobby and this room will be fine. Herbert will make sure of that. Everything will be perfect for Daddy's little girl.''

''We'll need the kitchen, too,'' I said, ignoring her sarcasm, ''and restrooms and rooms to change in. . . .''

''Don't sweat it. Herbert will get the kitchen and restrooms down here whipped into shape, and as for changing rooms, a couple of the top floors are already just about finished. All they need is some furniture. Trust me,'' she added, perhaps responding to my dubious expression. ''When it comes to Dunn's construction projects, I know what I'm talking about.''

''What do you do at Dunn?''

''A little of everything. I started out as a data-entry clerk five years ago. Now I handle the project management software, making sure projects stay on schedule, and that supplies purchased for specific projects end up where they're supposed to go.''

''Ah. Like marble fireplace mantels.''

She arched an eyebrow. ''I'll find it. A ten-foot slab of pink marble isn't something a workman's going to carry out in a lunch box.''

3

"BONNIE! IS IT REALLY YOU?"

The sound of that voice made me want to turn and run away. I looked around, and for a heartening second didn't see her. Was it an aural hallucination?

No. It was reality, in the short, plump, obnoxious form of Elsie Scott, hurrying across the street toward me.

I glanced back at the hotel's entrance. Courtney and Tiffany were still inside, Courtney in the ballroom, Tiffany talking to the assistant foreman, Neil Howard. If I dashed back into the hotel, maybe Elsie would think I hadn't heard her and go away.

"It is you!" she screeched, pushing her hefty self between two cars parked at the curb. "I can hardly believe it! What a small world! I just love the way people in New York City seem to find each other. One minute you're alone and the next you've found a dear, dear friend."

Elsie had mounted the hotel's steps but I didn't realize she was going to fling herself at me until it happened. I

couldn't extricate myself from her bear hug fast enough.
When I'd finally put a foot or so of air between us, she
jutted her face toward me, jaw protruding. I never know
what to expect from Elsie, but for a second it looked as if
she might dare me to take a punch at her.

"Look how swollen my jaw is," she said from between
half-shut lips. "Can you tell?"

When you have a face shaped like a pie plate and you
wear your hair like Buster Brown, a swollen jaw is hardly
remarkable. I shook my head.

"Of course you can!" Elsie retorted. "That man is a
beast. An absolute beast."

"Who?" Had someone . . . beaten me to the punch?

"My oral surgeon." Elsie nodded toward the white brick
building on the other side of the street. "I'm having gum
surgery. I'm not sure I need all the work he's doing, but—"

She gave a "What's-a-poor-girl-going-to-do?" shrug,
though in my experience Elsie is anything but helpless.

"—that's how I am. Dedicated to my art. I'll happily
endure any amount of pain for a good story."

Including gum surgery? Maybe so. A wonderfully bizarre vision flickered through my head: a heavily sedated
Elsie collapsed in one of those curving dental office chairs.
A perverted, sex-crazed dentist, tapping his foot to the Mu-
zak humming in the background as he reaches for a tray of
pointy little instruments . . .

I stared at Elsie and blinked. The vision disappeared. No
dentist on this earth could be that perverted.

"You're working on a story with your oral surgeon?"

"Don't be ridiculous! I only chose him because of the
location."

Her sharp answer must have caused her a twinge of the
pain she claimed to be happily enduring. Wincing, she
pressed a chubby hand to her jaw, which made me feel
better immediately.

"I'm interested in doing a story on this hotel. Not this
new Dunn Ambassador," she added contemptuously. "I'm
not interested in some junky renovation. What I want to
write about are the celebrities who died violently in the old

Ambassador. There were a number of them. And guess what I've already discovered.''

''What?''

''Several of them happened to be staying in room eight thirteen. That's got to be significant. I was going to call my piece 'The Ghosts of 813,' but now I'm thinking that 'The Curse of the Old Ambassador' might be better. What do you think?''

For some reason Elsie, who is superconfident about her articles, turns into quivering jelly when it comes to giving them titles. Knowing that it was one of her few vulnerable areas, I exploited it like crazy.

''It sounds like an old movie. *The Revenge of the Mummy*, *The Village of the Damned*, *The Perils of Pauline*.''

''Well, you don't know the first thing about writing!'' Elsie snapped. ''Why were you taking those pictures, anyway?''

''What?''

''I saw you taking pictures of the Ambassador. Don't deny it. You better not be trying to move into my territory, Bonnie. I'm suffering for this story.'' For effect, she pressed her hand against her jaw again. ''No one else is going to get it.''

Deep in her heart Elsie Scott must entertain the notion that some day her ridiculous column—It's called *Inside Elsie*, a sickening notion when you think about it—will win her the Pulitzer prize. Okay, so Elsie can put together a few catchy sentences. She knows her celebrities, too, and when it comes to digging up dirt about them, she is tenacious. Give Elsie a whiff of smutty soil and she'll push her nose into it and root with the ferocity of a French farmer's prize pig grubbing for truffles.

She is, however, at least in my opinion, quite crazy. Not wanting to antagonize her, I shook my head.

''I'm not interested in the old Ambassador's curse, Elsie. I'm helping out with a wedding. The reception is going to be held in the hotel ballroom.''

''You have access to the Ambassador?'' she asked, managing a puffy smile. ''You know, Bonnie, I would give anything for a teensie look around inside there, before Dunn Construction completely ruins the place.''

''No, no,'' I said quickly. ''I don't have free run of the place. I just stopped by today. The bride-to-be—she's . . .''

Midsentence, I hesitated. Among Amanda's endless instructions there had not been a word about confidentiality. Understandable. Who would have thought it would be an issue? But with Elsie around, anything can become an issue.

One of Elsie's eyebrows had lifted. If I didn't tell her who the bride was, she was going to ask. And if there was a hint, a suggestion, that I was holding something back, her gossip-hunting nose would be sniffing around in an instant.

''. . . Herbert and Kitty Dunn's younger daughter is getting married. We're going to have the reception here. I'm simply looking the hotel over to see how we'll deal with food and dancing.''

Very little that Elsie does surprises me, but her reaction to this information did.

''Well,'' she said, hands going to hips, ''you won't find me publicizing that in *Inside Elsie*! Herbert Dunn is a spoiler. He has no feeling for history, no sense of what New York—''

I broke off this diatribe by raising my palm and holding it inches from Elsie's face. ''That's fine. Courtney isn't interested in publicity. She just wants to have a nice traditional wedding.''

''Courtney. That's a stupid name. She's probably spoiled rotten. I'll bet she doesn't even have a job. Right? Or if she does, it's the kind of job Daddy got for her. And she's probably got tons of designer clothes and a sports car. . . .''

Elsie never fails to bring out the worst in me, even when she's thinking along the same lines that I am. ''Right,'' I said. ''All those nasty luxuries you and I wouldn't touch.''

''Oh, don't misunderstand me, Bonnie. I enjoy the finer things in life, but I pay my own way. I don't mooch off my parents.'' She jutted her chin toward me again. ''And I'll bet you don't mooch off yours, either.''

Elsie Scott, champion of the working-class. Considering what she does for a living, this seemed hypocritical, but then, we're all complex creatures, aren't we? Nevertheless, reluctant to give her any satisfaction, I pretended to think the matter over for a second. "If my parents were wealthy, I could see mooching a sports car," I finally said.

At that moment Courtney Dunn, the object of Elsie's wrath, emerged from the shadowed entrance of the Ambassador and happened to pause where a beam of sunlight had poked its way through the scaffolding. For a moment she seemed to be standing in the midst of an almost celestial glow.

Elsie responded to this vision with, "Oh, spare me."

A second later Tiffany had joined her cousin.

"I don't have to ask which one is Courtney," said Elsie. "She's the one who looks like a princess. The other one is obviously a slut."

I had no intention of introducing either the princess or her slut cousin to Elsie, and told her that I had to be going. It was too late, though. Tiffany had started toward us, a dumbfounded expression on her face.

"Is that really . . . ?"

When she's not writing a special series, Elsie's column runs once a week, and her picture appears at the top of that column. If I looked like Elsie, I would have worn a heavy veil when that photo was taken, or maybe had the photographer do something arty with deep shadows, but Elsie is nothing if not honest. What you see in the flesh is what you get in the tabloid.

". . . Elsie Scott, the columnist?"

I had no choice but to introduce the two women. Elsie, who for understandable reasons has suffered during her life from a lack of attention, put out her hand like a star greeting her public. And Tiffany, slut or not, clearly was her natural audience.

"I just loved your Dancing Fool series. I couldn't stop reading it. When you talked about the way he died, I was, like, you know, sobbing. I couldn't stop myself. It was like, you know, profound."

"Like, you know, thanks," responded Elsie.

Courtney had joined us, and Tiffany, who didn't realize

Elsie had ridiculed her, grabbed her cousin's arm and steered her closer to Elsie.

"Courtney. This is Elsie Scott," Tiffany said, proud of her new acquaintance. "Elsie writes a fabulous column for *The Herald*."

Courtney repeated the name of the paper with a clear curl to her lip and asked, "What kind of column?"

"Celebrity gossip. Elsie knows everything. It's called *Inside Elsie*."

Hearing that, Princess Courtney dismissed Elsie's achievement with a thin smile that reminded me of her mother's.

"Oh. Well, I seldom read *The Herald*," she said, "but I'll certainly look for your column when I do."

Elsie is many disgusting things but she isn't stupid. She had just been insulted and, from the way her lips narrowed until they almost disappeared into her fleshy face, I could tell that she knew it. A tremor of anxiety played with my nerves, but I recovered almost immediately. If the wrath of Elsie Scott descended, it wouldn't land on me.

Courtney, unaware that she'd just antagonized a lunatic, said to me, "If we're going to meet Amanda at two o'clock, shouldn't we be going?"

Courtney flagged a cab while I said a hasty goodbye to Elsie and Tiffany. There was no danger of Tiffany trying to accompany us to Bloomingdale's. As we climbed into the cab, I turned and saw that she and Elsie had crossed the street and were heading into the coffee shop. Elsie led the way with a queenly step and Tiffany followed, supplicant-like. I glanced at Courtney to see if she'd noticed, but she was busy examining her engagement ring.

"Justin and I are going to pick our wedding bands this weekend. We should be able to do it without Amanda's help."

How very adult of them.

The promised hors d'oeuvres were hard to come by, but Courtney and I snatched glasses of champagne from a passing waiter.

At two-thirty the bridal spectacular was going full force.

Activities extended far beyond the small area normally assigned to the bridal registry. Romance had, in fact, taken over much of the floor. From Photographs by Philippe to Caketalk, everything was weddings.

Champagne glasses in hand, Courtney and I made our way through the diaphanous lingerie in an area that had been sectioned off with pink velvet ribbon. "For That Special Night," a small, tasteful placard read. Courtney held a white silk negligee and nightgown in front of her, and examined her reflection in a mirror. I checked the price tag and felt giddy. Courtney didn't bother looking at the tag.

"When Amanda gets here, let's be sure to show her this," she said.

In the next ribboned-off area, a woman with a high-pitched voice from a company called Flower Power snipped stems from white flowers and speared what was left of the blossoms with short wires. To me it looked like an awfully tedious job, but what do I know? A rapt audience watched her every move. Across from the Flower Power woman, a man with an English accent was talking about invitations to a smaller but no less interested audience. "London Script is one of the oldest and most formal typescripts. It is especially popular for the traditional wedding."

Taking in all of this were not only brides-to-be, their friends, and their mothers, but who-knows-how-many aunts and cousins and sundry relations. The business of getting married properly—and by properly I mean with gown, guests, and gifts—seems to bring out the herd instinct. Nothing is done alone, no decision is made without consultation. Two, three, even four companions are normal and perhaps even necessary. Marriage is, after all, an occasion that calls for a lot of emotional support, and sometimes, as in my case, even some nudging.

The mostly female crowd was of all ages, and multiethnic. I sipped my champagne and watched, fascinated, as a Chinese foursome—grandmother in traditional loose black pants and smock, mother in an unstylish brown suit, and two exquisitely modish young women—debated crystal patterns. Three African-American women escorted—perhaps "pushed" is the better word—their lone male com-

panion from one exhibit to the next, ignoring him when he
said, "Man, I've had about enough of this." America's
great melting pot may not always work so well, but it was
sure cooking at that bridal show.

What wasn't working was Amanda, and being kept waiting a half-hour did not sit well either with her young client
or with me. Our registry consultant, a matronly woman with
a friendly air but eyes definitely on her commission, had
deserted us immediately upon hearing that our party wasn't
complete. There were brides who were ready to register,
and time is money.

Courtney's disposition wasn't quite as sweet as it had
been. "Amanda should be here," she grumbled. "That's
what Daddy is paying her for."

I couldn't have agreed more. "I'm sure she's on her way.
Would you like to get a cup of coffee?"

"No! There's a phone over there." Courtney indicated
a desk at the back of the registry. "I think you should call
Amanda."

The desk was occupied by a woman with steely eyes.

"That phone may not be for the public," I said.

"Just tell her who my father is," Courtney replied impatiently. "She'll let you use it."

The woman at the desk answered my initial request—
"May I make a quick call?"—with, "Sorry, but . . ."

"I need to reach Courtney Dunn's bridal consultant to
discuss some purchases. You've heard of Herbert Dunn, the
builder? That's his daughter."

I nodded toward Courtney. When the woman glanced at
her, the dear girl smiled that same thin smile she'd given
Elsie. Yes, the dimpled sweetheart was growing peevish.

The woman graciously dialed Amanda's home number
for me.

"You've reached Amanda LaMarca, for the elegant wedding. I can't answer your call right now, but—"

"Amanda? Are you there? I hope not, because—"

"Bonnie, is that you? Oh, Bonnie. Guess what! This is
the most unbelievable thing."

"You're not here at Bloomingdale's. That's the most unbelievable thing! You wanted this ridiculous job, and—"

"I'm going to have a baby."

Amanda's message really had come through loud and clear, but nevertheless my mind swirled around her words. Had she actually said *that*? Or had I misunderstood?

"A what?"

"A baby. It's wonderful, isn't it Bonnie?"

That Amanda really intended this as a question, and not a statement, became apparent a second later when the sound of her choking sobs traveled through the receiver. "Tony's going to die. He's so glad his kids are almost through college. He's been looking forward to having some extra money, maybe being able to take a trip to Italy, and now I'm pregnant."

Pregnant. It took several seconds for me to digest that word and even then the concept of it—of Amanda pregnant—didn't fully sink in.

Why was I having such a hard time with this? Perhaps because my friends—and I'm not talking only about Amanda and Tony—have sex like crazy, but they don't have babies. At least not very often. And Amanda seemed even less likely than the others to have a baby. How could she possibly get involved in the messy business of giving birth, this woman who had been known to spend her rent money on a makeover at Elizabeth Arden? And what about the even messier business of raising a child? Sure, somebody's got to do it, but not Amanda LaMarca.

But who am I to talk? I top Butterfly McQueen—not only have I kept the birthin' part a mystery, but as for raising them, please!

While Amanda went to get a tissue, I looked out across the floor. The woman with the flowers had worked up a real head of steam. ". . . and by using stephanotis blossoms you can create your own charming dome-shaped bouquet."

Her voice was loud and distinct above the general pandemonium, but then it was drowned out by the voice of the invitation man, who was getting some giggles from his audience: "Because of their heavy three-ply weight, the invitations used by the British aristocracy are called stiffies."

"Roses are lovely, too," the flower woman trilled, "though

these Sally Holmes pink-flushed roses will only last a few hours. . . .''

Voices and subjects were tangling into a confused knot. A waiter went by with a tray of what looked like tiny crab cakes. He wasn't a dozen feet from me, but it might as well have been a mile for my chances of catching up with him.

A man had joined Courtney. He looked stiff as a . . . stiffie, and was no doubt that personal-trainer's delight, Justin. He sported a gray suit, a white shirt, a rep tie, and a plastered-down haircut that made him look like a nerd. *She'll never have to worry about any funny business with this one*, I said to myself.

I watched as Courtney pointed me out to him. Justin, after regarding me for a moment, bent to his fiancé—he was half a head taller—and said something. She said something in response. This is pure paranoia on my part, but I imagined her saying, with a trace of contempt, *Bonnie's only the secretary.*

I didn't realize that my hand holding the phone had dropped to my side until I heard Amanda shouting my name through the receiver. Raising the phone, I said to her, ''Let's talk about this later. Right now I've got your client and her fiancé staring at me.''

Amanda had pulled herself together. ''The registry is the least of our problems. You do exactly what I say and everything will be fine. The most important things in the registry are the dinnerwear patterns, because they're the most visible. After that you choose crystal and flatwear. Don't bother registering for bed and bath linens. Courtney will be getting those at her shower.''

''Did you say dinnerwear patterns *plural*?''

''Of course. Formal and informal. Courtney may already know what she wants but if she doesn't, steer her toward traditional. The same for the crystal and . . . if she's in doubt about anything and the registry consultant doesn't help, suggest that she go for the most expensive as long as it doesn't have big aqua flowers on it. Pots and pans should be chef quality.''

''I don't think she can cook. She told me she's hopeless in the kitchen.''

"It doesn't matter. You can't go wrong with quality. We'll talk tonight. Bye."

You can't go wrong with quality. Those words echoed as I replaced the receiver. I'm not a complete disaster in the kitchen, but I'm about as equipped to suggest cookware and formal china patterns for someone else as I am to mount the stage at La Scala and sing *Madame Butterfly*. And what's wrong with big aqua flowers, anyway?

I made my way back through the milling shoppers. When I reached Courtney, she glanced at the gold watch on her wrist and then at me, accusingly.

"So? Where's Amanda?"

I shrugged. "She's still in Connecticut, but I can fill in. You're Justin?"

The man at her side nodded as he looked around the floor. "I left the office for nothing?"

"I've worked with Amanda for years," I said to Courtney. "When it comes to taste, she and I are"—I touched my hand to my heart—"the same person."

Courtney looked almost frantically at her fiancé. "But Amanda promised!"

I wouldn't have been too surprised to see her eyes fill with tears. When it came to setting up her new household, Courtney might have wanted to be led, but not by a secretary.

Justin, though, was prepared to believe me. He was probably prepared to believe anything that would hurry this process along. In any event, the reappearance of our registry consultant took care of Courtney's doubts.

"Are you ready now?" the woman asked.

"I suppose so," Courtney said once she had let out a sigh. "I've got some ideas about what I want."

"Let's just get this over with," said Justin.

A waiter was suddenly blocking my field of vision. Yes, that looked like crab cake canapés on his tray. In a flash I'd grabbed two of them. I wolfed one down immediately. As an afterthought I took a third before the waiter escaped.

You know my mixed feelings about housewifery. Yet strangely enough as our foursome made its way from delicate bone china to pottery, from white linen damask table-cloths to flowered place mats, I experienced the same thing I had in the hotel earlier, and found myself becoming increasingly involved. I'm not suggesting that this was an intellectual challenge, but I've sure had worse jobs. And when that registry consultant made the faux pas of suggesting an informal dinnerware pattern with—horrors!—big aqua flowers, I scored a couple of points with Courtney by shaking my head and saying prissily, "Oh, no. Not aqua." After that, whenever she was in doubt, Courtney glanced at me and asked, "What do you think?"

Getting through the list took almost two hours, and like most of the other male captives on the floor, Justin fell apart early on. After a half-hour or so he gave up looking at his watch. For a while his complaints grew in frequency and volume but then, finally defeated, he simply followed along, offering an occasional opinion but never pressing it too vehemently.

I actually liked them as a couple. They seemed happy to be together, and in many ways complemented each other. Where Courtney wavered, Justin was more definite, but where he was too definite she offered compromises. They were affectionate, too, exchanging lots of brief hand touches and quiet smiles. Between them there seemed to be a gauzy romantic glow that Sam and I had never experienced. Was this amorphous glow a vital ingredient for a good marriage? Probably not, but it would have been nice, anyway.

By the time we had worked our way down to the most prosaic items on the list—the home stretch of juicers and toasters—I was acting, and even feeling, like an expert. When Courtney wavered over a coffee maker, I pointed a firm pinky at one so ludicrously expensive that it should have come with its own Central American coffee plantation.

"You can't go wrong with quality," I said.

"You're so right, Bonnie."

These mundane small appliances were conveniently located, from my point of view, not far from a swinging door the waiters were passing through as they carried trays of food and drinks to the shoppers. I caught Justin as he tried, unsuccessfully, to stifle a yawn.

"I know where we can get a glass of champagne and maybe a bite to eat. Are you interested?"

"God, yes."

Leaving Courtney in conversation with the registry consultant, he followed me to the swinging door. Sure enough, a few seconds later a waiter emerged, his tray loaded with pigs-in-a-blanket. I took a napkinful and passed some of them to Justin. When the door opened again a moment later, Justin managed to snag two glasses of champagne.

He'd loosened his tie and unbuttoned the collar button on his shirt, and he'd run his fingers through his hair enough to make it look a bit less bankerlike. This rumpled Justin was more appealing than the one I'd met two hours before.

I shook my head when he offered me one of the champagne glasses.

"Good. I need them both." He polished one off in a couple of swallows. "This is murder. How do you stand doing it for a living?"

I answered truthfully. "Oh, it's never bothered me at all."

"She can't keep this up much longer," he said, glancing at his fiancée. "Maybe I can talk her into going to the club for a game of tennis."

So you can beat her again. "I understand that's where you met."

Justin hesitated a moment before responding.

"That's right. We met at a club tennis match. I better get back."

Tennis match? Courtney had said a dance. Had love muddled their minds? Oh, well. What did it matter where they'd met?

Finally the last item had been approved and the last blank on the list filled in. Outside Bloomie's I said goodbye to Courtney and Justin, promised Courtney yet again that Amanda would call her that night, climbed into a cab, and said to the cabby, "Penn Station."

He drove along Central Park South. I knew the leaves

on Long Island were the same green as the leaves shading the carriage horses across the street from the Plaza Hotel, but when the cab turned south I felt a tweak of regret at leaving the city. And, of course, on the heels of that tweak of regret came a smattering of guilt. There I was, engaged to a man most reasonable women would have followed to the Yukon Territory, and I was sulking about traveling to a comfortable house in the suburbs.

4

ELSIE'S COLUMN RUNS IN A TABLOID that is one step above the slander sheets I leaf through while waiting in grocery store lines. In my Manhattan life, when I read *The Herald* at all, it is usually over someone's shoulder on the subway. I would never have subscribed to it, and only bought it when the headline was especially lurid. At Sam's house, though, *The Herald* showed up on the doorstep every morning, at just about the same time that Moses showed up on my pillow demanding breakfast.

Weekday breakfasts followed a set routine. First Moses, who is unbearable when he's hungry, got his Finicky Feast, and then, not being much of a breakfast eater, I stood at the kitchen counter sipping coffee and making sandwiches for Sam's and Billy's lunch while they ate. Sam always read *The Herald* at the table, and when he finished he always handed it to Billy with a comment about something in the sports pages.

Billy wasn't much of a reader. I don't recall ever seeing him open a book, but he did scan the sports pages. I'm not sure whether he was interested or whether he pretended to be for his father's sake. Left to his own devices, Billy probably would have read nothing but rock-and-roll magazines and the captions in *Playboy*.

A few days after my Bloomingdale's experience, Sam's comment as he handed the paper to his son was, "The Knicks sound serious about getting rid of Patrick Ewing. Too bad. He holds them together."

Billy disagreed. "Ewing's had it."

As Sam finished breakfast, Billy flipped through the sports pages and then, keeping to the routine, handed me *The Herald*. I opened it on the counter.

I would almost prefer a session on the rack to admitting to Elsie Scott that I read her column. And really, I don't read it. I scan it for familiar, interesting names. The unfortunate subjects of the tripe that she writes get their names printed in bold black ink, so that if you're only interested in Brad Pitt you don't have to waste your time reading about Sharon Stone. That morning, *Inside Elsie* began with a blow-by-blow account of a Broadway leading lady's tiff with her director, something which I cared nothing about. My eyes ran down the column, not pausing until, suddenly, they were slowed by Elsie's last paragraph.

Dear Readers: What **Fifth Avenue lovely** stole her older sister's fiancé? If all goes as planned—and having seen this young lovely I suspect that it will— she will marry her sister's ex-intended on the same June day and in the same church her sister had reserved for her own wedding. Need a hint, readers? **Daddy's a high-profile real estate biggie**. Stay tuned. There may be more as the big day approaches. The path true love follows is often rocky.

"How many real estate biggies can you name," I asked Sam as he put the sandwiches into the cooler he and Billy take to work.

"Well, there's Donald Trump, and . . ."

Through his business, Sam has enough contact with builders to be familiar with the major players. He reeled off a couple more names, then added, " . . . and of course there's your employer, Herbert Dunn. He's big."

He sure was, and he lived on Fifth Avenue and had a lovely daughter planning a June wedding, and a not-as-lovely older daughter. It seemed as if my snap judgment of Justin had been wrong. He was capable of some funny stuff indeed. He'd switched sisters.

It was crystal clear where Elsie had gotten this information. Tiffany. I'd seen the two of them—awestruck Tiffany and crafty Elsie—heading into that coffee shop. It wasn't hard to imagine Elsie steering the younger woman into a booth and plying her with a hamburger or a BLT.

But why had Tiffany disclosed such a hot family secret? Had she been trying to impress Elsie with her insider scoop? Had she been naive enough to think Elsie wouldn't print it? I had a hard time believing that Tiffany was that dumb. Her appearance may have said "dumb," but she'd seemed sharp enough to me.

Whatever the explanation, Amanda was going to kill me when she found out.

"Oh, by the way, Bonnie," Sam said. "Rosaleen left a message at the warehouse yesterday. I haven't called her back yet, but her message mentioned visiting over Memorial Day. You want to see if you can reach her this morning? Maybe we can firm up some plans."

Rosaleen. Oh, terrific. If I didn't want to worry about whether I had ruined my best friend's chance for success in her new business, I could worry about a visit from Sam's late wife's sister.

"Sure," I said, trying to sound enthusiastic.

After breakfast, when Sam and Billy had gone, I got out the Finkelstein Boys checkbook. It was hard to concentrate on bookkeeping, though, with both *Inside Elsie* and Rosaleen to worry about.

One thing at a time, and Amanda came first. After weighing whether I should do the noble thing and confess, or the sneaky thing and wait to see if she found me out, I decided to call her.

Like Billy, Amanda isn't a newspaper reader. Tony is, but his bible is the *Daily News*. The LaMarcas don't subscribe to *The Herald*, and don't generally buy it, either, so I thought I might be able to break the news gently.

Things didn't work out that way. The first time I dialed their number it was busy. When I tried a few minutes later, Amanda picked up on the second ring, and her first words on hearing my voice, were "Courtney Dunn says that you introduced her cousin Tiffany to Elsie Scott. You're supposed to be helping me, Bonnie. Instead, you're getting my only client . . . slandered! I shouldn't have to deal with this in my condition!"

The best defense is often a good offense. Ignoring Amanda's "condition," I counterattacked. "I didn't introduce them. First Elsie cornered me, and then Tiffany introduced herself." That wasn't true but it was close enough. "How did you find out about it, anyway?"

"I was still in bed this morning when Courtney called me from her gym. Her personal trainer had already read the column. He told her about it. I just can't wait to hear what her mother's going to say. I'll probably be fired by my first client!"

"So the next time you get a client, do the work for yourself instead of imposing on me!"

I slammed down the phone. A moment later it rang. As I answered, I used my robe's sleeve to wipe away the tears that had clouded my eyes.

"Bonnie? I'm sorry."

"Me too, Amanda."

Neither of us can stay mad for very long.

I was to be the bearer of explanations, olive branches, peace pipes. Whatever it took to pacify the Dunns, that was what I'd promised Amanda I'd do. If necessary, I would grovel on their wall-to-wall carpeting.

Before I got around to groveling, I was going to pick up the invitations from the engraver and, after groveling, deliver them to the lucky secretary who was going to address them.

Why was I doing these things? There were a couple of

reasons. For one, Amanda had agreed to give me a big piece of the action—half. That was a large part of it, but the other part was, I like the rhythm of going to work in the morning. I like feeling productive and, for me, that means contributing to an end product that isn't a casserole. Sure, paying the Finkelstein Boys bills was a job of sorts, but I like to produce things that earn me a paycheck. Crass? Maybe, but I'd been supporting myself so long I didn't know how else to live.

That said, I've never had a job I couldn't complain about, and this one was no exception.

The invitations were the easier part of the job I did that day. Never mind that along with this rush order for which he was being paid an exorbitant sum, the engraver gave me a stern lecture about planning ahead, or that the bus I caught outside his door went out of service a block later, just as an unexpected shower started to fall, and I had to huddle in a doorway for fifteen minutes before another bus came along.

Compared to what happened at the Dunns' apartment, all that was a piece of cake.

Kitty Dunn's face was a study in stone as she examined one of the invitations, but it didn't begin to equal her older daughter's. Maryann looked as if she were sucking on a lemon.

Kitty laid the invitation aside. "They're perfect."

"I wish everything else was." That was Courtney.

Maryann, who until then had been sitting in a silent funk, looked at her sister. "What do you have to complain about? I'm the one who's going to be the laughingstock of Manhattan."

Knowing what had happened to Maryann, I felt sorry for her. Nevertheless, it was hard to imagine this dour woman provoking so much as a giggle, much less laughter. For all I knew, Maryann was a brilliant lawyer destined for great things, but I didn't have any doubt about why Justin had taken up with her sister. Courtney may have had her grumpy moments, but Maryann seemed to be having a grumpy life.

"It's not as if I even cared about Justin by the time you two got together," she continued. "I've told you that I was going to break things off myself. He just beat me to it."

I doubted that, but how Maryann dealt with Justin's defection was her own business.

Kitty was looking at me. "I understand you are somewhat responsible for . . . that, Bonnie."

"That" was the copy of *The Herald* on the glass-topped coffee table. Whoever had last read the paper had rolled it into a tube but, though *Inside Elsie* wasn't visible, out of sight was not out of mind.

"When we hired Amanda, we hardly expected to end up in a gossip column."

Courtney came to my defense. "Bonnie didn't do anything. It was Tiffany. The second she recognized Elsie Scott she rushed at her. Bonnie didn't have any choice but to introduce her."

Maryann shifted in her chair to face me. "How can you justify being on speaking terms with someone like that?"

My promise to Amanda flew right out that terrace window.

"I don't have to justify it. I often speak to people I'm not particularly fond of."

This tense moment was interrupted by a maid in a white uniform. "Tiffany is on her way up."

"Thank you," Kitty responded.

Courtney jumped to her feet. "I don't want to see her."

"I do," said Maryann.

Having said that, a venomous smile spread across her face, and I saw that she, too, had those deep dimples in her cheeks.

"We'll handle this calmly," Kitty said to her daughters.

When it came to groveling, Tiffany put me to shame.

"I'm so, so sorry," she wept. "Please forgive me. Elsie Scott is just so charismatic I couldn't help myself. Her personality is magnetic."

Hearing that, I gaped. No one noticed.

"It was like she made words just . . . fall out of me. I thought she was being nice because she liked me. I mean, she was so friendly and sweet that I never realized I was being manipulated until it was too late.''

"Do you think this Scott woman had heard rumors?'' Kitty Dunn asked her niece.

"Oh, yes,'' Tiffany responded. "She had to know something. She kept dropping these hints and saying things like that line in her column. You know: 'The path true love follows is often rocky.' ''

I could easily imagine Elsie spouting those words over a bowl of rice pudding, but not in the exact context Tiffany was suggesting. Yes, Elsie Scott is a first-class manipulator, and she isn't above pouring on the honey to get what she wants. But Elsie had expressed adamant noninterest in the blushing bride-to-be when I'd mentioned the upcoming wedding. What on earth would have made her do such a fast about-face?

One of the Siamese cats climbed onto the sofa and into Kitty's lap. "So it seems the news was already out,'' she said, rubbing the cat's head. "In any event, it was no secret.''

Maryann stood, straightened her skirt, and said, "It was a secret as far as my professional life was concerned. Now even my secretary will think that I was dumped. I told her I'd broken off the engagement myself.''

"If you hold your head up and act like a lady,'' Kitty said to her daughter, "the gossip will die quickly.'' She flicked her hand carelessly at *The Herald*. "Even the little people take that sort of nonsense with a grain of salt.''

Kitty walked Maryann to the door, then returned to the living room.

"What we have to think about now, Bonnie, is damage control. You should contact this Scott woman and tell her the information she got is wrong. Tell her she misunderstood. . . .''

I told Kitty that that wasn't a good idea, and explained why. With Elsie, who can be nourished for weeks by a bit of gossip, the less she is given to chew on, the better. Denials would inevitably bring questions: *But then why did Tiffany say . . . ?* she would ask. And telling Elsie she'd misunderstood would make her return to her source to double check the story.

"I don't think Tiffany should be put in that position again," I said. "Elsie is very shrewd, and it's easy to slip up. I believe that the best thing to do is ignore her story."

Kitty glanced at her niece, who looked terror-stricken.

"If I have to talk to her again, Aunt Kitty, I'll be a nervous wreck."

After a second, Kitty nodded at me. "All right, then. We'll let it die a natural death. By the time this awful woman writes her next column, something else may have diverted her. Maybe Hillary Clinton will have taken up with . . . Woody Allen. Now, Bonnie, about getting these invitations addressed," Kitty went on, changing the subject. "I mentioned that one of Herbert's secretaries would handle that. Violet."

"Oh, yeah? Has anyone told Violet that?" asked Tiffany.

"Herbert spoke to her," her aunt responded. "She has that lovely handwriting. Palmer penmanship."

"They must've taught that in the nut house."

Courtney ignored her cousin. "I have our list, and Justin's family sent theirs. A few addresses are missing, but . . ."

"I'll call Maryann later and take her to lunch," Kitty said. "She loves The Four Seasons' poached scallops. She'll feel much better afterwards. This is her birthday month anyway. May is a big birthday month for our family," Kitty added conversationally, smiling at me. "Pookey was born two years after Maryann, almost to the day."

And the potential scandal, the column that had caused such an uproar, was dismissed. That was one way in which these rich people really were different. They could sweep their problems under their expensive rugs and pick up where they'd left off as if nothing ugly had happened. Kitty and Courtney Dunn were carrying on as if Palmer penmanship and poached scallops were the most important things in their world, and as for Tiffany, she was carefully cradling one of the engraved invitations between her now magenta fingernails.

"These are so classy."

Maybe the things that Amanda and I had obsessed about earlier that day—scandal, loss of a client, income, maybe even a career—were so trivial to this family that such matters had no place in their reality.

Pookey Dunn wasn't what I had pictured, but then it's hard to know what a Pookey is going to look like.

It was obvious that the coupling of Herbert and Kitty had resulted in Pookey. Somehow, though, the whole of Pookey was less attractive than the sum of the parts that had gone into forming him. The heavy lips which gave his father a sensual but decidedly masculine appeal made Pookey look slightly dissipated, and the dimples, so charming on the women in the family, contributed to the effect.

Pookey had inherited his father's height and physique, but had added an un-Dunn-like touch, a slight layer of fat around his middle. This fat didn't appear to have attached itself anywhere except at his waist, and as a result, although Pookey's shoulders and legs were of normal size for a man of his height, he seemed to me to be shaped oddly, like an egg standing on end.

When Tiffany and I arrived at Dunn Construction's third-floor offices, we found Pookey stooped over a desk gazing at a computer monitor. The desk was in a cubicle that had Tiffany's nameplate mounted at its entrance.

"Can I help you, Pookey?"

He didn't seem disconcerted by his cousin's belligerent tone. "Just looking over the schedule for the Ambassador Hotel."

"Fine," responded Tiffany. "By the way, any word on those firewalls for the Bronx project? That was some terrific publicity we got when that fire broke out."

"The firewalls should be in by the end of next week. There was a problem with the supplier."

"Right, *Poo*key."

Tiffany seemed to take a special pleasure in repeating her cousin's nickname slowly, drawing out the "Poo." He didn't appear to notice, nor, as he made his way past her, did he seem to notice me.

Once Pookey had disappeared into a private office with

his name—Paul Kenneth Dunn—on the door, Tiffany said softly, "Watch him. He's a groper."

I nodded. "He looks like one."

"He's harmless, though—at least in that respect."

"In what respect *isn't* he harmless?" I asked.

Tiffany gave a noncommittal shrug. "Violet's eating lunch at her desk. She usually does. I'll introduce you once her lunch hour's over, but I better tell you about her first."

That made me nervous. It's bad enough giving someone you have no authority over a job they don't want to do. If the person is unpleasant . . .

"What's wrong with her? You said something about a nut house."

"I was kidding. Violet's okay. She's just . . . strange. A space cadet. You'll see. Her clothes are dumpy and her hair's a mess. . . ."

Considering where these grooming criticisms were coming from, I couldn't take them too seriously.

". . . lives by herself in some New Jersey suburb."

I giggled. "That's a sure sign she's unbalanced."

"What I'm saying is, Violet's young enough, and she makes a decent salary, but she's like, you know, isolated."

"What does she do around here?"

"General clerical stuff. She fills in for me when I'm on vacation. I've always suspected that she wouldn't mind having my job. As if she could deal with the construction crews! Violet can hardly talk to a man without stuttering. I don't think she's ever had a date, but the really funny thing is"—Tiffany leaned nearer to me—"she's so hot for Neil Howard—that assistant foreman at the Ambassador—that she turns red as a tomato whenever he comes in the office."

"I can live with all of that," I said, "just as long as she doesn't mess up the invitations."

Tiffany shook her head. "She won't. Violet does her job okay. I try to be nice to her because I'm sure she hasn't got any friends. Not with her personality. I bring her books I've read. . . ."

There's a scene in the old movie, *Dinner at Eight*, when Jean Harlow mentions that she's been reading a book and

Marie Dressler does a classic double take. I didn't do a double take, but I did have to struggle to keep a grin off my face.

"Books you've read?"

"Romances. I like them. Violet devours them. If you ever want to get on her good side, bring her a few romances. Just 'cause she's never done it, doesn't mean she doesn't like to read about it."

Since interrupting Violet's lunch was clearly taboo, I asked Tiffany if there was a phone where I could make a personal call while we waited. She told me that I could use hers. As I sat down at her desk, Tiffany was walking into Pookey Dunn's office.

A screen saver—pink piglets dancing across a dark blue background—had come onto Tiffany's monitor. I tapped the space bar, and while I waited for my calling card number to go through the system and connect me with Rosaleen, I looked at the screen Pookey had been studying. It didn't mean much to me, but I recognize a timetable when I see one. This one had "Ambassador" across its top, and under that were columns indicating types of equipment, the date that equipment was to arrive on site, the installation date, etc.

"Hello," said the lively female voice at the other end of the phone line.

"Rosaleen? Hi! This is Bonnie! We got your message!"

Why, when speaking to this woman, did my simplest utterance sound as if it was followed by an exclamation point?

A little about Rosaleen: She is, or was, Eileen's younger sister. If Eileen is a ghost who haunts me when I'm feeling insecure, Rosaleen is alive and well and haunts me on major holidays.

Before I met Rosaleen, I had formed a mental picture of the woman Billy referred to as Auntie Rosaleen. I saw ruffled aprons and tins filled with home baked goodies. Now I know better. Rosaleen can hold her own in a kitchen but she is a lot more than oatmeal cookies. She's one of the most formidable women I know.

A couple of years ago she divorced the man she'd been

married to for ten years. I understand that another woman was involved. For him, not for her. Whatever the particulars of the divorce, Rosaleen got the two-story Cape-Cod-style house, an Acura Integra, and enough cash to take the edge off. With that cash, she bought a franchise in one of her many passions, a gym. She now handles not only the gym's purse strings, but a number of classes, and it is rumored that her backs-and-abs class turns healthy young men into puddles of exhausted flesh.

Rosaleen resembles photographs I've seen of Eileen, but she isn't the beauty her sister was. She'll never coax a sexy pageboy out of her dark red hair, and while she is easily as tall as Eileen was, her figure isn't lithe and willowy. Rosaleen is wide of shoulder, and despite working out, ample of hip. In another era she might have been called "a fine figure of a woman." A pioneer homesteader somewhere on the Great Plains would have been smart to marry her if his long-range plan was to have lots of children and his short-range plan was to get the back-forty acres plowed under before frost set in.

She's a tough competitor on the tennis court as well as on a golf course, but always kind, if vaguely condescending, when it comes to helping those less athletically gifted. She'd no doubt be happy to help me with any of my many sports deficiencies, except I'm not about to ask.

Rosaleen's also a seasoned traveler. So am I, but while two weeks of meandering around Tuscany is my idea of heaven, Rosaleen is a roughing-it, hut-to-hut type who has climbed mountains I'll never see except from a plane. But you can bet she'd do just damned fine in Tuscany, too, if things came to that.

On top of all this, Rosaleen has the disposition of a master yogi. She's invariably upbeat and good-natured. The sun always comes up and the cloud always has a silver lining.

Now that I've mentioned a few of the woman's many charms, you're probably wondering why I was upset about her visit. I could learn from someone like Rosaleen, improve myself, my disposition, my . . .

Yeah. Right. But the thing is, ever since Rosaleen visited us last New Year's weekend, I've suspected (1) that she was patronizing me, (2) that she was competing with me, and (3) that her "we girls have to stick together" attitude was a front because (4) she was after my fiancé!!

"I'm so excited that you're coming for Memorial Day! When do you arrive? Can I pick you up at the airport?"

"My plane gets in late Friday afternoon, but don't bother picking me up, Bonnie. No one should have to endure a trip to LaGuardia at rush hour. I'll grab a cab and get to Sam's around seven. And I'll bring a couple new wines I've discovered. There's an '87 Côte du Rhone that I picked up in the French Alps, and a . . ."

Wine is something else Rosaleen is good at. Not just drinking it. I'm good enough at that. Rosaleen knows vintages and vintners. No matter what she brought us in her tote, I knew it would slide over our taste buds like silk sliding over Teflon.

We said goodbye and hung up. I was staring into the monitor at the pink piglets, thinking various unhappy thoughts, when Tiffany looked into the cubicle.

"Did you see my database?"

"What?"

After tapping a key, Tiffany nodded at the screen. The Ambassador's timetable was again visible.

"I was thinking about something else." I brought my eyes into focus on the monitor.

"Our technical guy installed a network a couple months ago. I even had it put on my computer at home so I can work there. I was the first one to really get comfortable with the network," she added proudly. "Now we can all call up each other's data, as long as we have their password, that is. "Mine's 'Sextoy.' ""

I let that pass without a comment. "What's the point of a password if you give it to anybody?"

Tiffany shrugged. "The way I figure it, I'm here to do a job. There's nothing confidential about it. I lock my data so that most of the employees can't tamper with it, but if anyone wants to see it, that's okay with me."

"And this is for the Ambassador Hotel?" I asked, nodding at the screen.

"Yeah. This database tracks the inventory. Looking at

it, I can tell you what we've ordered, received, paid for, and used.''

"Like nails and two-by-fours?''

"Sort of, but we buy regular supplies like that in bulk and keep a big inventory in our warehouse. If a foreman needs nails, he just calls out there and asks for them. These things here''—she nodded at the monitor—"are special orders. I mean, for a specific project. Like this marble mantel.''

Tiffany tapped the monitor with the tip of her nail. "You saw the broken one a couple days ago at the hotel. Remember? This new one's going to replace it.''

I read the price listed after the item. "Expensive.''

"You want quality, you pay for it,'' Tiffany replied. "If I ever get a really big-time position in this business, you can bet that anything I build will be the best.''

I didn't doubt her. Tiffany had a chaotic look about her but when it came to business, she struck me as rock solid. So solid, in fact, that I had difficulty believing this was the same quavering, hand-wringing wimp who, earlier, had begged her aunt Kitty not to subject her to another meeting with Elsie Scott.

"Hey, Violet should be through eating. Come on,'' she said. "I'll introduce you.''

Violet's desk was in a tiny cubicle at the other end of the floor. As we approached, me with the boxes of invitations and the envelope of lists, she was staring down at a paperback book on her desk. Seeing us, her eyes flicked like a startled animal's, and with a sweep of her hand she slid the book into an open drawer.

"It's still technically my lunch hour,'' she said defensively.

Tiffany nudged me in the ribs and then introduced us. I couldn't read Violet's reaction when I put the invitations and mailing list on her desk. In fact, she seemed to have no reaction at all but simply stared vacantly at the boxes.

She was probably in her late twenties, with perfectly regular features, but she was so utterly unadorned that I was reminded of newspaper photos of women in isolated religious cults. Her straight brown hair was fastened with a red rubber band at the back of her neck, and her face was completely free of makeup. Some women can pull off a look like that and yet keep some spark about them. Others tend to fade into their surroundings. Violet was in the second category.

"Mrs. Dunn told me what beautiful handwriting you have," I said. "She and Courtney are so happy you've agreed to help. We're going to need these as soon as possible."

"I'll start them right away."

"Your name's on the list," Tiffany threw in, perhaps trying to sweeten the job.

"Oh."

Violet's voice, like her appearance, was flat, but that didn't bother me. She wasn't unpleasant. That's what mattered. Before I followed Tiffany from the cubicle, I mentioned that Kitty Dunn wanted her to use a fountain pen, with ebony ink, and that the invitations shouldn't be run through a stamp machine.

"All right," Violet replied.

Though there was no trace of enthusiasm in her voice, she sounded agreeable enough. However, just as I was about to step out of her cubicle, I glanced over my shoulder to say thanks. Violet's lips were pinched, and her eyes, which prior to that had shown all the emotion of two marbles, had been burning into the back of my head.

Her expression startled me so, that I stumbled over my "Thank you." By the time I got the words out, the blaze in her eyes had disappeared.

"It's no trouble at all," she said blandly.

5

GIVEN A CHOICE, I'D ATTEND A BRIDAL
shower sooner than a cockfight, but if the
choice was between a bridal shower and
an opera, I'd choose the opera. And I'm
not crazy about opera. Turning the Chrysler east toward Fifth Avenue, I resumed
the nagging I'd been doing on and off
since picking up Amanda at her house.

"I thought showers were supposed to
be given by the bride's friends. We're
employees."

"Bonnie," Amanda said in a long-
suffering voice, "this shower *is* being given by Courtney's
friends. We're merely helping with organization. And
please drive carefully. I don't want anything to spill."

Our cargo was indeed precious. The Chrysler's back seat
and trunk were piled with things Amanda and I had just
picked up from a caterer in Soho. We had ordinary items—
a forty-cup coffee maker, ice buckets, and the like—and
some things you don't see every day: three-dozen miniature
picnic baskets packed with sandwiches of either crab meat

and avocado on sourdough bread, or fresh mozzarella and
sun dried tomatoes on foccacia. Each basket also contained
a small Caesar salad, a piece of fruit, a rum-raspberry torte,
and the pièce d'résistance party favor, a little bottle of
Piper-Heidsieck champagne wrapped in shiny white paper
and secured at the neck with a gold ribbon.

"I still think it's a bunch of hooey," I said.

"You'll change your mind when you have your own
bridal shower, Bonnie."

That notion shot a lightning bolt of fear into my heart,
so strong that prickles of sweat erupted across my forehead.

I was once on the receiving end of a bridal shower. Most
of what went on there, and my reaction to it, has mercifully
faded into oblivion, but since I remained on good terms
with the friends who were responsible for the event, I must
have been reasonably gracious about the steam iron, the
mixing bowls, and the crotchless red panties. I'm not sure
what my reaction would be now. Over the years, I have
evolved.

I got snotty with Amanda, probably as a defense mechanism.

"I've had an account at J.C. Penney's for years. I can
buy my own sheets and towels."

"You *will* have a shower," Amanda insisted. "Noreen
and I have already talked about it."

Noreen? That did it! She's my brother's wife. Homemaker extraordinaire. The thought of her forcing her deadly
petits fours on all my calorie-counting friends was yet another reason not to set a wedding date.

Amanda looked at me across the car's wide front seat.
"Bridal showers are a tradition, Bonnie. They grew out of
the custom of dowries. If a girl's family couldn't provide
a dowry, her friends got together and contributed things for
her new home."

"I believe that in this case the girl's family can provide
a dowry."

"Courtney is a traditional young woman, and she's
having a traditional shower."

"Oh, sure."

The event that we were headed for was hardly your garden variety shower. The Dunns and Courtney's friends had been involved in the planning, but in only a superficial way. Amanda had orchestrated almost the entire event, from choosing the menu to inviting the guests.

And such a guest list! Reading it over that morning, I'd realized that about half of it was comprised of older women whose names continually flare up on the society pages. It had surprised me that someone Courtney's age would be chummy with so many grande dames.

"Kitty wanted to invite them," Amanda had said. She'd then allowed herself one of the few less-than-kind observations I heard her make about the Dunns. "I think she's trying to move into a higher level of society."

That explained the grande dames. If you're a social climber, who would you invite but high society?

The Dunns had arranged for us to park in their building's garage. As we pulled up to the driveway, Amanda was already slipping into her commander-in-chief role. She'd dressed the part in a pewter-colored silk pants suit with a vaguely military look to it. At the same time she'd asked me—ordered me, if you want to get technical—to wear a waiterlike starched white shirt and black pants—which will give you an idea of where I stood on her company's organization chart.

"Now, Bonnie. You and I have to make sure everything is perfect. Every guest who walks in the door must be greeted and seated. I don't want anyone to feel left out."

"Aren't these things supposed to be informal?"

"It *is* going to be informal," she responded. "What could be more informal than picnic baskets?"

In theory she was right, but in practice this event was as managed as a High Tea with the Queen.

One of the building maintenance men was waiting in the garage with a dolly. As he loaded our cargo onto it, Amanda continued with her instructions.

"Kitty Dunn will have a full bar, and tea and coffee too, but she's not having a serving staff. That's up to us. You make sure no one ever has an empty glass. And I don't want to see dirty dishes anywhere the guests congregate. . . ."

I took hold of Amanda's arm. Respect for her very delicate condition kept me from yelling, but I said, emphatically, "I will make drinks, and serve them, but I am not, repeat *not*, the cleaning lady."

She shook her arm free. "I didn't suggest that. The maid is going to be there. You just work with me to keep on top of everything. A lot of women from old money families are attending." Straightening her shoulders, Amanda added, imperiously, "My professional reputation is at stake."

Courtney and some of her young friends sat on the floor among reams of torn wrapping paper. On Courtney's head was a paper plate adorned with ribbons and bows taken from the gifts. Her complexion was flushed, and a wide purple bow teetered off the edge of the plate and hung over her forehead. A camera's flash caught the bride-to-be looking decidedly looped.

As Amanda passed me with a bucket of ice, I nodded toward Courtney and whispered, "I will never wear a paper plate on my head."

She whispered back confidently, "That's what you think."

It was three hours since we'd arrived, and Amanda's professional reputation was assured. Her picnic baskets had been pronounced "marvelous," and the red-and-white-check tablecloths and napkins she'd gotten from a rental service "too too perfect."

The mountain of beautifully wrapped gifts that Courtney had started opening an hour earlier had dwindled to one medium-sized package. Yet another sheet set, or more bath towels, I figured. After the first few 200-thread percale sheets and comforter and Sea Island cotton towels had been pawed over, the thrill was gone for me.

Courtney read the card from her cousin Tiffany aloud. "To Heat Things Up On Chilly Nights."

That got one or two giggles, but when the red satin sheets were released from the box and fell in a lustrous pool across Courtney's lap, there were some real "Aahs" and some genuine peals of laughter.

"Well, somebody had to do it," Tiffany said. "I mean, you've gotta be a little bit trashy."

Courtney gave her cousin that thin smile she was cultivating. "Thank you, Tiffany."

I don't know how it happened that Tiffany had ended up sitting on one of the sofas rather than in the circle of young women sprawled on the floor among the gifts and discarded wrapping paper. Had she been subtly snubbed because of her too-loud voice and her too-tight purple suit? Or had it been Tiffany's decision to sit among the grande dames and not with her contemporaries?

Thinking about it, I decided there *was* something of an informal caste system operating at the party. The center of attention was the circle of youth and beauty on the floor near the picture windows. Courtney I've already described. Her friends Taylor and Alex—I was having a hard time telling them apart—didn't have Courtney's dimples, but they had shiny, well-trimmed hair, tasteful makeup, trim figures, and stylish but quiet clothes. Stacey, the third bridesmaid-to-be in the group, was a true brunette, with hair that was almost black, olive skin and large dark eyes that, in another setting, might have been called smoldering. With her bright red lipstick and nail polish, she deviated from the pattern the other bridesmaids had been cut from, but not by much. At least I didn't think so at the time.

This circle of young women was not easily breached. Kitty Dunn moved in and out of it, but if she hadn't been Courtney's mother and this hadn't been her home, I doubt that would have been the case. There were other, equally stylish, well-kept women of Kitty's age present, but early on they had flocked together on the sofas, from where they made appropriate noises about the gifts.

A gathering like this can make for strange pairings, too. The two grandmother-age women at the shower couldn't have been more different. One was wearing a black suit appliquéd with huge yellow sunflowers. I thought it was one of the most profoundly bizarre things I'd ever seen, but Amanda told me, in an awed whisper, that the suit was a Missoni. This woman's heels were high and her hair was pale red bordering on pink, a color that does not occur in nature. She was not going gently into the good night. The other woman of about the same age was plump and gray-haired, and dressed in a polyester pants suit that I wouldn't have been surprised to see my mother wearing. Yet, for the duration of the party, these two women were inseparable.

As at almost every gathering, there were those who didn't fit into any of the groups. Maryann, looking harried as always, arrived late, disappeared into another room to make some phone calls, and then was the first to leave, slipping out before the last of the gifts had been opened. Considering the circumstances, I didn't blame her.

Then there was Maddie, who also was in a class of her own. A daughter of the deep South, Maddie spoke with an accent thick as molasses, her voice rising at the end of every inane utterance and turning it into a question: "These picnic baskets are just too precious?" "Ah just adore that bath set?" Maddie would have been a standout, though, even without the accent. She was quite tall, and so thin that her collar bones jutted like drawn swords above the scooped neckline of her little black dress. If it hadn't been for her minuscule biceps, her arms could have been those of a starving waif. She had probably put in some hard time at a gym, but if she were held up to a strong light, I'm sure you could have seen through her from sternum to spinal column.

Maddie's hair was a tumble of dark curls, and her skin so pale it might never have been exposed to the sun. I wasn't surprised when Amanda whispered to me that this woman had briefly worked as a model, but I could hardly believe it when she added that this ethereal creature, who looked as if she would blow away in a crisp breeze, was married to Pookey Dunn.

"You're joking," I said.

"Keep your voice down! Why would I joke about that?"

It seemed obvious to me but for a woman with a past that is even more interesting than mine, Amanda is some-times annoyingly prissy.

"Can you imagine them in bed together?" I whispered back. "The Blob meets Tinkerbell."

Amanda responded sanctimoniously. "I think they complement each other perfectly."

Right. Pookey had the money, or at least the promise of it, and Maddie had the style.

"What ever happened to her modeling career?" I asked.

Leaning closer, and briefly forgetting her holier-than-thou act, Amanda told me that Maddie's career had fizzled out. "She's older than she looks, you know. Five or six years older than Pookey. Anyway, I hear she's a real homebody. She has her own interior decorating business. I can't wait to see their duplex on Sutton Place. Apparently it's fabulous."

The homebody in question stretched up a bony arm to flip an errant curl off her skeletal shoulder. The thick gold band of her watch, caught in the rays of afternoon sun streaming through the window, glimmered like neon. Her wide wedding band was encrusted with diamonds, and the single diamond of her engagement ring looked like something you'd see locked in a museum case. Pretty fancy for a homebody, but no one ever said homebodies have to be low end.

And, as I've said, there was Tiffany, too young for the grande dames, too trashy for the sweet young beauties. I felt kind of sorry for her, until she pulled a stunt that wiped out every trace of sympathy. If Tiffany was an outcast, she deserved it.

It happened as the event was winding down. Kitty, who until then had been circulating breezily among the guests, sat on one of the sofas and gestured for Amanda, who had not stopped moving for three hours, to join her.

"You are a treasure," Kitty said to her.

Sitting, Amanda refused a glass of champagne from a tray that had been left on the coffee table, but accepted a cup of tea from our hostess. As she lifted the porcelain cup to her lips, she looked every inch the treasure.

Kitty's kind gesture hadn't included me, but I hadn't stopped moving either. I perched myself lightly at the edge of a nearby chair and reached, ever so furtively, for the glass of champagne Amanda had passed up.

Whoa! The bubbly that Bloomie's had served had been fine with me. This was . . . sublime.

Tiffany was sitting across from Amanda and Kitty. A number of the guests had already gone and others were preparing to leave, but there were easily a dozen women within earshot when the subject of Courtney's visit to the bridal registry arose.

"I couldn't have done it without Bonnie," Courtney said. "She's an awesome shopper."

Awesome!

"It's such a wonderful way to shop," the woman with the sunflowers on her suit said. "Such a time saver."

"And couples get what they want that way," Kitty put in. "Herbert and I didn't register anywhere when we got married, and you wouldn't believe some of the things we got. A wok, but no frying pan. No coffeepot, but two coffee-bean grinders."

"How come you didn't register anywhere?" Courtney's friend Stacey asked.

"Well, that was a long time ago. I'm not certain department stores had registries. Not where I lived, anyway."

"You could have registered at K-Mart."

Every head in the room turned toward Tiffany. I couldn't imagine what had provoked her comment. On the surface it was inane, a nonsequitur tossed out for no reason. Some of the other women must have agreed. One of them had tilted her head quizzically, and another said "Pardon me?"

It occurred to me that Tiffany might have a neurological disorder—something like that syndrome that causes people to burst unprovoked into obscenities. But why didn't this disorder affect her performance at work? Are there thought disorders that flare up only in family situations? Granted, family situations can bring out the worst in anybody, but that notion seemed unlikely.

Tiffany was smiling at her aunt. "K-Mart. Don't they have them in Florida?"

Florida may be thick with K-Marts, but the idea of Kitty Dunn having ever shopped in one seemed ridiculous. That is, until I caught Kitty's expression. The cordial smile she'd worn all afternoon was struggling to stay put, but her eyes had widened and her mouth hung slightly agape as she looked at her niece. I didn't understand what had happened, but Kitty appeared almost . . . frightened.

"I don't believe there's a K-Mart in Boca Raton," a woman in a pale pink suit said as she rose from her chair. "I must be going, Courtney. I'll look forward to seeing you at the wedding. This has been lovely, Kitty."

Standing, Kitty started after the woman. Tiffany's next comment followed them.

"But Aunt Kitty wasn't living in Boca when she met Uncle Herbert. She lived in Orlando. What was the name of that restaurant, Aunt Kitty? The one where you were a waitress?"

The woman in the pink suit turned back to Kitty. "Oh. You waitressed during summer vacations. I was a receptionist at my father's law firm during school breaks. I was the only one of the girls in my crowd who worked, and I resented . . ."

As Kitty and the pink-suited woman left the room, another woman began talking about a summer job she'd had—something at a yacht club that didn't sound so awfully back-breaking, and one of the grandmotherly women mentioned helping out in her father's brokerage.

Both Amanda and I could have contributed much on the subject of summer jobs, but Amanda chose not to mention feeding the chickens on her parents' farm in Mississippi, and I kept my mouth shut about my summer in a dermatologist's office located in a New Jersey strip mall where I learned things about rashes I hope I never need to remember.

This was hardly a gathering of the exploited workers of the world, and if it hadn't been for Tiffany's persistence, the subject would have died.

"But your mom's job couldn't have been just for the summer," she said to Courtney. "Because Uncle Herbert met her when he was on vacation down there in the winter. She was his waitress."

Tiffany's voice had taken on a little-girl quality, high and giddy. If I hadn't known who the speaker was, I might have thought she was a child, embarrassing her aunt with a child's unwitting candor. It was the same innocent tone she'd adopted when confronted about the item in *Inside Elsie*.

Courtney, who hadn't developed her mother's composure under fire, had turned pink. She lifted her shoulders self-consciously, then got to her feet and began picking up some of the scattered wrapping paper.

Oh, well. Tiffany was the Dunns' problem, and not mine. I finished my champagne and stood, intending to use the bathroom and then start packing the things Amanda and I would be returning to the caterer.

At that moment Kitty called from another room, her voice light and cheery. "Tiffany. Could you help me here please?"

The bathroom we—the staff—had been using was down a short hall behind the kitchen. There were two doors into this bathroom, one from the hall and one from a room which Kitty used as an office, and sound which might have been muffled by the apartment's walls carried through these doors. Eavesdropping wasn't my intention, but when the volume of Kitty's and Tiffany's voices increased, I did what had to be done in the bathroom very quietly, and took my sweet time about it too.

"I don't know what you mean, Aunt Kitty. It's just conversation."

"It's not *just* conversation. It's malicious conversation. You are trying to embarrass me and my family."

"What? You know I wouldn't do that, Aunt Kitty. I'm part of your family. What did I do wrong?"

Tiffany sounded as if she was about to cry, but her aunt didn't seem to think that was the case.

"You know exactly what I'm talking about," Kitty said. "First you revealed a very personal family matter to that horrible columnist, and now you're making an issue out of the fact that I once worked in a restaurant."

"But what's wrong with being a waitress?" Tiffany asked plaintively. "It's a perfectly respectable—"

"Of course it's respectable!" Kitty snapped. "But it's

not something I want to discuss with these people at this function.''

"I'm sorry. I didn't know it would embarrass you."

Kitty's sigh was so clear that I knew she was just on the other side of the bathroom door.

"Let's go back and join the others," she said after a moment. "But if there are any more indiscretions on your part, Tiffany, you will not be included in the wedding or at any of our other functions. Do you understand?''

"Yes. Please forgive me, Aunt Kitty. I just didn't realize what I was doing. Sometimes I say things without thinking.''

"Tiffany's up to something," I told Amanda as we waited for the building maintenance man to load the coffee maker and the other things back into the Chrysler.

Amanda was rummaging through the box that contained the table linens. "Tiffany's too dumb to be up to anything. She must have a brain the size of a peanut. You know what, Bonnie? I left a couple of the napkins on the kitchen counter. I'll be right back.''

We agreed to meet in front of the building.

The maintenance man opened the car door for me, and then closed it when I was settled. I backed out of the parking spot and drove to the garage door. In an instant an attendant was there to open it. "Have a nice afternoon, miss," he said as I pulled through. I thought, *I could get used to this.*

An empty parking spot on Fifth Avenue would have been nothing short of a miracle. I pulled into the loading space in front of the Dunns' building. The doorman approached me immediately, ready to object.

"I'm waiting for someone from the Dunns' apartment."

"Oh." He backed away. "No problem."

At that time I was driving a big white Chrysler that Sam had bought for Eileen. A few months before, I'd had an accident in it and had hoped that the insurance company would decide it was totaled. Unfortunately, they'd paid to have it fixed good as new. It was a fine car, but not one I would choose for myself. I felt lost in the thing. I *was* lost in the thing. I'm five foot four inches tall. In the Chrysler you had to be five foot eight inches to clear the steering wheel.

On the other hand, the seats were comfortable. I leaned back into the leather, shut my eyes, and spent a moment obsessing about my problems.

What was I going to do about Rosaleen? Nothing, I decided. If there had been any spark between her and Sam, it should already have ignited. They were friends, they had a lot in common, but that was all. I didn't have anything to worry about there. A far bigger worry was my own ambivalence. Why couldn't I just bite the bullet and marry the man?

Bite the bullet. What an odd choice of words. You bite the bullet when your leg's about to be amputated without benefit of an anesthetic, not when you're about to be joined with the perfect man. Unless the perfect man isn't perfect for you.

God, this was depressing. I forced my eyes open and willed myself out of my funk. Sam was the best. Reliable and hardworking. I'd be a fool . . .

Fifth Avenue is a heavily traveled street. On a weekday the little bit of the conversation that I overheard through my open window might have passed me by, but this was a Sunday. Buses run less frequently, and automobile traffic isn't so thick. A familiar voice broke through my thoughts.

". . . wasn't a fancy restaurant at all. It was like, you know, a joint. Tacky. You know what I mean?"

Tiffany, whose spike heels gave her a walk that was a combination wobble and flounce, passed the Chrysler without noticing me. The older woman, in spite of the sunflowers galloping amok over her suit, was not the flouncing type and had been wearing spike heels long enough to conquer wobbling. She had perched a yellow straw hat atop her pinkish hair. I'm never sure whether women who wear hats are on the cutting edge of fashion, or throwbacks to the forties, but I knew that this woman would prefer to be thought of as cutting edge.

Looking at her companion, she said, "Really!"

They passed out of earshot then, but not out of view. I

watched their heads bend toward each other. At that moment an automobile passing on my right stopped short, its tires squealing against the pavement. The noise caused Tiffany to glance back. For a moment our eyes locked.

She seemed startled at first, though I may have imagined what I took to be a guilty flinch. In any event her guilt, if it was there, didn't last long. She leaned toward the other woman again and resumed speaking.

Seconds later Amanda emerged from the building, a bag in her hand. As she stepped off the curb to cross in front of the Chrysler, I said quite loudly, "What a sneak!"

Amanda is probably the most generous woman friend I've ever had. Still, she knows a sneak when she sees one. She looked down Fifth Avenue as she slid in beside me.

"That moron Tiffany?" She let out a little puff of breath. "What's she done now?"

"She's still going on with that waitress nonsense."

As I looked over my shoulder for traffic, Amanda was frowning.

"Do you think it's true about Kitty waitressing?"

"Probably, but what difference does it make? It's not the same thing as working Tenth Avenue at midnight."

"I know," said Amanda. "But it might make a difference to the people Kitty is trying to impress. Frankly," she added with her voice lowered, "I'm a little disappointed myself."

Hoping that this was one of Amanda's rare excursions into irony, I glanced across the front seat. From the set of my friend's jaw I knew she was dead serious.

"Why?" I asked

Amanda shrugged. "I guess I wanted her to be someone special. Now she's just a working-class girl who married up."

Funny how easily perspectives can change. A week and a half before, Herbert Dunn had been a builder who had married up. Now it was Kitty who had climbed the matrimonial ladder.

I pulled to the curb in front of the two-story house in Queens where Amanda and Tony live.

"Don't forget, Bonnie," Amanda said, opening the car door. "Tomorrow we meet the girls in midtown to choose their gowns."

There was that "we" again. The girls surely were capable of choosing their gowns without my help. I started to object, but as Amanda slid from the car she crossed her forearm over her abdomen protectively. She didn't look any more pregnant than she'd looked six months, or six hours, before, and it may only have been a practice-pregnant gesture. Whatever it was, though, it worked on me.

"I'll be there," I said.

6

THE PHONE IS ON SAM'S SIDE OF THE BED but he slept through two rings. On the third ring I lifted my head and wormed my arm across his chest.

"Hello?" I said groggily into the mouthpiece.

"Bonnie? We're at the hospital."

"Tony? What's wrong?"

"It's Amanda. She was having cramps. Her doctor told me to bring her here. She's all right now, but she has to stay on her back for a while."

It was morning, but very early. Only a thin sliver of gray light showed under the curtains in our bedroom window.

"When can she go home?"

"In a few hours if she's still okay. She wanted me to remind you about picking dresses. You're going to have to do it without her help. She said to make sure that everything they choose is in stock. And she said—"

Tony hesitated here. I imagined him taking a long breath, but couldn't be sure. He might have been sipping from a container of coffee. For that matter he might have been thinking of dropping the phone, walking out of the hospital, and never looking back. I used to think that Tony was easy to read but I can't tell about him anymore. Not long before, under the influence of too much sun and a couple of beers, he had told me that he felt like running away from home. He was kidding, of course, but sometimes he seems on the verge of doing just that.

"Yes?" I asked.

"Amanda said to tell you a couple of other things. 'Less is more.' That's one of them."

"What's that supposed to mean? No feather boas?"

"Beats me."

"What else did Amanda want to tell me."

"She said you should 'Think Audrey Hepburn and Grace Kelly.' "

"Thank Amanda for her words of wisdom." She must have thought that left to my own devices I'd walk into that chichi bridal salon thinking Cher, or even Roseanne!

"I'm just passing on messages," Tony said.

He sounded awfully tired, and there was no reason for me to give him a hard time anyway. He was merely the messenger. You're not supposed to kill the messenger.

As I hung up, Sam stirred beside me and asked sleepily and without opening his eyes, "What time is it?"

"Almost time to get up. But we have a little time," I added.

Less may very well be more where clothing is concerned. The famed "little black dress" can certainly hold its own against any amount of chiffon and rhinestones. With sex, however, less is less and more is, indisputably, more. For some time I'd felt as if our sex life was moving into "little black dress" territory. I slipped my fingers across Sam's bare chest. Opening one eye, he looked at me and said, "Hum," which in these circumstances translated into *Good idea*. We had about a half-hour before he would have to get up, and that gave us enough time for a few rhinestones.

Tiffany McKinney wasn't having any of that "less is more" business. The car she was attempting to pull into what may have been the only empty parking spot on the Upper East Side was bright metallic blue and adorned with all sorts of gizmos—a spoiler, gold-rimmed hubcaps, darkened window glass.

The driver who was attempting to back a dirty white van into the same parking spot clearly wasn't impressed by all this glitter. Even if he had been, I don't think he would have been happy about giving up that parking spot. Leaning through his window, he shouted, "I was here first. Gotta use the phone booth at the corner. You can find yourself another spot, lady."

He didn't know the lady he was dealing with. She responded with "No way, fucker!" and nosed the front of her car closer to the curb. The other driver, in response, cut his wheel sharply and backed up until the van's dented fender tapped the car's pristine bumper.

Tiffany was out of her car in a flash. "You're going to pay for any damage, asshole," she yelled, surveying the front of her car.

The van driver threw open his door and stepped into the street. He wasn't the hulking monster I'd half expected. In fact, I'd be surprised if he was much taller than five six or seven. You have to watch those short ones, though. It's that Napoleon thing.

"I'm paying for nothing. You can either move your car or you can stay here all day stickin' halfway out in the street."

A black stubble showed across his jaw, and his black hair could have used a trim. He wore a green-and-brown camouflage T-shirt and pants. His black boots had steel insets at the toes, and looked like the footwear of choice for members of a violent paramilitary group. A diamond stud glittered in one of his earlobes. I don't understand tough guys with earrings, but then my understanding probably isn't important to most tough guys.

Tiffany was no more impressed by this man's pseudo-military regalia than he was by her flashy car. She rested her Lycra-encased bottom—Did this woman realize that clothing was available in fabrics that weren't elasticized?—against the car's hood and put her hands on her hips.

"I can wait all day."

A cabbie, forced to stop behind the two jackknifed vehicles, blew his horn. The van driver glanced his way and
snarled, "Get out'a my face."

For a moment I thought the cabbie might jump from his
taxi and, in typical Manhattan style, join the fracas. He
eased out into traffic, though, and whatever he yelled back
at the van driver was lost in another blare of horns.

The guy in the camouflage outfit turned back to Tiffany.
She was examining her fingernails—they were painted
deep, deep purple, almost black—and seemed prepared to
spend the day perched on the hood of her car.

The driver took a couple of steps, which put him within
inches of Tiffany. "Move your car or I'll move it for you."

Tiffany looked up very slowly. "Try it and you'll get
more grief than you ever knew was possible." She glanced
at the logo on the van's side. "Cutter's Plumbing Supplies.
I know the owner. I do business with him sometimes."

I'd been standing, agog, in front of one of Zoe's mini-
malist windows during this entire standoff. Seeing the van
driver's hands draw into fists, I tried to say something
soothing.

"Hey, Tiffany. It's not worth it."

The van driver, after giving me a long, hard glare, turned
back to the lady in front of him.

"It is to me," she responded.

Tiffany's street-brawler instincts were more finely honed
than mine. The man stared at her for a few seconds more,
then backed down abruptly, though not gracefully.

"Fuck you, bitch. Don't ever run into me when I'm not
feeling generous." Circling to the front of the van, he
climbed back inside and blasted into traffic.

Tiffany bent and examined her car's fender and, apparently satisfied that no damage had been done, got into the
driver's seat and pulled into the empty spot. When all that
was done and she had put some change into the parking
meter, she walked up to me.

"Did you ever see such an asshole? I set him straight."
Her cheeks were pink and her eyes bright. The fight had

agitated her. It had agitated me too, but in a different way. Tiffany had enjoyed it.

"That was crazy," I said. "He might really have gotten violent."

"I can take care of myself. Actually," she added with a sly grin, "since Dunn's offices are across the street, the company has some reserved parking spots in a garage not far from here. I could have parked there but you gotta stand up for yourself. Know what I mean?"

Without waiting for an answer, she glanced at the bridal salon's window display. "So what's the program here, anyway? We're supposed to choose all the dresses?"

I nodded. "We'll choose Courtney's gown first, then the bridesmaids' and Kitty's. That way, we'll be sure the wedding party complements the bride."

"Great." Noticing that the panty portion of her pantyhose showed beneath her hem, Tiffany tugged at her miniskirt and snapped the Lycra down an inch or so. "We'll all get to look dull."

Rummaging through her handbag, she pulled out a pack of cigarettes.

"I'll bet they won't let me smoke in there," she said, offering me one.

I shook my head. "No, thanks."

"No bad habits, huh? Everyone should be virtuous like you, Bonnie."

She seemed ready to turn her anger on me. "What's with you, Tiffany?" I asked.

Striking a match, she lit the cigarette. "Nothing much, except I saw the snotty look you gave me yesterday after the shower. You know. When you heard me talking about Kitty's secret life."

"Not snotty, Tiffany. Surprised. I'd just heard you promise Kitty you'd keep quiet about her waitressing, and there you were—"

She finished the sentence for me. "—blabbing to one of the biggest blabbermouths in New York," and blew a cloud of smoke into the air between us. "So what? Why not tell it like it is? I can't believe *you're* crazy about my aunt Kitty. Haven't you noticed what a snob she is? How she can hardly look at you if you're not wearing the right clothes?''

I wasn't about to get into a debate concerning Kitty Dunn's virtues and vices with her niece, whose resentment obviously ran deep.

"I have no problems with any of the Dunns."

"Yeah? Well, I do. Sometimes I feel like screwing Aunt Kitty big time. All I'd have to do is dig through some of my parents' old photo albums." She glanced at her watch. Like everything else about her, it was gaudy—fat silver links, a huge blue face. "We've got a few minutes," she said. "Want to learn a little family history?"

We were in the middle of a busy sidewalk, groups of pedestrians breaking stride to make their way around us. I moved closer to Zoe's window. "Sure."

"Okay. About thirty years ago my father and his sister—that's Aunt Kitty—inherited a piece of property near Orlando. They wanted to build on it. A small apartment complex. Okay, so they had problems getting financing, and the Florida economy wasn't doing so well, and maybe my dad drank a little too much and wasn't a very good businessman. Whatever the reason, they went broke.

"Then Kitty happened to meet Herbert in that restaurant where she was waitressing. He already had a reputation as an up-and-coming developer. Anyway, Kitty talked my father into selling Herbert his share of the piece of property. After that, the property sat undeveloped for a year or two. And then guess what happened? Disney announced that it was going to build an amusement park near Orlando. The piece of land that my dad had sold Herbert Dunn for almost nothing happened to abut Disney's property. Not just abut: it turned out to be right outside Disney World's main gate."

"Do you think Herbert and Kitty knew this before they bought your father's share?"

Tiffany shrugged. "My dad's always refused to believe that Kitty knew anything. But Herbert? He knew for sure. He was already a big enough deal in real estate to have gotten inside information.

"Herbert and Kitty—they were married and living in New York by then—held on to the property until every hotel chain in the country was ready to throw money at them. They sold to the highest bidder. Got millions for it.

"My dad got a consolation prize: a second-rate office job with Dunn Construction Company. He and my mom moved up north, to Riverdale. And that's the family history. While my Dunn cousins were going to the most exclusive private schools in town and having their birthday parties on yachts, I was in a girls parochial school. My bedroom was about a quarter the size of Courtney's, and instead of looking out on Central Park, it looked over an old-age home and a highway."

"Your dad still works for Herbert?" I asked.

"No. About two years ago he took a cheesy buy-out Herbert offered him and retired. He and my mom live okay, you know, but not in a dozen rooms on Fifth Avenue."

Everything is relative. Tiffany had gotten a decent, if not fashionable, education. And how many people *do* live in a dozen rooms on Fifth Avenue? I might have mentioned these things, but looking at Tiffany, at the harsh way she drew on that cigarette, at the angry lines creasing her forehead, I knew that she had been nurturing her resentment of the Dunns for a long, long time, and that nothing I said was going to make a difference.

"And so," she went on, "do you think I should be grateful to the Dunns for including me in their boring parties? Or for buying me a dress that I'll never wear after Courtney's wedding? Screw that! They've been looking down their noses at me for years. Now it's my turn. But—"

She had glanced across the street. I did the same and spotted Courtney and Stacey walking toward the corner opposite us. Tiffany was smiling when I looked back at her.

"—let's talk about something else. I've got a date with Mr. Wonderful this Saturday night," she said. "Neil Howard."

"That sounds promising."

Considering the way she had salivated over Neil not two weeks earlier, the long face she pulled surprised me. "I'm not sure about Neil anymore," she said. "He looks good but I've developed some major doubts about him."

"Such as?"

"Let's just say I've been doing a lot of homework." Tiffany drew deeply on the cigarette one last time, and then, as Courtney and Stacey approached, tossed the butt into the gutter.

Courtney, even in jeans, was the picture of good taste—quietly expensive tweed jacket, quiet hair. Stacey's veneer was quiet, too, but not as hushed as her friend's. There was a quality about her that pushed at the edges of good taste. She didn't approach Tiffany's territory, but once again I noticed the lipstick that was more red than pink, the glossy dark hair falling a little provocatively across the side of her face, the jeans decidedly tighter than Courtney's.

In the few seconds it took the new arrivals to join us, Tiffany seemed to have undergone a mood swing. As I pressed the door buzzer, she was smiling at the sketches in Zoe's window.

"You'd never know this place sold gowns. I mean, like, where's the fluff?"

My feelings too, but with the others there I wasn't about to admit to that bourgeois sentiment. "Sometimes less is more," I said as a smartly uniformed guard opened the door from the inside and ushered us into the shop.

"Yeah," said Tiffany, eyeing the gold braid on the shoulder of the man's navy blue jacket, "and you can be sure that in this place less is going to cost more, too. Glad I'm not paying."

Neither Courtney nor Stacey made any response, but as they preceded us into the shop they exchanged the kind of glances that said, Isn't she an embarrassment!

As I started in after them, Tiffany put her mouth close to my ear.

"They all hate my guts. If I ever end up with my throat slashed, tell the cops to take a hard look at the wedding party."

On that beautiful spring day, entering one of Madison Avenue's most elegant stores, in Manhattan's safest neighborhood, in the presence of a six-foot-plus guard who, though well past middle age, carried himself with great authority, I didn't give that statement a second thought.

*   *   *

Kitty and the remaining bridesmaids-to-be had arrived, the shock of Amanda's absence had passed, and the girls were finally in the hands of one of Zoe's salesladies. She wasn't called a saleslady, though. Like the woman at the bridal registry, she was called a consultant. Consultants tend to be thinner than salesladies, and better dressed.

Courtney's consultant had achieved skeletal perfection. Whether viewed straight-on or from the side, the woman had scarcely a bump to disturb the flow of her mauve knit dress. Though her eyes were brown, her hair was blond, and not a black root showed. It wouldn't have dared, any more than a strand of hair would have dared stray from the ballerinalike knot at the back of her head.

With the consultant in firm control, it appeared that I was going to be ignored. That was just dandy with me. I had my own clothing dilemma to deal with.

My outfit—gray sweater worn over a long-sleeved blouse, and tweed slacks—was a mistake, too warm for this May afternoon, and much too warm for Zoe's. There were air conditioning vents in the ceiling, but not a whiff of air seemed to be coming through them. I tugged at the band of my sweater's neck. When had it gotten so tight, anyway? Or was my neck getting fatter? There was a happy thought.

Maybe if I got rid of the sweater . . .

Interrupting our consultant as she was steering Courtney into a dressing room, I asked where the restroom was. She nodded toward a closed door at the back of the salon. "Through that door, and on the right."

"You'll be back soon, I hope."

That was Kitty. So much for my being superfluous. I might not have any useful function at Zoe's, but the Dunns were paying for my presence and they wanted what they paid for.

I peeled the sweater over my head, shoved it into my tote bag, and splashed cold water over my face. Relief. After drying with one of the soft folded guest towels supplied by Zoe's, combing my hair, and straightening my blouse, I left the small, windowless but pleasant restroom. I wasn't especially eager to resume my vague duties with the bridal party, but I didn't want to irritate Kitty by disappearing for too long.

It was cooler here at the back of the shop, something that had been apparent the moment I walked through the door separating it from the selling area at the front. I was headed back to the front of the shop when a lovely breeze drifted across my face. Somewhere nearby was an open window or door.

Just a minute more, I decided. They won't miss me.

I wandered in the other direction, past a small, unoccupied office at the end of the hall. Its door stood open, revealing an old-fashioned roll-top desk. Around the corner from this office was a big stock room. The door there was also open and though the lights weren't on, I made out racks of clear plastic garment bags brimming with gowns.

At the end of this short hall, I found the open street door that had let the breeze into the rear of the shop. In New York City, unattended open doors are unusual, but this one led into a driveway surrounded on three sides by buildings and on the fourth by a tall gate of iron bars. The gate wasn't topped by the razor wire or spikes you find in less posh neighborhoods, but the padlock dangling from the latch looked formidable.

Past the gate, on the far side of the street, were Dunn's offices. I glanced at a third-floor window but wasn't certain whose office or cubicle it belonged to. When I'd dropped off the invitations, I hadn't paid attention to the office layout.

A wobbly cement step brought me into the alley. After I recovered my footing, I took in a long breath of the spring air. It would have to do me for a while.

I was turning back toward the entrance when a white van pulled into the driveway and nosed up to the iron gate, to the point of actually touching it. Though I wasn't wearing my glasses, I thought the van resembled the one that had nudged Tiffany's bumper on Madison Avenue.

Squinting, I peered at the driver. Sunlight was glinting off the van's windshield, and though I could make out the shape of a man behind it, his features weren't clear. Regardless, I assumed it was the guy in the camouflage outfit.

He gave the horn two quick blasts.

What was he doing here? Still looking for a parking space after that fight with Tiffany? Impossible. But was he just going to park there in the driveway, with the van's rear sticking out into the street? That was impossible too. It meant an immediate ticket. Maybe even a tow truck, which would mean a visit by the irate driver to the dreaded car pound.

Kitty was no doubt missing me but not really needing me, so I stayed there for a few seconds, partly hidden by the shop's door. Soon enough, the mystery was solved. A man in a gray workman's uniform hurried from the back door of a building catty-corner to Zoe's. I heard him say, "How come you didn't call first?" as he unlocked the gate.

7

AS I'D EXPECTED, MY BRIEF ABSENCE hadn't made a bit of difference. A couple of the girls were sitting in Queen Anne chairs with pink brocade upholstery, picking at a dish of mints on a mahogany coffee table and critically eyeing the gowns being shown to them. I joined them, and for about ten minutes attempted to be useful. Most gowns got head shakes and were returned to the racks. A few got nods and were hung in nearby dressing rooms.

Stacey, who had struck off on her own, finally appeared in front of a full-length mirror, holding up a brocade dress in a dark cream shade. With her dark hair and olive complexion it would be beautiful, but then most dresses would be beautiful on Stacey. I didn't see Maryann at first, but then spotted her in a niche between a dressing room and a rack of gowns. She was speaking into her Dictaphone, her face partly turned to the wall. As for Tiffany, she was near the shop's entrance. I couldn't begin to guess what her mood was, and whether—or better put, when—she would again say something to embarrass the Dunns. From the way she was pawing through her handbag, though, I knew it was time for another cigarette. For a moment I thought she was headed out the shop's street door, but then, apparently changing her mind, she headed for the rear of the shop.

I didn't see Kitty for a while, but recall hearing her voice at some point from inside one of the big dressing rooms:

". . . will take care of that when they fit it to you, Courtney."

"But Mom! What if it still gapes and everybody . . ."

Oh, the anxiety of the big choice. Sometimes it seems that choosing the gown is more worrisome than choosing the groom, which, when you think about it, makes some sense. Generally you're only going to get one shot at marching down the church aisle in the long white dress with the trailing train surrounded by attendants, but you can have as many husbands as you can get.

This was not by any means my first foray into the frothy world of wedding gowns. From the time I was eighteen until I was perhaps twenty-four or twenty-five, I took part in a number of weddings, my own included, underwritten by a variety of budgets. Most of those budgets were pinched, and certainly none of them approached the abundance Courtney Dunn had at her fingertips. Still, every bride is special, or shops as if she is. Not a New Jersey mall was left unexplored as my friends and I searched for perfect headpieces and for bridesmaid dresses that flattered the willowy, the Rubenesque, and every body type in between. A corner display of designer shoes at Zoe's reminded me of dyed-to-match pumps, and how we had agonized over the swatches we brought to our local Chandlers. What if they didn't get the color right? What if we, dazzling in royal-blue taffeta, followed the bride down the aisle in three-inch peau de soie heels that looked something less than royal?

Playing with the idea that I might find something for my second wedding here at Zoe's, I flipped through a rack of cocktail dresses. A peach-colored one, flapperlike, with beads on the bodice and a scooped neck, captured my eye.

There was no price tag—in Zoe's, if you had to ask, you couldn't afford it. I ran my hands covetously down the smooth silky fabric. The dress was short, the skirt flippy. Perfect for me. The legs are the last thing to go.

And my bridal party? Would I even have one? According to Amanda, matrons of honor and bridesmaids originated in our pagan past when a bride-to-be, considered defenseless against evil spirits, not to mention men other than her betrothed, was isolated from the community and looked after by female friends or relatives. Later, in medieval times and into the seventeenth century, bridesmaids decked the marriage bed, and helped get the couple into it.

Since Sam and I were already sharing the Serta Posturepedic that would be our marriage bed, it was unlikely we would be needing help getting into it. You never can tell about those evil spirits, though, so a matron of honor was probably going to be necessary. Amanda would be my first choice, of course, but my sister-in-law was sure to be upset. Maybe if her kids got to be ring bearers and flower girls . . .

Flower girls? For a second wedding? For me?

Here's a confession. Deep in my heart I've never found the trappings of the wedding ceremony an especially exciting part of the mating game. My first wedding—the only one so far—was a church affair mainly because it was the thing to do and my mother loved the idea. A tight budget sent us speeding to wedding gown outlets in run-down New Jersey strip malls. Why the speed? I can't remember. I wasn't even pregnant.

"I see you're engaged. We don't usually show that particular dress to our brides, but . . ."

My engagement ring had caught the eye of an idle consultant. Elizabeth Taylor probably wouldn't give the ring a second glance but by ordinary standards it was impressive, a brilliant one-karat oval bordered by trillions. During the five months I'd been wearing it, though, I'd come to realize that my standards are not ordinary. Like the Chrysler that was too much car for me, this ring was also too much. Self-conscious, I removed my hand from the dress and lowered it to my side. The woman pressed on, undeterred.

". . . it is lovely for the bride who is more mature."

At least she hadn't said "older." This woman was about my age but taller and thinner, with a short, stylish cap of ink-black hair. She spoke with a slight, unfamiliar accent. I initially assumed that was an affectation; nevertheless, the woman struck me as intimidatingly cosmopolitan.

Taking the peach colored dress from the rack, she held it out to me. "You know we show dresses by appointment only, but while the shop is quiet for a few minutes, why don't you try this? You can get an idea of how it will look, though I'm sure you will take a smaller size," she added, almost flattering me into submission.

As was the case with many of the dresses in the shop, the neckline was stained. These garments, regardless of how beautiful, are samples. Once the bride and her attendants decide on styles, the brand-new gowns are brought in and fitted.

Looking at me critically through narrowed gray eyes, the woman persisted. "When is your wedding date? If you ordered a size eight, alterations should not be terribly extensive."

Flustered, I took the dress from her. It was one thing to daydream about it, another to confront reality. I didn't plan to try it on, but inexplicably found myself moving ahead of the consultant toward the dressing rooms at the side of the store.

I was only vaguely aware of the sound of the buzzer, and of the guard opening the door for a number of women. Their rapid-fire chattering in a foreign language caused my consultant—How quickly I'd started thinking of her as mine—to veer away from me. I was left alone, holding the dress over my arm and gaping at the sudden throng at the front of the shop.

There were eight new arrivals—all female, most of them young, a couple middle-aged. They were all rather tall, and not stylishly svelte. Their voices carried, Valkyrie-like, through the salon, and their laughter was louder than good manners allowed. By the standards I'd come to associate with wealth, their clothing was dowdy and their abundant jewelry gaudy.

Glancing out the shop window, I saw a black limousine,

long as a city bus, parked brazenly in the illegal zone near the corner. A man, his eyes hidden by dark glasses, was sitting in the driver's seat.

The language spoken by the new arrivals sounded to me like German, yet the physical gestures that accompanied their chatter seemed more dramatic—an Italian slicing of the air with the hands, a Spanish fling of the head. The consultant who'd been attending to me seemed to have no trouble communicating with them, and she supplied the dramatic body language as well. One or two of the group lapsed into English, and one of the middle-aged women said, "But Zoe, you are so kind to fit us in."

Zoe. And for a moment she'd been mine. I examined the dress hanging over my arm once again. If Zoe thought it was lovely for me, then who cared what it cost! I could skimp on the shoes, maybe. I pictured myself gliding across the floor, past throngs of friends, past my mother, teary-eyed with happiness, past my sister-in-law, sobbing just because she likes to make a scene, toward . . . Toward what? A minister? Or a judge? It was unlikely a priest or rabbi would have us. And if I was going to do much glid ing, then Sam's living room wouldn't be big enough. . . .

Funny, looking back on that visit to Zoe's, how Sam scarcely entered the picture. The scene I had constructed in my head included a dress, guests, a matron of honor, some kind of officiant, and even bargain-basement shoes, but no groom.

I was completely lost in thought, and wasn't aware Kitty was behind me until she whispered harshly in my ear, "This won't do. Take care of it."

Looking around, I saw Courtney alone in front of her dressing room examining an ivory gown, and her brides-maids scattered all over the shop. The girls' consultant had deserted them, at least momentarily, to join the happy crowd that had just arrived.

"We had an appointment," Kitty said.

This was the kind of thing I was expected to handle. Hanging my prize, the perfect dress, over a mirror, I wandered into the midst of the newcomers and plucked at the errant consultant's sleeve. When I had her attention I nodded toward Courtney.

"Excuse me, but Ms. Dunn . . ."

"Oh, certainly," the woman said. "I just wanted to meet the princess."

Looking at the rather bulky young woman who was at the center of all this attention, I whispered, "You mean she's a real princess?"

"Austrian royalty."

Since when did Austria have a monarchy? The consultant answered my unspoken question. "She's a member of the Hapsburg dynasty. The family was deposed many years ago, of course, but that doesn't make her any less a princess."

It certainly didn't in the eyes of Zoe and her staff. This consultant told me that the princess's party hadn't made an appointment, *de rigueur* for us nonroyals, but had simply called a half-hour before their arrival.

"Zoe was thrilled to take care of them, though. After all, Zoe herself is of Hungarian descent, and as I'm sure you know, the Hapsburg empire extended into Hungary."

If I'd ever known that, I'd forgotten it. Royalty, whether deposed or otherwise, is something I can't get excited about. Others do, though, and there's no arguing that from the moment this new party arrived the dynamics in the shop changed. I'm not suggesting that the Dunn party was treated like poor cousins. They got all the attention they needed. But they were treated like . . . regular people. All the fawning, bowing, and scraping was directed toward the new group.

I made sure the sales consultant returned her attention to Courtney before going to retrieve what I was now thinking of as my dress. It had disappeared. I spent about five seconds looking for it before Kitty emerged from one of the smaller dressing rooms wearing the peach-colored dress.

"What do you think of this, Bonnie? It's not really a mother-of-the-bride kind of thing, but I do like it. Maybe for the rehearsal dinner. It's not too youthful, is it? I think peach is always flattering, and when you get to be my age, flattery is such a comfort."

She said this with a rueful smile. I'm not sure whether it was that smile or simply the fact that I was getting to know her better, but at that moment I decided that I liked Kitty. Yes, she was a social climber. Yes, she was sometimes arrogant when dealing with what she'd called "the little people." At the same time, though, she operated in a sensible, down-to-earth way, the way a woman who had waited tables in a tacky restaurant in Florida might operate.

But as to her question. Was the dress too youthful for her?

How would Amanda have responded? Amanda certainly wouldn't allow her own lust for the dress to influence her answer. But I'm not Amanda. "Maybe it's a little . . ."

My words were lost in a gale of high-pitched laughter which floated across the shop.

The deposed royalty was having a downright boisterous time of it. Maybe that's customary with deposed royals. Their rung on the social ladder is assured, yet they have nothing to live up to, no reason to worry about the incensed proletariat dragging them to the guillotine. Though the social-climbing commoners might *tsk tsk* at their behavior, they can whoop it up like nobody's business and get away with it.

Kitty had fixed her gray eyes on me. "You were saying something about this dress?"

I made a split-second decision. This was a case where discretion was better than valor. "It may be a little . . . costumy."

"Yes, but . . ."

Kitty had begun examining her reflection in a mirror, when a chorus of gasps and *oooh's* filled the shop. Courtney had emerged from her dressing room in the gown she'd been looking at a few minutes before. It was an almost perfect fit, and the style was perfect, too. The bodice was tightly fitted, the short sleeves puffed, and the long skirt hung from wide pleats. Clusters of seed pearls punctuated the sweetheart neckline and the edge of the sleeves, and there was a cathedral train at the back of the gown. The fabric, ivory silk brocade, was stunning.

Courtney looked a little awkward as she stood there, but

she had captured every eye in the salon. "Perfect!" Kitty and Zoe said at the same time. Maryann lowered her Dictaphone to stare at her sister, and Stacey exclaimed, "That's it!"

Courtney had even attracted the attention of the princess. The chunky girl stared critically, and after a moment turned to one of the middle-aged women in her party and said something behind her hand. That woman, in turn, said something to the shop owner, who was at her side. Zoe nodded toward the closed door at the back of the shop, and the woman immediately headed in that direction. As she disappeared through the door, Zoe called, "I'll be right there, Baroness."

As Stacey joined us she was rolling her eyes. "Baroness? I'll *bet* she's a baroness!" When Zoe had trotted away after the woman and was safely out of earshot, she added, "The princess is a cow. That back area must be where they keep the chubby—"

She was interrupted by a series of eerie, high-pitched squeals. Shoppers turned, almost in unison, toward the door at the back that had closed behind Zoe seconds before. Voices—and there had been many of them working at once—quieted, the better to listen to footsteps falling hard and quick against a wood floor. Stacey gasped when the sounds of a brief struggle were heard. It sounded as if bodies were colliding against the other side of the door. All the while, the short, shrill cries continued.

The uniformed guard had left his post near the front of the shop. As the squeals rose in volume, he moved more quickly and, though he never did exactly run, by the time the squealing had lengthened into a scream he was pulling the rear door open. He didn't get through it, however, because at the same time he pulled, Zoe was bursting through from the other side, pushed by the baroness. The door crashed into the wall behind it, and the guard was shoved back into the shop.

The baroness ran through the selling area, shrieking so, that I clapped my hands over my ears. Arms stretched wide, she rushed toward her companions. Zoe raced behind her, shouting in a foreign language, perhaps Hungarian, and flinging her hands into the air. When she caught up with the baroness, the other woman brushed her away and stopped shrieking long enough to tell the others something in words that absolutely flew from between her lips.

I didn't understand a word of what she was saying but it sure impressed her party. Eyes grew wide, hands were clutched over mouths. The princess/bride-to-be whimpered delicately and pressed her wrist to her forehead as if she might faint.

Zoe began making soothing gestures, trying to calm the hysterical woman while at the same time questioning her. After a minute of this, Zoe signaled to the consultant in the mauve dress.

"Please call the police and tell them to come immediately. There may have been a—"

She paused, her gaze sweeping around the shop. I can't be sure, but it seemed she took a second to reconsider what she'd been about to say.

"Just tell them there may have been some unpleasantness in the back of the salon."

The baroness reacted violently to that statement. Her shrieking started anew and she swayed as if about to collapse. Members of her party helped her onto a settee. The princess began fanning the woman's face with a satin bustier that had been on the counter, and at the same time started crying in earnest. Seeing that, several other members of their party burst into tears.

The guard, who was still standing near the door at the back of the shop, was looking questioningly at his boss. He didn't seem particularly eager to find out what had caused Zoe's customer to become hysterical, but when he finally did reach tentatively for the doorknob, Zoe stopped him.

"Stay out of there, and don't let anyone else through until the police arrive! The baroness thinks she saw a—"

The baroness half rose. She was pale to the point of appearing blanched, and still terribly shaken. Nevertheless she managed, in accented but understandable English, to say what Zoe was having such problems with.

"Think? Not think. I know! A woman is murdered. Raped. Dead."

She collapsed back onto the settee. As her companions hovered over her, the baroness added, "There is a madman in here!"

8

UNLESS ONE OF THE WOMEN IN THE SHOP
was actually a man in drag, the only con-
ceivable madman was the poor guard,
who by now was looking almost as upset
as the sobbing woman on the rose settee.
Regardless, those of us whose hysteria
had been held in check by either our re-
pressed upbringings or the fact that we
hadn't seen what lay behind that door,
moved en masse to cluster around the
baroness and join the pandemonium.

"Murdered? Are you sure?"

"A girl? Did you recognize her?"

"Raped? She was raped?"

Courtney was finding maneuvering difficult. She stood
clutching the gown's bodice to her chest and saying,
"Someone was raped and murdered? Is that what she's saying?"

Through all this, Zoe was shaking her head and repeating, "I don't know. I didn't see anything."

I was as curious as everyone else, but it happened that

as I tried pressing closer to the shaken woman, an especially stout member of her party shoved me against the counter. From that vantage it was impossible to avoid glancing out the window and into the street.

A black-and-white police cruiser had pulled in front of the royals' illegally parked black limousine. One policeman was still in the cruiser but another was at the curb speaking with the limo driver. This police car obviously wasn't responding to the call from the shop, but it was there in any case.

I opened the street door and immediately attracted the attention of all the women in Zoe's. Once again heads turned and voices stopped, and Zoe herself looked at me with alarm, as if I were the madman himself escaping the scene of the crime. Attempting to explain myself, though no explanation was necessary, I nodded in the direction of the police cruiser.

The women inside the shop, who did not have my view into the street, must have assumed that my nod meant something like, See you later, ladies. I'm out of here.

The notion that they too could—and should—escape the madman seemed to strike everyone simultaneously. By the time I was through the front door, Zoe's customers were headed, en masse, toward it.

Cops look younger and younger to me. The one on the sidewalk looked about eighteen, and was no taller than I am.

"I understand there's a murdered woman in the back of the bridal shop," I told him.

That in itself was a jaw-dropper of a statement, but I doubt if it fully accounted for the cop's stupefied expression as Zoe's customers erupted from the shop and poured fast as molten lava onto the sidewalk. Next-to-last out was Courtney, in partly pinned bridal regalia and trailing six feet of silk brocade. Behind her came the guard, who helped her wrestle the train through the door.

I repeated what I'd said, louder this time, so that the cop's eyes were forced away from the crowd and back to me.

"Did you see the alleged body?" he asked, as though reading from a police procedures manual.

"No, but that lady did." I nodded toward the baroness.

The young policeman walked to the cruiser and said something to his partner, who took the radio from the dashboard and spoke into it. A moment later he joined us on the sidewalk.

"Is someone the spokesman for this group?" asked this second policeman, who looked almost as young as the first, though he was taller.

"I am Zoe," was the imperious response to that question. She pulled herself up to her considerable height, which put her at about the same level as the taller cop, and about a foot above the other one, but before she was able to enjoy that advantage for long, the royal personage who claimed to have seen the body attracted everyone's attention by crumpling to the sidewalk in a dead faint.

Giving a little yelp—"Oh, Baroness!"—Zoe knelt at the woman's side. So did several other members of the group. The taller policeman, after mumbling something to his partner, joined the women huddled on the sidewalk.

"You say you know where the alleged body is located?"

The first policeman was looking at me. I hadn't said that at all, but I locked onto the word *alleged*. Was there really a body? Zoe hadn't seen one. Of course, she hadn't been in the back area for more than a few seconds, but might this possibly be a case of mass hysteria brought on by the stress of planning a wedding?

I'm not an especially brave person, but seeing is believing and if I was going to believe in a body, I wanted to know it was there.

"I'll show you," I said to the cop.

As the policeman and I started into the shop, my eyes briefly scanned the gathering on the sidewalk. It was growing, attracting the attention of curious passers-by. Kitty and Stacey were with Courtney, who was still confused about what was going on. Kitty was talking to her daughter, while Stacey was doing something to the back of the wedding gown. And there were Taylor and Alex, speaking excitedly to two young men, joggers, who had joined the group. Maryann had edged out of the crowd and stood apart from them, but for once she seemed more interested in what was going on around her than in getting her work done.

But where was Tiffany?

Making my way through the door and into the warmth of the store, I was inexplicably chilled, as if an icy hand were creeping up my spine. It can't be Tiffany, though, I told myself. She's too streetwise, too tough a cookie to . . .

As the cop followed me through the door into the back of the shop, I heard the wail of sirens. Glancing over my shoulder, I saw other police cruisers pulling up to the curb. I looked questioningly into the young policeman's face. Perhaps he wanted to wait?

No. He stepped toward me, up the corridor, and indicated that I should move on. I opened the door to the restroom first, and found it as pristine as it had been when I'd last seen it. I then led the policeman around the corner and glanced into the small office. Only a vertical dead body or one seated in the swivel chair could have fit into that room. No body.

The door to the storage room was half open now. When I'd been back here earlier, hadn't it been open wide? Nudging it with my knee, I pushed it further and said to the policeman, "She might have come in here to look for a gown."

The incandescent ceiling lights were turned off, and I couldn't find a switch at the side of the door, but two barred windows high on the outside walls allowed beams of afternoon sun to cross portions of the room.

The racks standing against the wall to the left of the door held gowns intended for bridesmaids and other members of the wedding party. Though almost all these gowns were protected by garment bags, the bags themselves were translucent plastic, revealing a gardenlike array of colored fabrics. At the other side of the room, separated from the colored gowns by a narrow aisle, racks of white wedding gowns stood side by side. These gowns were also in plastic bags, but you had to peer closely to make out a pattern of lace or beadwork on a bodice.

The dress the baroness had been looking for was a wedding gown, ivory, with a row of seed pearls along its heart-shaped neckline.

With watchful eyes I went through the closest rack of white gowns. The garment bags were tightly packed and unwieldy, and shifting them to reveal the floor beneath took more strength than I would have thought. The sound of footsteps moving up the hall reached me but I paid little attention.

"Officer?" a man called. "Found anything?"

"No."

By then I had found something, though. The dress with the seed pearl neckline was the last one on the rack. The plastic bag covering it should have been pressed flat between the bag in front of it and the wall, but someone— probably the baroness—had pulled the bag free and manipulated the hanger so that the dress faced front. The plastic case had been partly unzipped, exposing the top of the gown.

What had the woman seen that frightened her so? The dress, with its long train tucked into the plastic bag, was exceptionally heavy. It took all my strength to shift it.

Reaching down, I clutched at the bottom of the bag. My fingers brushed against something furry. Startled, I pulled my hand back.

Other uniformed policemen had moved into the room. Light flooded the area suddenly. My hand felt sticky. I looked at it, at the deep red smear shining across the tips of my fingers, and then looked down and saw the terrible thing that had been revealed when I pulled the bottom of the bag away from the rack.

Tiffany's body lay crumpled against the wall, a grotesque parody of a smile on her face. One side of her forehead looked raw, and a glistening trickle of blood had zigzagged down her cheek and across her chin. A pool of it had gathered in the dimple on her cheek.

Humpty Dumpty. A drawing of the nursery rhyme character that I'd seen as a child flashed through my mind. Humpty Dumpty's head had been split apart too, zigzag like a cracked egg. Only there hadn't been blood in that drawing.

I blinked, trying to bring the scene on the floor into focus. This was no fairy tale. Blood and thick white clots
were coagulated in Tiffany's mass of chaotic blond curls.

Feeling a rising nausea, I bolted for the door, at the same
time wiping my bloodied fingertips against the fabric of my
slacks. Men called out to me but I didn't stop moving until
I was in the alleyway behind the building, crouching on the
wobbling step and retching onto the oily broken pavement.

When the churning in my stomach had calmed and the •
bitter taste in my throat lessened, I straightened and leaned
back against the rough brick of the building.

The storage room and hall were busy now. Police officers
came and went, some issuing commands, others following
them. The wail of another siren brought an officer to the
door I was blocking.

"Excuse me."

Another young one. I hadn't seen him before, nor had
he seen me. He seemed surprised to find me on the back
step. I looked up at him, then rose and moved away from
the door. As he bounded down, skipping the wobbling step,
the ground under my feet seemed to undulate. I leaned my
shoulder against the building, took a deep breath, and
closed my eyes.

When I opened them a few seconds later, the policeman
was at the entrance to the driveway. A key ring dangled
from one of his hands.

I was still in a fog, but when his hand stretched toward
the lock, a fragmented memory made me call out to him.

"There may be fingerprints. You shouldn't—"

Too late. He had opened the padlock and was pulling the
gate wide. Within seconds an ambulance pulled into the
driveway, lights on top whirling and siren screaming. The
cop motioned it on through the gate, then ran back past me
and into the building.

The ambulance driver and the woman riding alongside
him were already out of the vehicle and opening its rear
doors. I moved away from the building and toward the rear
of the ambulance, keeping close to the wall in case I needed
something to collapse against.

The attendants had lowered a stretcher to the driveway.

One of them raised a pole attached to the stretcher's side, and at the top of that pole hung a plastic container. The space was very narrow and I pressed myself against the building as the two attendants rolled the stretcher quickly toward the door. When the stretcher had passed, I stepped away from the wall. One of my heels rocked over something. Looking down, I spotted a small black object, not much bigger than a deck of cards, partly hidden by a patch of weeds growing against the building.

It was a tiny tape recorder. I examined the machine without touching it. It lay face up, and the clear plastic window that would have shielded a tape was open. There was no tape in the machine, though, and none on the ground near it.

I glanced around for a policeman but saw none. The ambulance attendants had stopped in front of the wobbling step. They looked at the doorway, and appeared to agree that the stretcher wouldn't fit through it. The woman hurried into the building, calling out to someone inside, while the man maneuvered the stretcher alongside the door.

I was to learn, later, that only ten minutes passed from the moment the first shrieks tore through Zoe's shop until that ambulance pulled into the driveway. For me, though, time crawled. It felt as if I'd been living with chaos, fear, and violence forever. I waited, endlessly it seemed, for whatever would happen next. The rational part of me knew that Tiffany was dead, that she would never again paint her fingernails purple or tug an elastic skirt over her hips. The irrational part of me looked at the white-coated attendant fiddling with the tubing running from the bottle that hung over the stretcher, and thought that maybe there was a chance they could revive her. Her eyes had been open. Was it possible I was mistaken about how still they'd been?

The woman attendant appeared at the door and, blank-faced, she said something to her partner. He, equally blank, began reversing the process he'd gone through moments before, removing the tube from the bottle, and then the bottle from the pole.

My irrational notion that Tiffany might still be alive had passed by the time her body was carried from the back door of Zoe's on a small stretcher borne by two policemen. A white sheet covered her completely, but when her body was shifted to the larger stretcher, her right hand suddenly came into view. I couldn't tear my eyes away from her fingernails. One of them was broken down to the quick. Tiffany would have hated that.

"There you are! The lieutenant wants to talk to you."

It was the short cop. His walk reminded me of a rooster's: chest puffed out, feet splayed. As this bantam strutted toward me, my head began clearing. I had a lot to tell the lieutenant.

"What's your lieutenant's name?" I asked.

"LaMarca. Lieutenant Anthony LaMarca."

Hearing that, I was torn between giggling hysterically and bursting into tears. Controlling myself, I told the cop about the recorder in the weeds, adding that there was a good chance it had belonged to the dead woman. He strutted over to the little black device and stooped to gaze down at it for a second. Then he pulled a plastic evidence bag from his pocket and slipped it around the recorder.

"And what's your name?" the cop asked me.

Could I possibly give an alias, and then invent an excuse to divert his attention and sneak away. No. I wouldn't have dared. The gods were playing rough that afternoon.

"Indermill," I said. "Bonnie Indermill."

9

"I DON'T UNDERSTAND HOW THAT could have happened with you there," Amanda said as we talked in her bedroom.

Over the years Amanda and I have had a few ups and downs but our friendship has remained solid, rooted in mutual regard, sympathy, and our ability to keep criticism of each other to a minimum.

That's why her reaction to Tiffany's murder caught me off guard. It might have upset me even more than it did if I'd been able to give her my full attention, but downstairs in the kitchen Tony was on the phone with someone from his precinct. What was he learning? Had the van driver been found? How about the man in the gray work clothes? How about a missing tape?

"My being there didn't have anything to do with it, Amanda," I responded, one ear tuned toward the open bedroom door. "I'm not a bodyguard. Tiffany and I weren't even in the back of the store at the same time."

"That's my point, Bonnie."

Pausing, she took a glass of milk from the bedside table and sipped delicately. I thought I heard Tony hang up.

"If you had been doing your job..." continued Amanda.

It wasn't my job. That was one thing. And even if it had been my job, no reasonable person could have expected me to plaster myself like a sheet of flypaper to every member of the wedding party.

But reason and Amanda were in two different galaxies.

She was propped up on a bunch of down pillows in the bedroom she and Tony share on the second floor of their house in Queens. The room is old-fashioned and sort of cramped, with a slanting ceiling at one end that makes standing impossible for most adults. Amanda's done a lot in there with wallpaper and paint, but I know she'd still like to knock a wall or two down.

For a woman who had spent the night before in the hospital, Amanda looked fine. Her hair didn't have that flattened look mine always gets when I spend too long in bed, and her coloring was good. Strangely, though, she suddenly looked pregnant, as if she'd puffed up during the last twenty-four hours. Her face was fuller, and her abdomen seemed to push at the blue and white quilt that covered her.

It doesn't happen overnight, though, does it? Maybe I'd been fooling myself a few days earlier when, to me, Amanda had looked like her stylishly slender self. Maybe I'd seen the heavier jaw and the growing tummy and hadn't wanted to believe my eyes. Why not? A psychiatrist could probably take a stab at answering that, but I'm not going to.

Putting the issue of my mental health aside, Amanda was visually pregnant now, and taking advantage of her bedridden condition. She knew I would have difficulty counter-attacking.

"If you had been doing your job," she repeated, "Tiffany would have been in the salon with the other girls, not out in the alley smoking a cigarette. I just hope"—leaning into the pillows, she looked up as if praying to the nondescript ceiling fixture—"that this hasn't ruined the wedding for the others. What do you think, Bonnie?'' she asked, looking back at me. ''Do you have any idea how Kitty and Courtney feel?''

All I knew was that *they* hadn't blamed me for Tiffany's death. ''I only spoke to them briefly after . . .''

It had been after the ambulance bearing Tiffany's body had left, siren quieted but lights still spinning.

A forensics team was in the storage room when the young police officer and I walked back into the building. I recall how the flash of a camera brightened the room as we passed it. My urge had been to pause there, to listen to the team's murmured comments, and see more clearly that space where Tiffany's body had lain.

The officer—I was starting to think of him as my personal officer—would have none of that. He herded me along like a sheltie nipping at the heels of a reluctant sheep.

The police had taken over Zoe's office. ''When I heard where this happened, I figured it might involve you,'' was Tony's comment when he saw me. He'd seemed about to add ''again'' to that sentence—I've been involved in several other homicide investigations—but he was kind enough not to do it in front of the other policeman, who was still hovering.

After telling Tony how I'd discovered the body, and then backtracking to tell him about Tiffany's fight with the van driver, and about that same man's presence in the alley, Tony had glanced at his watch.

''I have to talk to a couple of other people, but if you'll wait around a few minutes I'll drive you home,'' he said. ''That will give us more of a chance to discuss this.''

He turned to my policeman escort. ''You've gotten the names, addresses, and phone numbers of all the women who were in the shop?''

''Not . . .''

''Well then you'd better get on it. I don't want any names to get lost in the confusion. Eventually we're going to have to interview everyone who was here.''

''Yes, sir. After that maybe I should start questioning people in the buildings that look out on the driveway.''

"Right, but first the people in the shop."

The young policeman followed me back into the salon.

The royals were considerably more subdued than they'd been earlier. They had circled their wagons, so to speak, around the baroness, who had originally discovered Tiffany's body, and who was now back on the pink brocade settee she'd occupied before joining the stampede from the salon. The rest of the group, princess and Zoe included, surrounded the lady, generally being sympathetic.

Kitty, Courtney, and the others in our party had commandeered the chairs in front of the coffee table, and pulled a couple of extra chairs around to close their own circle.

Courtney was more upset than the rest, quaking as tears rolled down her face. Kitty, shiny-eyed, comforted her daughter while Taylor and Alex, who both had puffy red noses, took turns thrusting tissues into each other's hands.

Stacey wasn't reacting so moistly to Tiffany's death. She was balanced on the edge of a chair across from Kitty. On her lap was the cream-colored gown she'd admired earlier. I watched her flip the neckline to examine the dressmaker's tag, study it, and then look toward Kitty as if poised to ask a question. I could well be wrong about this, but Stacey seemed about to bring up the subject of the bridesmaids' dresses. It was sheer chance that our eyes met. She looked away immediately and, with me still watching, stood, hung the dress back on the rack and returned to the group.

Maryann was in a chair slightly apart from the others. There was nothing unusual about that, nor was there anything out of character about her behavior. Her briefcase was propped open on her lap, and I noticed that her tape recorder was tucked behind the strap that secured it. After leafing through some papers in the case, she fingered the machine as if considering getting some work done. Then, apparently reconsidering, she slammed the briefcase shut.

Stacey had settled back into a chair. "Isn't this terrible?" Though she wasn't crying, she swiped at her eyes with the back of her hand.

"Yes, it's terrible," I agreed, though for all I knew she could have been referring to the gown which was temporarily out of her grasp.

"Poor Tiffany," sobbed Courtney.

Either Taylor or Alex said, "I can't believe it."

"Can't you?"

Everyone pretended they didn't hear Maryann's comment, except for Kitty, who frowned at her older daughter and said softly, "Please."

"Sorry. I'm just wondering how long we're going to have to stay here."

I nodded toward the police officer, who was making his way through the other group. "As soon as he gets your names and addresses, you can go."

Maryann immediately rose and headed for the policeman. Nothing, including a murder, was going to get in the way of her billable hours.

"And that was it," I said to Amanda. "Tony was ready to leave, and here I am."

"Maybe Maryann did it," Amanda said. "She had every reason to hate Tiffany. But then, so did everyone else."

I shook my head. "There's a suspect. The cops are looking for him now. He and Tiffany had a fight over a parking space. . . ."

The phone rang. A second later Tony called from downstairs, "For you, Amanda. It's Mrs. Dunn."

Hearing that, Amanda raised her hands, crossed her fingers, and chanted, "Please, please let everything be all right."

Everything was far from all right, but as Amanda spoke to Kitty I began to realize that a little thing like a murdered bridesmaid wasn't going to get in the way of Courtney's wedding. Still, there was no getting around the unpleasant subject, at least at first, and Amanda did her part.

"So horrible," she said into the phone. "Tiffany's poor parents. They must be devastated."

From the way the conversation progressed I could tell that Kitty was keeping up her end. It wasn't too long, though, before a slight but noticeable smile brightened Amanda's face.

"Yes," she said. "Bonnie did tell me about the dress Courtney found. It sounds perfect. We're so lucky it's in stock.'' After hesitating for a second to listen, she continued. "And Bonnie also mentioned a cream-colored bridesmaid's . . .''

Getting up from the corner of the bed where I'd been sitting, I waved goodbye. Amanda flicked her hand my way, but otherwise ignored me. I had reached the bedroom door when she said, "We'll have to get the girls back to Zoe's for fittings right away. I'll call Zoe and make an appointment. My obstetrician insists I stay in bed for a couple of . . . Oh,'' she said after a pause, "you didn't know. Yes, my first. We're thrilled. But don't worry about the wedding. Bonnie will help out. It's too bad everything couldn't be done today, but—''

"—but unfortunately one of the girls got her head bashed in.''

I said that in the same airy tone Amanda was using, which may have been what diverted her momentarily from her client.

"Excuse me one second,'' she said to Kitty before putting her hand over the mouthpiece.

"You have to be realistic, Bonnie. Nobody liked Tiffany. Nobody at all.''

"What about her poor 'devastated' parents?''

Ignoring me, Amanda returned to the important business at hand: a veil for Courtney? Of course. But what kind of headpiece? A tiara? "Kitty? Do you suppose she'd like an ornament of flowers woven into her hair? That's always lovely, and Flower Power does a beautiful job—''

"By the way—'' My voice was pitched loud enough to make Amanda look up. "Bonnie isn't going to be helping out anymore. No way. Bonnie quits!''

"It'll probably be two years before I get laid again,'' said Tony. "I'm not kidding.''

I didn't suppose he was, though considering Amanda's condition, sex hadn't disappeared entirely from their marriage. I didn't want to discuss their marriage with Tony, though, and I especially didn't want to discuss their sex life. The subject can easily turn into a minefield. I changed it abruptly.

"Any ideas about how Tiffany was killed?"

"You know we won't have the medical examiner's report for a while."

"But what's your guess?"

"My guess? My guess is that somebody bashed her head against the concrete wall near the storage room door. There's evidence of what looks like blood there. Another guess—You want to hear another guess?"

"Sure."

"She had that mess of long hair. Someone could have gotten a good grip on it and swung her into the wall. Build up a lot of force that way. There wasn't much external bleeding," he added, "but the ME may find a lot of internal damage."

"And then the murderer hid the body behind the gowns?"

"Possibly. Or maybe the blow to the head didn't kill the victim. She could just have been weakened or unconscious. The perpetrator could have shoved her onto the floor and finished the job by smothering her with that plastic garment bag."

"The woman who found the body kept saying Tiffany had been raped. If she was weak . . ."

Tony shook his head. "She'd be the first rape victim I've ever seen whose undergarments hadn't been disturbed." He glanced at me across the car seat, and then looked back at the road. "Did the victim have any enemies that you knew of?"

"I told you about the van driver."

"Besides the van driver. What about the bride's sister? Amanda mentioned last week that there was some kind of trouble. And didn't Mrs. Dunn have a problem with her?"

I told Tony about the two incidents where Tiffany had purposely embarrassed the Dunns, and also about what Tiffany had said to me not long before she was killed. *They all hate my guts. If I ever end up with my throat slashed, tell the cops to take a hard look at the wedding party.*

"But did you see those Dunn women?" I asked. "They're not exactly the type."

"What type is that?"

"The type to slam someone's head into a wall, and maybe finish the job with a garment bag."

Lifting his shoulders, Tony said, "You never can tell."

"But what about the van driver? Have you learned anything?"

Tony nodded—"Yeah"—but was diverted by a slow-moving car ahead of us in the passing lane. He turned on the revolving light on his dashboard, which must have scared the devil out of the other driver. The man, who was maneuvering a big brown four-door gently over the potholes that dot the highway, hurriedly pulled into the right lane.

Once he had sped past the brown car, Tony went on. "I put one of my men on him right away. He's already talked to him."

"And?"

"The guy says he wasn't there."

I made one of those back-of-the-throat noises that translates, roughly, into "Baloney."

"He admits to the fight over the parking space, but claims he found a parking place on the street around the corner. Says he never turned into the driveway, that no super or maintenance man opened any gate for him, and that he never drove into any alley."

As Tony pulled off at the Huntington exit, he glanced across the front seat again. "You weren't wearing your glasses, were you, Bonnie."

He intended that as a statement, I think, and not as a question. Whichever, I took it as an insult.

"I saw him very clearly, in bright daylight."

"Were you wearing your glasses?"

This time it was a definite question.

"No, but . . ."

"Did you see him get out of the van?"

"No."

"Could you see the Cutter's Plumbing logo on the van from where you were?"

"No," I admitted, growing less sure of myself.

"Could you see a camouflage shirt on the driver sitting in the van?"

"Well, no."

"So all you really saw in the alley was the front of a white van and someone driving it. Half an hour earlier what you'd seen was the back and side of a white van. When you were on Madison Avenue, you never saw the front of the van at all. Am I correct?"

"Umm." He was right, but I was still convinced it was the same van driven by the same man.

"What about checking with that porter? Has anyone . . ."

"Gee," Tony said, tapping his forehead with the heel of his hand. "Thanks for reminding me. Otherwise I might have forgotten about him."

"Sarcasm does not become you, Tony."

"Okay. Then I'll stop it. Yes, someone talked to the porter. He was the only one in the building. It's empty, and about to be renovated. The porter says he only opened the gate once today, and that was for a trash collection service. He claims he never heard of Cutter's Plumbing."

I shook my head. "I was so sure."

"To put your mind at rest, Bonnie," Tony said, "this driver who had the parking space fight with Tiffany McKinney is named Robert J. Annessi. Allegedly called Bob by the dozens of people he swears will vouch for his good character. Annessi's thirty-four, lives on City Island with his wife and three kids. He's worked for Cutter since he was twenty. No prior arrests. Not even a speeding ticket. Annessi and his family live with his in-laws. He has a ten-year-old Honda, three maxed-out credit cards, and a bank loan for an aboveground pool. One of his kids has Down's Syndrome and goes to a special school."

"Hmm."

"Annessi's father-in-law has Alzheimer's. The family can't afford to put him in a home, so Annessi's wife helps her mother take care of him."

The Annessi family sounded like candidates for a *Times* Christmas season Most Deserving column. Accusing him of murder, I sounded like a real bitch. I clutched, desperately, at the one thin straw left to me.

"What about that jungle fighter outfit he was wearing?"

Tony shrugged. "The guy can wear anything he wants. Annessi apparently had a brother injured in Operation Desert Storm. Maybe the camouflage belongs to him."

Patriots yet!

Tony pulled up in front of Sam's house and turned down the cup of coffee I offered him. As I was opening the car door, it occurred to me that he hadn't said anything about the Dictaphone I'd found in the weeds.

"That was Tiffany's tape recorder that I found in the alley, wasn't it?"

"Looks that way."

"What about a tape?" I asked. "Did one turn up?"

He shook his head. "Not so far, and keep quiet about that."

"Why?"

"We're not going to release anything to the public about the tape recorder, or the possibility of a missing tape. It's always a good idea to keep a few things quiet. You never know when you might need them."

"Okay," I said, "but you should know that there was something wrong with her recorder. It was hard to get the tapes out."

"So?"

"So why didn't the murderer take the entire machine, rather than struggling to remove a tape?"

"Who knows," Tony responded. "Just don't mention it anyway."

"All right." I pushed the door open.

"Hey, Bonnie."

Tony put his hand on my shoulder.

"I've been telling you about this case for a reason. There's something I'd like you to do."

Turning to face him, I braced myself. Tony had been awfully forthcoming, but I expected his usual, "Stay out of police business" speech.

"You're probably going to be spending a lot of time with the Dunns. Keep your eyes open. Let me know if you find out anything you think would interest me."

I was flabbergasted and probably looked it. Maybe I looked excited, too, because Tony quickly qualified what he'd said. "Don't play detective. That's not what I want. All I want you to do is be your usual observant self."

If Robert J. Annessi, a candidate for sainthood, hadn't killed Tiffany, who had? In less time than it had taken Tony to say "Don't play detective," my usual observant self was putting together a mental list of suspects.

Any of the women who had been in Zoe's Bridal Salon could have followed Tiffany into the back of the store and, realizing that they were unobserved back there, could have grabbed Tiffany by her hair and swung her into the wall.

Yes, any one of the women might have had the opportunity to kill Tiffany but when it came to a motive, that was another matter entirely. Sure, Tiffany could be awfully confrontational, and it wasn't hard to imagine anyone getting into a fight with her, but the salespeople, including Zoe, hadn't had time to decide they couldn't stand her, and as for the royals, they hadn't even met her.

Which left the bridal party.

It was possible that either Stacey, Alex, or Taylor might have been more closely linked with Tiffany than I realized, but they scarcely entered my mind that evening. Neither did Courtney. I'd seen her lose her temper when dealing with Tiffany, but that had been a short spat, quickly ended. There hadn't appeared to be any ongoing anger on either side. On top of that, Courtney hadn't had the time to kill her cousin. She'd been center stage at Zoe's almost continually.

Maryann Dunn was another matter. She had a disagreeable disposition to start with, and Tiffany had done something truly nasty to her. Would Maryann harbor a grudge to the point of killing Tiffany?

And then there was Kitty Dunn. Elegant, sophisticated Kitty. She hadn't made it into Elsie Scott's gossip column, but Tiffany had still managed to cause her painful social embarrassment.

Contacting Elsie Scott isn't something I do on a whim, but she seemed as good a place as any to start. Later that night, while Sam was in the shower, I called Elsie at home. I didn't try to pretend this was a friendly social call. I'm not that good an actress. Elsie wouldn't have believed me, anyway. People don't call her for friendly chats.

"I'm curious about what went on when you and Tiffany McKinney had lunch," I said. "How did you get her to talk so openly?"

"Why do you want to know?"

Elsie doesn't give without getting. Though it seemed unlikely, it was possible she didn't know about Tiffany's murder. I decided not to mention it. When dealing with Elsie, it's wise to hang on to any carrot you might be able to dangle.

"I've gotten to know Tiffany pretty well," I began, "and—"

"Oh, Bonnie. Don't insult my intelligence."

"What do you mean?"

"You're still doing it. I don't know why you try. I was at the paper when the report came in over the wire."

There went that carrot.

"So why are you asking about our lunch? Oh, I've got it," Elsie continued, not giving me a chance to come up with a response. "You were there. At that bridal salon. Right?"

"Well, yes, and—"

"So who do you think did it? One of the Dunn girls? Is that why you're snooping around asking questions?"

"I'm not snooping, Elsie. I'm . . . curious."

"Humph! Remember when I was curious about the Ambassador Hotel? Remember how I asked you for a tiny favor. How I wanted to take just a teeny look around room eight thirteen? Remember that? And remember how you wouldn't help me?"

If Elsie Scott is ever found dead under suspicious circumstances, the police can come question me. It's possible I won't have done it, but by God! I want to be one of the first to know, and I want to hear every gory detail.

"Where I come from," she said, "we believe in tit for tat."

Tit for tat? That was one I hadn't heard since about fifth grade. There was no dealing with this woman. We hardly spoke the same language. She was going to be going "Naaa naaa naaa naaa naaa" at me next.

"Fine."

I was getting ready to cradle the phone when she sent a zinger through the wire.

"And you know what, Bonnie? There was a lot more that Tiffany wanted to tell me. She called me last Friday and wanted to meet with me. She said she had—"

I put the phone firmly to my ear.

"—brand new information about the Dunns. Tiffany said some of this was . . . 'hot.' "

"But she didn't give you any details about this 'hot' information?"

"Not in so many words. She did drop hints, though. We talked about having lunch one day this week, and then visiting the hotel, but we hadn't firmed anything up."

Hot information? The fact that Kitty had been a waitress in Florida was already old news, and even when it had been new news, only someone with a thoroughly lukewarm life would have considered it 'hot.' I had a feeling that if Tiffany considered something hot, it was probably scalding.

Across the hall, the water had stopped splashing in the shower. Sam would be back in the bedroom any minute now. He didn't like it when I became involved in police investigations, even when the police requested my involvement. "Meddling," he had called it during a heated discussion we'd had the last time I'd helped solve a crime. If I was going to fling myself into investigating Tiffany's murder without Sam knowing about it, then I had to do it quickly.

What it came down to was this: Elsie had hints, and I had access to the Ambassador Hotel.

"Elsie? If I were to take you on a tour of the Ambassador . . ."

Seconds later she was telling all, or at least more.

"I didn't have to pry the day Tiffany and I went to lunch. She simply opened up to me. People often do, you know."

I'll bet! "And you didn't do any digging, or maybe bribe her with something?"

I was pretty sure what Elsie's answer would be, but I had to be certain.

"Bribe? Hardly, Bonnie. Tiffany even paid for our lunches, and promised that she'd show me around the Ambassador herself, as soon as she got a chance."

Aha. It seemed as if Tiffany might have been using Elsie, something Elsie would never admit was possible.

"It was one of the easiest stories I've ever gotten," Elsie said. "Not that the Dunns' family problems are especially interesting to my readers, but heck! It was a slow week for celebrity gossip. I'm not going to look a gift horse in the mouth."

"And what about the hints she dropped last Friday when she called you."

"Oh, no you don't," Elsie said. "Remember? Tit for tat. I answered one of your questions. I'll answer the next one when we're inside The Ambassador Hotel. And not on the ground floor, either. I want to see room eight thirteen."

She had figured, correctly, that I might try to get away with trotting her through the lobby. The crafty devil.

As soon as Elsie and I had hung up, I called Amanda and signed back on as her assistant. She was happy about that. Too happy. She offered to cut back on my workload. It seemed that she and Courtney had already chosen a band, and had decided to leave the flowers to Flower Power. As for the dresses . . .

"Zoe is going to stay open late on Wednesday so Kitty and the girls can have their fittings. You don't *have* to be there if you don't want to."

By then I'd blown Tony's request completely out of proportion. If I wasn't with Kitty and the girls, how would I keep an eye on them?

"I *want* to be there," I insisted. "They might need me."

If Amanda wondered what had caused this sudden enthusiasm for the job, she didn't mention it.

"That's up to you," she said. "Since I'm supposed to stay off my feet as much as possible, I think the best way for us to work is . . ."

We decided on a division of labor that suited me and my purposes fine. Amanda would handle most of the things that

could be done by phone—the menus, the limousines—
while I would do the things that required legwork. She and
I would speak several times a day. "Phone conferences,"
she called our anticipated conversations.

"That way," Amanda said, "there won't be any problems. Everything will run smoothly."

I thought she sounded more confident than the situation
warranted, but didn't say so.

"One thing you're going to have to do," she added, "is
meet with the caterer who's handling the rehearsal dinner
and the reception. He wants to see the reception space. You
should meet him at the Ambassador around seven-thirty
Wednesday evening. His name is Jeffrey Phipps. Whatever
you do, Bonnie, treat him with kid gloves and don't antagonize him. Jeffrey is terribly temperamental. Just last week
he threw an entire blancmange at the chairwoman of the
museum . . ."

This wedding planning wasn't turning out to be quite as
dainty a profession as I'd imagined.

10

THE AUTOPSY OF TIFFANY'S BODY, which had been detailed in the morning papers, revealed that Tiffany had been stunned, but not killed, by the blow to her head. It was the plastic garment bag over her face that had killed her.

No matter. The wheels of commerce at Dunn Construction's Seventy-fourth Street office kept turning. I got there shortly after most of the employees had returned from lunch. Phones were ringing, fingers were clacking against keyboards, and two fax machines were churning out reams of paper.

Violet had eaten at her desk, as was her habit. When I rounded the partition that gave her a semblance of privacy she was just finishing her sandwich. Tuna. The smell permeated the cubicle.

Rendered momentarily speechless by the look of total indifference she gave me, I glanced out the window that overlooked the street. The driveway behind Zoe's Bridal

Salon was in plain view, and with one step forward I was able to see Zoe's back door. Unfortunately that one step forward brought me right to the edge of Violet's desk, a spot I would just as soon have avoided.

She was still staring at me vacantly. I cast around for an innocuous comment.

"Tuna's one of my lunch staples, too."

Though Violet's expression didn't waver, my comment seemed to ruin what was left of the sandwich for her. She dropped the bit of remaining crust onto a napkin, then wadded the napkin up and tossed it into the trash can beside her desk.

"I mailed all the invitations out last Friday, if that's what you're worried about," she said.

"Thank you, but I wasn't at all worried." In fact, I hadn't given the invitations a thought since dropping them off.

Violet nodded, perhaps assuming that I was complimenting her work ethic rather than confessing my own slovenly approach to this job.

"I'm sorry about Tiffany," I said.

For a second it seemed she hadn't heard my comment. Her eyes were focused beyond her partition and across the room. Glancing that way, I realized that she was staring at a young blond secretary who was at the desk directly outside Herbert Dunn's office. The young woman was huddled over her phone, cupping the mouthpiece to her lips, her eyes smiling.

"She's been on a personal call for twenty minutes," Violet said, not taking her eyes off the other woman. "She's a temp. They're useless." She shifted her gaze to me. "And of course I'm sorry about Tiffany, too. I can't be a hypocrite, though. I warned her."

"Of what?"

"I told Tiffany she was asking for trouble, the way she went out on construction sites with all those men around and her skirts up to you-know-where. She was asking for it, you know. Sometimes people get what they ask for."

It was doubtful that the length of Tiffany's skirt had gotten her killed. However, I saw no point in pursuing the subject with Violet, who was turning out to be a little too sanctimonious for my taste.

"I understand that I can get the keys to the Ambassador Hotel from you."

The almost invisible threads of hair that served Violet as eyebrows drew together into one long, suspicious streak. I didn't owe her an explanation, but rather than let her think I planned to relieve the Ambassador of its valuables, I provided one.

"Later today I'm meeting the caterer there to look over the ballroom. The construction crew will probably have gone, and I understand that the night watchman doesn't get there until about eight."

Violet took a key from her top drawer and unlocked the cabinet beside her desk.

"Here you are. This one"—she indicated a big key with a square back—"opens the street door. The other big one opens the door inside the vestibule. The public rooms on the first floor won't be locked," she added.

"And how about the guest rooms? Or are they open?"

One of her eyebrows tilted up a millimeter. "You need to get into a guest room? Only the ones on the top floor are finished."

I couldn't very well tell her that a gossip columnist would be joining me at the hotel. "We're going to want some changing rooms for the bridal attendants. I want to check out a couple of them."

It sounded reasonable to me, and must have made sense to Violet too, because when she handed me a master key for the guest rooms, her eyebrow had returned to its normal position.

"Thanks," I said. "I'll give them back to you after the wedding."

"Fine," she responded.

She was once again looking past me, and her lips had drawn together into a scowl. Following her gaze once more, I saw that Herbert Dunn's blond secretary was not only still on the phone, but was now filing a fingernail.

"They'll probably offer her Tiffany's job."

If anyone else had said that, I would have considered it

black humor, but with Violet there was no humor intended.
I got out of her cubicle even more quickly than I ordinarily
would have.

The cubicle that had been Tiffany's was between Violet's
workspace and the office's main door. It was unoccupied,
but the computer had been turned on. I'd been planning to
leave the office, but the sight of the screen saver raining all
those pink piglets made me pause.

Stepping into the cubicle, I tapped a key on the computer's keyboard. The piglets disappeared, replaced by rows
of columns. Many things confuse me, but for some reason
most computer software doesn't. This was part of the project management program Tiffany had shown me during
my earlier visit to the office. I scrolled to the top of the
document, and saw from the heading that this was the
schedule for the renovation project going on in the South
Bronx. Escaping to an earlier menu in the program, I found
a listing of other Dunn projects that Tiffany had been tracking. The Ambassador Hotel was on the list, but I didn't
access the file. It had nothing to do with me, or so I thought
at the time.

Shifting in the chair that had been Tiffany's, I looked
out the window at the back of the cubicle. Like the window
near Violet's desk, it had an unobstructed view of the alley
behind Zoe's Salon. I sat there so long, staring out the
window, that when I looked back at the screen the piglets
had returned.

How cute they were, with their fat pink bellies, but had
Tiffany been thinking "cute" when she installed the screen
saver? Or had she been thinking "pig," as in greedy or
perhaps dirty. With Tiffany it was hard to say.

What a contradictory person she'd been. Sneaky and con-
niving, and yet, with me at any rate, upfront about the rotten things she was doing. And her appearance! A mess, but
yet she had a good enough head on her shoulders to do a
responsible job for a big-money company.

Another contradiction was Tiffany's reaction when Neil
Howard had asked her out. What had caused her to hesitate
when the "awesome babe" had come through with a bona
fide invitation? What was the "homework" she'd done? In

the end, weren't awesome babes like Neil the reason for the Lycra skirts and the stiletto heels? Otherwise why bother? She might as well have worn sweats and running shoes. Sex symbol paraphernalia isn't all that comfortable.

Thinking about it, maybe we're all contradictory creatures. I don't have the money or the inclination for social climbing, but I do have my pretensions. About theater and some forms of dance I can be a tremendous snob, and though I'd made fun of the Dunn women's penchant for non-color clothes and furniture, given a trust fund and a personal shopper, I might become one of those non-color women myself. But the thing is, given the right kind of party, I'd still have to fight the urge to wrap a turquoise sash around my middle, dangle feather earrings from my earlobes, and do the hootchy-kootchy on a tabletop.

Where is this leading? To this: while my idea of a hellishly embarrassing evening would have been to attend the City Ballet opening with Tiffany McKinney, I could still imagine the two of us hitting a couple of First Avenue bars after a day at the office, and getting a little tipsy together and revealing bits of our past to each other. That's because, in her gritty dedication to doing her job well, and—heaven help me!—even in her appearance, Tiffany McKinney sort of reminded me of where I'd come from, and also of where I still might end up.

I had started crying. Not openly sobbing, but my eyes had blurred until the piglets seemed to fall across the monitor in continual pink streams.

"Hey! Look at you. Bonnie? That's your name, isn't it? I know you're working on Courtney's wedding. You want to come in here for a second?"

A moment later I was on my feet, and a hand on my shoulder was steering me into a private office.

I looked at Pookey Dunn through a waterfall of tears. As he pushed me toward a chair, though, my eyes were already drying. In spite of his dimples, his pillowy middle, and his puffy lips—even in spite of his silly name—Pookey didn't have that piglet thing that had moved me to tears in Tiffany's cubicle.

Nevertheless he was kind, and that goes a long way with

me. The first thing he did was close the door behind us; then he handed me a nicely pressed and folded white linen handkerchief. Under ordinary circumstances I try not to go to pieces in front of virtual strangers, but these circumstances weren't ordinary. After a few more sniffs I shook the sumptuous fabric free of its folds and dabbed at my eyes.

"I never cried when I found her body."

Pookey took a chair next to me rather than the boss chair on the other side of his desk. A nice human touch, although it put him a little closer to me than I was comfortable with.

"Go ahead," he said sympathetically. "Have a good cry."

My reluctance to cry in front of an audience had kicked in. Muttering that I was all right, I refolded the handkerchief. It no longer looked freshly laundered, but I laid it on his desk anyway.

"I'm okay. It was just for a minute or two there . . ."

"That's all right. I've been doing that sort of thing for the last day and a half. Tiffany and I may have argued a lot, but it was all good-natured. We were buddies. I loved her like a sister."

And probably groped her like a cousin, if what Tiffany had said was true.

Pookey's face was only inches away from mine. I tried to move slightly in my chair, and one of his legs brushed my knee. He appeared not to notice, but I was sure that he did. A heroine in a romance novel with a liking for men bordering on pudgy might have found herself turning pink and growing breathless, but I'm no romantic heroine. Straightening, I pushed my chair back until I was able to move my knees without touching his, and stood.

"You know that project management program on Tiffany's computer?"

If Pookey was surprised by this change of direction, he didn't let on.

"She had started explaining it to me," I said. "It doesn't seem that complicated. Since I'm in this neighborhood almost every day, I was wondering if I could stop by here occasionally and use the program to keep track of the wedding. I could take care of wedding correspondence, too,'' I added, although what that correspondence would consist of I didn't have the foggiest idea.

"I don't see why not," Pookey said.

"Thanks. The way things are now, I keep jotting notes on scraps of paper, and end up losing half of them."

"Then feel free to stop by whenever you want. We open about nine, and someone's usually around until seven or eight at night. If you don't have time to do your own typing, you might be able to give it to one of the secretaries. I hear Violet's been helping you."

He didn't offer me a key to the offices, but at least I now had access. You can pick up all kinds of information around an office, and a lot of it doesn't have anything to do with the work supposedly being done there. Spending a few hours a week at Dunn Construction, I might pick up bits of gossip about the family, or learn more about Tiffany's background, or find out what made the decidedly weird Violet tick. I could even keep an occasional eye on that driveway. Perhaps the maintenance man who swore he had only opened the gate for a trash collection service would show his lying face, or maybe the saintly Bob Annessi, or whoever that guy in the van was, would pay a return visit.

Or maybe none of this would happen. A few hours a week doesn't constitute serious surveillance. At the very least, though, even if I didn't pick up one iota of valuable information, I'd be able to get my notes about the wedding into some order.

It looked as if Amanda had been right. During the fittings at Zoe's I was not needed.

There was nothing partylike about the atmosphere in the fitting room on the second floor of the salon. The subject of Tiffany's murder was gotten out of the way early. "Terrible," everyone agreed in hushed voices, after which no one mentioned it again. The next hour and a half was spent on serious wedding-type business: put on the dresses, pin the dresses, get out of the dresses, choose the shoes and get out of the store. No one, but no one, wandered downstairs and through that white door to the rear of the shop. A part of me—the snoopy part that Tony LaMarca had asked to "keep an eye on things"—wanted to. All it would have taken was a mumbled excuse about using the restroom. Another part of me, though, the hysterical part that had pulled its blood-stained fingers from Tiffany's hair, was firmly in control. I stayed put on the second floor and, in a pretense at earning my keep, offered an occasional comment about a bust dart or a hem.

Maryann, who actually had a nice figure when she wasn't slumped over a mass of papers, was the first fitted and the first out of the place. During her brief time in the shop I heard her speak exactly two sentences to the people around her: "I have to get to a deposition, so fit me first" and "This is taking a ridiculously long time." Everything else she said—and she said quite a lot—was spoken into her hand-held tape recorder, which she had mastered to the point where she could flip a tape with one hand while tugging a gaping neckline with the other.

Kitty Dunn, having been fitted for a silvery mother-of-the-bride number and for that flapper-type dress I'd had my eye on, was next to leave the salon. She was in a rush—some committee couldn't start its meeting without her—but on her way out she bent over me and said softly, "The service and wake for Tiffany are tomorrow. Call Herbert's secretary and she'll give you the church's address. It's somewhere in Manhattan."

Which meant that my presence was desired at that unhappy event. Desired, but not required. I couldn't be forced to go. For a while I deliberated, but an hour later, when the rest of the fittings had been finished, right down to the pantyhose everyone would wear, I had decided to attend. Though my eyes had been wide open for signs of guilt and my ears primed for incriminating comments, I'd learned nothing new during my time at the salon.

Which of these women had gone to the back of Zoe's, ostensibly to use the restroom, on the day Tiffany was killed? Had any one of them disappeared for more than a minute or two? Had any one of them returned flustered and red-faced? Had any one of them noticed a dark stain on another's clothing?

Wouldn't that have been nice! If anyone had seen anything, though, it wasn't being discussed, and while it would have been interesting to play around with some paranoid notions about a conspiracy, common sense told me that the Dunns and their friends were reacting to Tiffany's death with an unconscious, upper-crust restraint. Simply put, personal matters aren't discussed in front of outsiders. Though they might gossip like crazy among themselves, and entertain all sorts of notions about Who Done It, I was going to have a real hard time getting through that wall of restraint.

Stacey and I were the last to leave the shop. She was too well-bred to say, Why are you still here? but when she walked from the dressing room in her street clothes and spotted me still parked on that chair, she did give me a curious look.

Standing, I said to the fitter, "Well, I guess that's it," as if the woman needed my permission to put her pins and measuring tape away.

"Are you going downtown? We can share a cab," I said, hoping that, separated from the others, Stacey might be more given to small talk.

She didn't reply. As I followed her down the stairs to the salon's ground floor, she was looking at her watch. Before I could repeat the question, one of Zoe's sales consultants had planted herself in front of me.

"Will you be seeing Mrs. Dunn? She left this behind the counter."

A black tote bag with a museum logo swung from the woman's hand. I hadn't planned to see Kitty until the following day, but at least this "task" sort of justified my presence in the store.

Stacey had glanced at her watch again, indicating that she was in a hurry. I looked into the tote to see if there was anything in it that Kitty might need immediately—a wallet or a prescription drug or the like. My quick examination revealed a packet of tissues, a perfume sample, a library book not due back for ten days, and a small umbrella. Nothing she couldn't do without for the next twenty-four hours.

Kitty's tote fit easily into my own. I asked the consultant

to call the Dunns and leave a message that I'd bring it to the funeral service the next day.

Stacey followed me onto the sidewalk. "Actually I'm going uptown," she said immediately. "Better run. I'm meeting a friend. See you."

She rushed off, heading north on Madison Avenue. Without really intending to, I found myself staring after her. She was dressed simply in a longish print skirt and flat shoes, but every man she passed looked her way.

11

"SO THERE YOU ARE," SAID ELSIE IN that scolding tone that grates on my nerves something fierce. "I've been waiting . . ."

After looking at her watch, she made one of those little *tsk* sounds to let me know I'd wasted even more of her valuable time than she'd realized.

". . . almost ten minutes."

"The bridal party fittings took longer than expected," I said, though they hadn't. The truth was, the idea of meeting with Elsie, even when I had something to gain from the meeting, had filled me with such distress that every store window I'd passed had pulled me like a magnet pulls a nail. I hadn't stopped with window shopping, either. The sales racks in a couple of those stores had been downright fascinating.

It was now just after seven, an hour since I'd left Zoe's shop. The sun was setting later every day, but we still hadn't reached those wonderful few weeks when daylight lasts far into the evening and then fades suddenly over the Hudson in glorious bands of red and gold. Some New York City residents of certain ages—mine included—were still stuck in that wintery emotional place where, at eight o'clock on weeknights they start looking around for their slippers and the *TV Guide*.

Looming above, the Ambassador's turret cast a long, eerie shadow on the street, and though lights showed on the bottom floor and in some of the higher windows, the old hotel was hardly inviting.

"I'm a very busy person, you know," Elsie said, refusing to let me off the hook.

"I'm busy too, Elsie. The caterer is due here at seven-thirty. You have exactly twenty minutes to see everything you want to see. And," I stressed, "to tell me everything Tiffany said to you."

She dogged my footsteps as I fitted the key into the lock on the hotel's street door. The door squeaked terribly when I pushed it open and entered the vestibule. Another few seconds and I had the inner lobby door open.

Elsie elbowed me aside, graceful as a rutting moose shoving aside a sapling.

"Oh," she gushed, "it's everything I expected."

Given the fact that a construction crew had been there every day since I'd first seen the hotel's lobby two weeks before, it was something less than I'd expected. The crystal chandeliers had been reinstalled and brass sconces replaced on the walls, but the wires that should have connected them to light switches poked unshielded from gaping holes. The marble floor was still chipped and dirty, and the varnish on the oak doors and trim was still grazed.

The dial above the elevator indicated that the car was on the eighth floor, something I might have paid more attention to had I planned on using the elevator. To me, though, the ancient contraption looked like certain death, and when it came time to get to the eighth floor the stairs would do me fine.

Elsie appeared overwhelmed to the point of ecstasy. Eyes shut, pie-shaped face raised to the heavens, or to the non-functional chandelier, she sighed.

"Aaaah. Their ghosts are speaking to me." For emphasis, she ticked her earlobe with her finger. "I hear the sounds of history. Stanford White is here, and Sara Bernhardt, and Samuel Clemens. Voices and footsteps from the past are all around us, Bonnie."

Breaking free of her trance, she stared at me. A second or two of that and I could sympathize with a germ on a glass slide under a microscope.

"If you listen very carefully, Bonnie, you might hear the voices, too. Those of us who don't heed the past are lost," she added.

If ghost voices aren't dead bottom on the list of things I want to heed, they are damned close to it. I nodded to placate Elsie, though. After she had closed her eyes and, I assume, resumed her tête-à-tête with history, I searched through my nylon tote and dug my note pad from beneath Kitty's canvas museum bag.

On one of the doors leading into the ballroom, someone had scratched an obscenity deep into the wood. I made a note of this for the Dunn crew working in the hotel, and once in the ballroom added notes about exposed wires and unpainted walls. The marble fireplace mantel still hadn't been replaced, and the old fixtures, frozen with rust, still secured the windows. Moving through the room, I noted everything that looked as if it needed fixing. I didn't have Tiffany's expertise, and I probably didn't have her flair with the construction workers either, but like it or not the success of Courtney Dunn's wedding was in my hands.

"If this fireplace could divulge its secrets," Elsie was saying, "we would have a chronicle of New York City. Deals were made here, fortunes earned and lost."

Arms extended, she performed a pirouette in the center of the room. She was an unlikely ballerina. A Lippizaner stallion would have done it better.

"This room has seen life, death—"

I interrupted before she could get started on birth. "Speaking of death, let's talk about Tiffany McKinney."

That ended the dramatic recital. Coming to an abrupt halt, Elsie crossed the floor and stopped in front of the huge fireplace. I couldn't see her face but I'm sure any number of disagreeable expressions crossed it during the several seconds that she seemed to contemplate the fireplace's cold walls.

"You're not going to get away with that, Bonnie," she said finally. "I'm not saying anything about Tiffany until I've seen room eight thirteen. That's the room of death, you know."

There had been at least three death's in that room, according to Elsie. The first had occurred in the early part of the century, when the French ambassador had discovered his wife in the room with her lover. The lover had lived to talk about it, but the ambassador's wife had ended up going out the window, either a suicide or a murder victim, depending on whose story you believed. The second violent death had also been the result of love gone wrong. An actor and his mistress had quarreled, and the actor, like the French ambassador's wife, had ended up splattered on the sidewalk eight floors below. The last death was that of an English rock star.

"He hanged himself in the closet."

"I remember that one," I said. "Nice change from going out the window."

"And so you understand why I must see that room, Bonnie. They say it carries the Ambassador's Curse."

" 'They' might have been stretching the truth, Elsie," I snapped. "I've never heard a single person say one word about room eight thirteen or the 'Ambassador's Curse.' "

Elsie faced me, arms crossed over her chest. The next thing I knew she had taken one step, and then another, and another. She was coming my way.

You must understand that when Elsie is bargaining, every position she assumes is well considered. Those crossed arms didn't indicate a defensive posture on her part. No way. They transformed her ample yet unattractive bosom into the fleshly equivalent of a medieval battering ram. As for her weighty steps echoing through the empty ballroom, they were the human equivalent of an axe chopping methodically into a log. Whomp! Whomp! Elsie Scott was going to see room 813 and anyone or anything in her way would end up in splinters.

Stepping aside, I allowed her to lead me to the ballroom door. Before leaving the room, she took a picture of it with a small, 35 mm flashbulb camera she carried in her hand-bag.

"I plan to use photos with my story," she explained.

"Just don't tell anybody how you got them."

"A good reporter *never* reveals her sources."

Five minutes later the good reporter's face was as red as my working-girl polyester dress.

"This is ridiculous!" she said, following me up the stairs. "The elevator seemed to be working fine when I pushed the button."

Maybe so, but even if the ghost of old Mr. Otis himself had stood at the bottom shouting encouragement, I wasn't desperate enough to use that elevator.

The Ambassador's upper floors, starting with the sixth, were in fair shape. The light fixtures were finished, and new carpeting, so thick that an army could have marched un-heard through the halls, had been laid. On the eighth floor, the landing had been decorated with ornate mirrors and chairs with delicately curved legs.

Upon reaching that landing, Elsie released her hold on the banister and collapsed into one of the chairs.

"My legs are quaking," she gasped.

My own legs were a little wobbly, too, but I wouldn't have admitted that for the world. Nor would I have gasped. I drew in a quiet breath before speaking.

"While your legs are recovering, tell me exactly what Tiffany said to you."

During our climb we had already determined that room 13 lay to the left of the landing on every floor. Elsie's eyes swung left and she braced her arms on the chair as if pre-paring to make a run for it. I shook my head.

"No way are you seeing that room before we talk about Tiffany."

Either I sounded tougher than I am or Elsie's legs were in truly rotten shape. She settled back down without a fight.

"Tiffany McKinney told me that the house of Dunn was going to fall like the House of Usher."

"Tiffany said that? It doesn't sound like her."

Elsie shook her head. "That's how I would have put it in my column. As a writer, I understand the importance of drama."

As a snoop, I understand the importance of accurate information. "What exactly did she tell you?" I asked.

"Nothing very much, actually," Elsie admitted. "She said there were things about the Dunns that nobody knew. 'Hot' information that was going to 'screw them bigtime.' That was how she put it."

"Screw them bigtime" sounded a lot more Tiffany-like than references to the House of Usher.

"But you said she had given you *hints*, Elsie. What exactly were those hints?"

I doubt if guilt is an emotion that often overtakes Elsie, but was that a guilty look that crossed her face before her gaze dropped? Had I brought someone whose company I could barely tolerate to a section of a hotel where I had no business being, for nothing? I began to fear that this was going to be a defeat for me.

"Elsie?"

Her eyes shifted toward the hallway on our left again. "There may have been—there was—one hint."

Ah, victory. I moved so that my body blocked her view down the hall. "Would you like to share it with me?"

She rolled her eyes as if she were dealing with the world's biggest pain in the neck. "The impression Tiffany gave me was that her 'hot' information didn't necessarily involve the Dunns as a family. I mean, it wasn't about adultery or drugs or nervous breakdowns or any of the other things my readers are interested in. My readers are very discriminating, you know."

"Then what was this so-called hot information about?"

"Business. Tiffany didn't come out and say it, but I'm sure she planned to reveal something about Dunn Construction that would hurt the business. I have a nose for news, Bonnie. When Tiffany said she planned to 'put the whole damned bunch of them out in the street, and maybe one of them in jail'—that's a direct quote—I said to myself, 'Aha! She's talking about the family business.'

"Now, Bonnie . . ." Standing, Elsie nudged her way past me. "Shall we move on?"

We started down the hall. "But that would have been self-defeating," I said. "After all, Tiffany worked for Dunn Construction too."

"Maybe ruining Dunn Construction meant more to Tiffany than her job. Some people don't have generous natures, Bonnie."

The master key slipped easily into the lock and the door to room 813 opened soundlessly. I half expected Elsie to start communing with the past again, but she must have felt pressed for time. Once I'd located a lamp on a dressing table, and figured out that you touched the brass base to light it, she immediately began snapping photos of the room.

Ghosts or not, I would have been happy to sleep in room 813. The carpet was the color of French vanilla ice cream and the wallpaper was a light floral print. The ornate furniture may have been through a lot, what with the violent guests who had stayed in this room, but it had been refinished to perfection and the dark wood glowed under the assault of Elsie's flash.

The pillows on the double beds were still wrapped in plastic and the mattresses draped with sheets. I tested one of the mattresses with my hand. A little firm, maybe, but I could have endured it.

There were two doors on the wall to our left. One opened onto a closet.

"This must be the bathroom," I said, opening the second door.

Elsie had focused her camera on that alternate route out of room 813—the window—and paid me no attention.

The door swung quietly, on well-oiled hinges. I stepped into the bathroom without flipping on a light switch.

The room was a little small, maybe, but the marble fixtures were sweet and old-fashioned, and the deep claw-foot tub looked like a great place for a long hot soak.

At the other side of the bathroom there was another door. Elsie hadn't said anything about a suite, but perhaps there was a living room. . . .

I opened that connecting door. No. It wasn't a living room. It was a second, smaller bedroom, lit by one lamp on a chest of drawers, with only one bed and . . .

What . . . ? Oh my! Oh no!

A little sound burst from my lips on a startled puff of breath. "Uh."

One or both of the people on the bed, who were partly covered by a sheet, responded almost as cleverly: "Wha . . . ?"

Talk about your coitus interruptus!

I stood stock still, gaping like an idiot for another second or two before pulling that door shut. As I hurriedly left the bathroom, I heard the lock click into place on the other side of the second door. If I hadn't been so undone, that might have been worth a giggle. The last thing in the world that Herbert Dunn and Stacey whatever-her-name-was had to worry about was a second appearance by me.

Once I got myself moving, I couldn't stop. Elsie was examining the inside of the closet. Why? Oh, yes. That English rock star . . .

". . . looped the strap from his guitar over the rod, and—"

I grabbed her arm. "We've got to go."

"I haven't seen the bathroom."

She tried to shrug my hand off. I not only held tight, but yanked her away from the closet and began steering her toward the door to the hallway. As we passed the bathroom she dug in her heels.

"There's nothing to the bathroom," I said.

"I want to see the connecting room."

Without my key she wouldn't have been able to get into it, but what if those lovebirds heard her rattling the doorknob? They didn't know there were two of us. They would think *I* was trying to pay a return visit. The notion was too horrible to think about.

"No. We have to leave right now! Go!"

Elsie is not as tall as I am, but she must outweigh me by thirty pounds. Nevertheless I was prepared to get into a full-fledged brawl if that's what it took to get her out of the hotel.

She glared at me, and perhaps something of the state I was in pierced her rhinoceros-hide skin. "All right. It's not necessary to shove," she added as I hustled her from the room.

Necessary or not, I shoved until we were on the stairs, and then hurried her all the way down to the first floor.

Our parting at the Ambassador's outer door was chilly. "Thanks for almost nothing," Elsie said.

She may not have heard my response—"Drop dead"— because she was already across the sidewalk.

Stepping back into the vestibule, I closed the street door and leaned against it. The run down the stairs, along with my anxiety, had left me breathless and sweaty. My back was damp and cold against the frosted glass.

Damn! Hell! I whispered all my usual profanities and some I don't normally use. One of New York's most sought-after, most temperamental caterers was on his way. I couldn't leave. Well, I could, but that wouldn't exactly amount to the kid-gloves treatment Amanda wanted this man to receive.

I was trapped with Herbert and Stacey, and they were trapped with me! I considered one horrible "What if?" after another. What if they thought I'd gone? If they'd looked out the window and seen Elsie leaving, that would be a reasonable assumption. What if they tried to leave and came face to face with the caterer?

Why did I care? Because I wanted Amanda's first job to be a success. Because I wanted to spare Kitty and Courtney, both of whom I had decided were okay people, public embarrassment. But I cared most of all because without this job there was no way I could keep an eye on the people who had been close to Tiffany McKinney.

I listened for the sound of the elevator rising, or of voices on the stairs. The old hotel was quiet. Was it possible Herbert and Stacey had picked up where they'd left off when I interrupted?

What was the matter with that old goat, anyway? He had to be well over fifty. That's too old for *me*. And what did Stacey see in him? He looked good for his age but let's face it: fifty-plus ain't twenty-something.

A knock right next to my ear sent me reeling away from the door. When I'd caught my breath, I positioned myself about four inches from the door frame. If Elsie was back, she'd never get past me. Gripping the knob, I cracked open the door.

"Ms. Indermill, I assume? Jeffrey Phipps."

He was wearing a white shirt with pleats and a red bow tie. His black jacket was open, and around his middle was a cummerbund. He could have been a member of the wedding party who had gotten the date wrong. I moved away from the door, allowing him to step into the vestibule.

He was tall and thin, with dark hair cut as if the barber—though I doubt that a mere barber had done this—had put a bowl on his head. Not a big mixing bowl. A little soup bowl. Jeffrey Phipps's bangs stopped about a half-inch down his forehead, and his ears were completely exposed. There was no hint of a sideburn or any other facial hair, except for a ratty goatee.

The effect was bizarre.

"Well, are you?"

"Are I what? Oh, yes. I'm Bonnie Indermill."

Tearing my eyes from the tuft of hair on his chin, I put out my hand. He shook it once, briskly, then marched through the inner door into the main lobby.

"No, no, no. This won't do."

"It's not finished."

"Not finished? It's hardly started. Typical. People expect me to handle everything. I want you to know, Ms. Indermill, that I handle food, linens, tableware, servers, and the wedding cake. And that is it! I do not do furniture, flowers, music, or"—he looked at the mess around us—"menial labor."

There was suddenly a loud clank from the other side of the lobby as the elevator began rising.

"The night watchman's upstairs," I said hastily. " He must be coming down. Maybe you'd like to see the ballroom?"

Phipps was staring at the ancient elevator—understandable, considering the awful racket the contraption was making.

"Is that thing safe?"

"Certainly. I must show you the ballroom." Hurrying up the half-dozen curved steps, I flung open the ballroom door.

He hadn't budged.

"NOW!"

That got him moving, but not in the right direction. Taking a step back, he put his hands on his hips.

"I am not to be spoken to as if I am a servant. I do not need this. I agreed to do this as a favor to Amanda La-Marca. *She*," he added, "is a lady."

The elevator was quiet now. The indicator on the dial above it had stopped on eight. Another minute and they'd be down.

Jeffrey Phipps was holding his ground. Barking commands wasn't going to work with him, and though he was hardly an Arnold Schwarzenegger type, he would probably put up quite a struggle if I tried dragging him into the ballroom. Since there was absolutely nothing with which I could bribe him, I was left with one option: groveling.

"I'm so sorry, Mr. Phipps. The pressure of this event is . . ."

High above us, the elevator clanked.

". . . ruining my disposition. Please forgive me. I've always admired your work. There's so much I can learn from you."

"I'm not here to teach, either," he snapped. "But all right. Your apology is accepted. And you may call me Jeffrey."

He joined me in the ballroom just as the elevator arrived in the lobby. I slammed the door so that Herbert and Stacey would know they were not alone. Unless they had screwed themselves witless—and if they had, after my surprise visit, they were about as sensitive as warthogs—they'd sneak out quietly.

"We must move with alacrity," Jeffrey said. "I have another appointment this evening. An engagement party. Austrian royalty. Long deposed, of course, but the family is still accustomed to the best."

Those royals again? It had to be the same ones. How

many engaged deposed Hapsburg princesses can there be running around Manhattan?

"The Dunns are important, too," I said, trying to score a point for American royalty. "Kitty Dunn is very particular."

"Kitty Dunn, particular? I can't imagine why. She's nothing but a waitress from Florida."

The street door opened, then closed with a bang. Whew! Jeffrey had just insulted American royalty, but I flashed him a big smile anyway, whipped out the instructions Amanda had given me, and proceeded to move with such alacrity that I surprised myself.

Twenty minutes later we had firmed up the menu for the reception—"Salmon yet again?" Sigh. "One does get so tired of it. And Cornish game hens? How original! Don't you dare suggest a salad of mesclun greens or I'll simply scream"—and table settings for the reception, inspected the hotel's kitchen—"This shambles *must* be put in order"— and agreed on a price—"A pittance, considering the circumstances."

Which circumstances? The quickie wedding or the half-finished hotel? Oh, I didn't care. I wasn't paying him. I signed my name on a contract which promised him an amount of money sufficient to support me in style for the rest of my life, and swore that a deposit check would be in the mail the next day.

"Have it delivered to me by messenger," Jeffrey ordered.

It had also been agreed that Jeffrey would handle the rehearsal dinner to be held at Pookie's home, but he preferred to wait for Amanda's input on that menu.

"Nevertheless," he cautioned, "prior to my preparing that dinner you *will* have a check for me to cover the unpaid balance. Otherwise I will not unpack so much as a stick of butter from my van. I have worked with these nouveau riche types for years. None of them can be trusted."

Oh, if he only knew.

The two of us were out of the Ambassador before eight o'clock. I would have been content never to see the wretched place again.

I flagged a cab at the corner. The words, "Penn Station," were already out of my mouth when I changed my mind. The day had exhausted me. At Penn Station there would be a long wait for the next train, followed by a long ride to Huntington. "No. I want to go to Washington Heights," I told the cabbie.

Twenty minutes later I walked into my apartment. After slipping off my shoes, I called Sam. He listened to my reasoning—that I was tired, that I had to be in Manhattan the next morning—quietly.

"So you'll be home tomorrow evening."

"Of course," I said. "The funeral service is at eleven. I should be home by three or four."

"Good. Oh, and Mrs. Dunn has been trying to get in touch with you. She called three times. Sounded worried. You have some tote bag of hers?"

I told Sam I'd call Kitty, and then told him I'd miss him. He said he'd miss me, too.

"And Bonnie? Don't forget that Rosaleen will be here this weekend. You might want to pick up some groceries."

"I'll do the shopping tomorrow," I promised.

"Okay," he said.

I thought he was going to hang up then, but he added, "I love you."

"I love you too, Sam," I said.

After we'd hung up, I experienced a rush of euphoria as strong as the rush I'd gotten from playing hooky in junior high school. Irrational though it was, I felt as if I were getting away with some mischief.

There was nothing to eat in my kitchen and nothing to drink but tea. I called the roach-hole Chinese carryout up the street and ordered a pint of cold sesame noodles, a pint of hot broccoli with garlic sauce, and a diet soda.

While I waited for my dinner I sipped tea at the table in front of my living-room window and enjoyed the view of the Hudson River. The night was crystal clear, and lights from the spans of the George Washington Bridge glanced off the water. There were lights at the marina over on the New Jersey side, too. In the winter I'm lucky to see a few barges or freighters on the river, but in the spring, cabin cruisers and tour boats, little sailboats and big schooners, begin to appear.

I was going to miss watching the river this year.

And forever.

From euphoric to maudlin in seconds. I was feeling downright miserable when I called Kitty Dunn.

"The Dunn residence."

The voice was unfamiliar. Probably the maid's.

"This is Bonnie Indermill. Is Mrs. Dunn there?"

"Yes, Miss Indermill. Mrs. Dunn's been trying to reach you."

Kitty must have been standing right beside the maid.

"Bonnie? I'm so glad you called," she said. "You got my message?"

"Yes," I said. "I didn't have time to bring your tote to your apartment, but it's safe."

"Of course. I knew it was safe with you. It's just that I was worried. Not worried, actually. There's nothing but a bunch of junk in it. I was a little concerned, though. You understand?"

I understood. A library book, an umbrella, a minuscule perfume sample. Not to mention the tissues. That's the kind of stuff you can't afford to lose, even when you're rich.

"Your tote is tucked into the bottom of mine. I'll bring it to the service tomorrow."

"It's inside yours. Good. We'll see you tomorrow then. Bye."

"Goodbye."

A buzz let me know that my dinner was downstairs. I pressed the button to let the delivery man into the building and then opened my door to wait for him. Across the hall the Codwallader sisters' television blared. A game show. As the sisters grow older, they play their set louder. A couple of apartments down a baby cried. New people. I hadn't met them yet. I couldn't hear anything of the soprano upstairs, but I would if I stayed here long enough. Death, taxes, and the soprano upstairs are inevitable.

The man who delivered my food was the man that the phrase "Just off the boat" was coined to describe. He bowed to me and stayed that way, as if genuflecting in front of a deity, during the exchange of brown paper bag for green dollars, and when I told him to keep the change, I could swear that he was truly baffled. He wouldn't be for long if he stayed in New York City.

Back inside I spread my dinner on the table. And then, I dug Kitty's tote from inside mine and dumped its contents onto the table alongside the little plastic bags of soy sauce and fortune cookies.

The sesame noodles were perfect—glompy, oily, pea-nutty. With enough soy sauce they went down like fois gras, like portabella mushrooms, like lobster. In the suburbs they just don't know how to make them. The broccoli was spicy and overcooked, just like I'd become accustomed to during my years in this neighborhood. My taste buds were in culinary paradise.

Once my physical hunger was sated, I ran my hand through Kitty's tote bag, going so far as to feel for a secret compartment sewn into its side. No secret compartment, no nothing. Next, bad luck or not, I opened the umbrella. No note fell into my lap, and no secret code had been jotted onto the nylon. As for the perfume, unless some fiendish chemist had found a way to make arsenic smell like Chanel No. 5, it was exactly what it appeared to be. So were the tissues.

Which left the library book. I'd glanced under the front cover earlier that day, but this time I did it more carefully, even looking behind the library card. After that I flipped through the pages.

I finally found the thing that Kitty was so concerned about, at the back of the book, tucked between the cover and the clear plastic dust jacket provided by the library.

It was a plain white envelope, addressed by typewriter to Mrs. Herbert Dunn at her home. Inside was a single piece of paper that had been folded three times like any ordinary letter. This was no ordinary letter, though. Between the folds of the paper was a photograph, slightly blurred and taken from a distance, but clear enough. There was Herbert Dunn, smiling at his female companion as they walked along a sidewalk bordered by sand and palm trees. Herbert and his companion were dressed for warm weather, he in shorts and a polo shirt, and she in a sundress. And the companion who smiled back at Herbert? Guess.

I tucked the photo back into the sheet of paper and slid it back inside the envelope, but before returning the envelope to its hiding place I examined the postmark. It had been mailed in Manhattan more than two weeks earlier, at about the time Amanda and I had met the Dunns. Herbert had mentioned just returning from Florida. What he'd neglected to mention was that Stacey had been with him.

It surely was Tiffany who had mailed this photo to her aunt. I'd heard her tell one of the construction workers at the Ambassador that she'd been in Florida, but I hadn't connected her trip with her uncle's. Tiffany had seemed more Fort Lauderdale than the Boca Raton type.

Offices being what they are, Tiffany wouldn't have had much trouble learning when Herbert was going to be visiting his home in Boca Raton without his wife. With a few calls to airlines, she could have discovered that Stacey planned to be in Florida at the same time.

Tiffany could have gotten herself to Florida in not much more time than it takes me to get from Long Island to my parents' place in New Jersey. After that, all she had to do was wait in the right place with a camera.

Kitty Dunn was no fool. After her recent experiences with Tiffany she must have suspected that this photo had come from her niece, and realized that it was only a matter of time before her husband's affair was made public. But would she have killed her niece to keep the details quiet? I couldn't see it.

12

THE NEXT MORNING, LOW GRAY CLOUDS hovered like a shroud over the city, threatening rain, and the air was cool. When giving me directions to the church, Herbert's secretary had assumed I'd be taking either a cab or a bus. I've known people who would sooner crawl than ride the subway, but I only take buses in the middle of the night and cabs in dire emergencies. When she told me the address, which was in the Inwood area, I realized that my subway line, the A train, stopped only a couple blocks away from the church.

Inwood, like all of upper Manhattan, is bisected by Broadway. Thirty years ago the neighborhood was almost completely Irish but these days most of the neighborhood's Irish contingent lives west of Broadway. On the east side of Broadway is a growing population of Dominicans. You can still find Irish bars in Inwood and hear Gaelic spoken, and there's still a shop that sells lace tablecloths and other Irish imports, but these days it's easier to find a plate of *arroz con frijoles* than a loaf of Irish soda bread, and Spanish is the lingua franca.

I exited the subway at 207th Street and Broadway and walked two blocks north to St. Margaret's. The wind had picked up since I'd left my apartment, and the old green trenchcoat I'd dug from one of my closets was no match for it. With most of my clothes at Sam's house, however, there hadn't been much choice. It was either the trenchcoat or a cherry-red blazer.

A small copper plaque mounted beside the church doors stated that it had been built and consecrated in the late 1920's. The late twenties were memorable for several things, including the Great Depression, but St. Margaret's didn't appear to have suffered from any financial stinting on the part of the builders. The stinting, I expected, had come much later. The massive blocks of stone that made up the outside walls were black with soot, and as I came nearer the building, I saw that portions of the stained glass windows had been replaced with something that looked suspiciously like plastic.

It was a big church for a neighborhood house of worship, so I wasn't surprised that it was only half full. Most of the attendees were seated near the front. I couldn't see many faces, but the NYPD was represented by the same young policeman who had hovered over me at the murder scene. He entered the church just after I did and remained standing next to the door through the entire service.

It was cold inside the church, not much more comfortable than it was outside. Wrapping my coat tightly around me, I sat in an empty pew near the rear.

A young priest, his English so tinged by an Irish brogue that I felt almost as if I'd been transported to Dublin, conducted the funeral mass. Midway through, when he stepped to the altar's side and began speaking about Tiffany's sweet disposition and her charitable nature, and alluded to her modesty—"In her manner and her dress, in the way she respected her family, her neighbors and her friends, Tiffany McKinney was a shining example of saintly womanhood"—I knew he'd never met the dearly departed.

When the service had ended I remained seated for a few

minutes. Curiosity. I wasn't surprised to see all of the Dunns there. Courtney, who was dabbing at her nose with a tissue, nodded my way, as did Justin, who was holding her other hand. Dry-eyed Maryann didn't acknowledge me and neither did Pookey, who walked past me with his wife, Maddie.

Kitty Dunn caught my eye but kept walking, while Herbert, who was beside her, saw me and looked away, an understandable response considering the experience we'd shared the evening before.

Behind the Dunns came a middle-aged couple dressed entirely in black. I guessed, correctly as it turned out, that they were Tiffany's parents. The woman was short, and graying brown hair peeked from under the scarf covering her head. The man who walked beside her was tall and red-faced, and what remained of his hair was light. There was a vague resemblance to Kitty Dunn in his high cheekbones, and maybe when he smiled, dimples would show up, but this was hardly an occasion for smiles. As he passed me he swayed slightly, as if his foot had slipped forward and he might topple back. Neil Howard, who was behind him, took his arm and held it until the older man was steadied, and as they left the church, Neil had a protective arm on the man's back. The kind gesture from the construction worker struck me as very sweet.

Neil himself looked awful, his red-rimmed eyes conspicuous against the pallor of his skin. For some reason, seeing him made me think of Violet, but I never did spot her in the crowd.

Stacey, in a stylish black hat with a short veil, came next, along with the two other bridesmaids. Stacey not only didn't look me in the eye, but when she passed she turned her head as if to examine the empty pews on the other side of the aisle. I followed the last of the congregants from the church.

Kitty was on the sidewalk talking with the middle-aged couple in black. I approached her as unobtrusively as possible and handed her the tote.

"Thank you, Bonnie. Have you met Tiffany's parents, Colin and Patricia McKinney?"

She knew, of course, that I hadn't met them. As she introduced us, she looped the straps of her tote over her arm with such apparent indifference that no one would have thought it had warranted three telephone calls the day before.

"You will be coming to the house, won't you?"

Patricia McKinney's question took me by surprise.

"We met so few of the friends Tiffany made once she went out on her own," she added.

Her husband, though not as composed as his wife, nodded. "Yes. Please join us."

"I wouldn't want to put you to any trouble," I said, glancing toward a coffee shop on the other side of the street. "Maybe I'll grab a bite of lunch and . . ."

"There will be plenty of food at the house," Mrs. McKinney assured me.

The wind wrapped my coat around my legs. A cold, misty rain had started to fall, and during the few moments we stood in front of the church it grew heavier. The only umbrella I'd had handy had now been returned to its rightful owner, and by the time I reached the subway I'd be drenched. It was something that Tiffany had said on the afternoon that she was murdered, though, that settled the matter for me: *Sometimes I feel like screwing Aunt Kitty big time. All I'd have to do is dig through some of my parents' old photo albums.*

A black limousine pulled to the curb. Kitty took my arm and said, "Here's our car. Courtney is riding with Justin, and I think Maryann brought her own car."

The chauffeur opened the limousine door, and as a wave of warmth from its interior washed over me, I smiled gratefully at the woman who just might be a murderer. Once I'd settled into a corner of the back seat, the soft leather seemed to mold itself around my body. This sure beat the A train.

Herbert, given the choice of sitting beside me or on the seat facing me, chose what he must have considered the lesser of two evils and sat across from me but at the other side of the car. Still, there was no way he could avoid looking at me, however briefly, as he stepped into the limo.

"We're glad you could make it today, Bonnie."

That said, he quickly discovered something else that held his attention. His fingernails.

Kitty slid across the seat until she was beside me, which must have made Herbert even gladder than he had been.

"Tiffany would have appreciated it," she said.

"Yes," Herbert agreed.

We pulled into traffic, and as the car made its way north on Broadway through a bleak stretch lined with filling stations and car washes, Herbert looked away from his hands to stare out the window, seemingly fascinated by the passing scene. After a few minutes of this he must have decided I wasn't going to squeal on him, at least not right then. He turned to Kitty.

"After I pay my respects I have to get going. I'll leave the car and take a cab."

"Fine."

Neither of them spoke another word until we reached our destination in Riverdale. The temperature in the limousine may have been toasty, but the atmosphere was glacial.

Although no one was going to mistake the house Tiffany had been raised in for a co-op on Fifth Avenue, it was hardly a shanty. It was two stories tall, with a high peaked roof, a small front porch, and a larger, screened-in side one. The yard that surrounded the house, though minuscule, was well-kept, as were the others in the neighborhood. The grass was green, hedges were clipped, and there were colorful spring blooms in flower beds and window boxes. The street itself, like many streets in the area, was shaded by tall trees.

Feeling a bit awkward, but not so awkward that I didn't want to be there, I followed Kitty and Herbert up a flagstone path and into the house. Inside, a man I didn't recognize took our coats and carried them out to the screened porch.

A small foyer led into a big combination living/dining room. In the living room, under a bay window that overlooked the street, a makeshift bar had been set up on a small table. Colin McKinney couldn't have been in the house for more than a couple of minutes, but he had already downed a good part of the drink in his hand. Kitty and Herbert both accepted his invitation to join him, as did Pookey, Neil, and most of the others who soon arrived. By then I was so hungry that a drink would have ruined me, and I shook my head when he offered me one.

While Colin mixed drinks, various women fussed around the dining room table. It looked as if there was enough food to feed everyone who had been at the service. Where the custom of the deceased's family entertaining the mourners originated beats me. If Amanda ever coordinates a wake— Do people hire consultants for that sort of thing?—maybe she'll do some research and fill me in.

I do know how wakes themselves originated. It seems that years ago people who were pronounced dead sometimes weren't. It must have been startling, to say the least, to be lowering Grandma into the grave and hear her pounding on the coffin's lid. And what about poor Grandma? What if she didn't snap out of her coma before the coffin was six feet under and covered with dirt? Just think about that. So began the ancient ritual of keeping watch over a dead body for a while, just in case. As rituals go, what with my fear of enclosed spaces, I find it a comforting one.

The McKinneys' doorbell kept ringing, and the house became more crowded. Everyone, except for me, seemed to know everyone else. Courtney was helping her uncle with drinks and Kitty had joined the women around the buffet. Herbert, moving with the efficiency I'd expect of a captain of industry, was already making his escape, patting shoulders, hugging, and inching toward the door.

I spent a few minutes wandering, unobtrusively as possible, around the first floor. There was a bookcase in the hall between the kitchen and a laundry room, but I didn't see anything like photo albums in it. Of course, the albums, assuming they actually were in this house, didn't have to be in a bookcase. They could be anywhere: on a table, in a drawer, under a bed. But not under the day bed in the little television room that I discovered during my wandering. I wonder what would have happened if someone had caught me in there on my hands and knees.

Back in the living room I sat down briefly, then gave up my chair to a man who was leaning heavily on a cane. I was feeling grossly out of place and beginning to wonder if I shouldn't follow Herbert's example and leave, when Colin McKinney thrust a drink at me, in a glass so big I could hardly get my hand around it. The liquid was deep amber and looked like undiluted bourbon. A lone ice cube clinked against the side of the glass.

It was only noon, too early by my standards, for even something like a wine spritzer. I was in a strange situation, though, and thoroughly uncomfortable. Lifting the glass, I took a long drink. Even before I'd managed to swallow, I knew it was a mistake. A waterfall of tears began gushing from my eyes.

"Oh, you poor thing. Take another drink. Try to calm yourself."

Colin McKinney pushed the glass to my mouth and I swallowed like an obedient child taking her medicine.

"You must have known my daughter well. She was such a darling girl."

The burning in my throat made any response other than a gasp impossible. Colin, misunderstanding, put his hand on my shoulder. "That's all right, dear. Monday afternoon when her mother and I got the call, we couldn't stop crying. Even now—"

His face, flushed to begin with, became inflamed. He flicked a finger at his eye, then wiped his nose on a cocktail napkin. "My daughter was such a darling. Did you know her from her work?"

Now I really did feel like crying. What in the world was I accomplishing by being here? Not only had I not found any photo albums, but I was misleading these kind people.

I shook my head. "I'm Courtney's wedding consultant."

He blinked, baffled, I suppose, by that statement. To get through an uncomfortable silence I took another long drink. This time the liquor was a little easier on my eyes but not on my throat or, for that matter, on my equilibrium. A second or two after it had made its fiery way down my esophagus, my legs seemed to weaken.

To my great relief some new arrivals had shifted Mr. McKinney's attention away from me. Setting the drink on a glass-topped table, I pushed through the crowd.

"Where is the bathroom?" I asked Courtney.

She nodded at the stairway. "You're better off up there. There's one behind the kitchen, but it's probably occupied. Are you okay, Bonnie? You look awful."

Shaking my head, which was growing lighter by the second, I made my way to the stairs and climbed them on legs that were as wobbly as two Slinkys.

Upstairs I wandered into two or three bedrooms before trying the knob on a door that was locked. "Just a minute," someone called from the other side.

I couldn't bring myself to stand there and wait. Backtracking down the hall, I stepped into a small bedroom which, even in my woozy state I immediately figured was the room Tiffany had described to me as hers. The west-facing window looked over the Henry Hudson Highway, and to the north were the grounds and brick buildings of the Hebrew Home for the Aged.

Locking the door behind me, I collapsed on the bed. Ten minutes later I was still there, telling myself that I was not only an incompetent detective but a disgusting creature to boot, collapsed in a woozy stupor on the deceased's childhood bed. Sitting up in a hunched-over posture, I planted my feet on the carpet beside the bed, and when my head stopped feeling as if it had been inflated with helium, I straightened and looked around.

There was too much furniture crowded into the room, which made it seem even smaller than it was. In any number of ways, though, it was more appealing than my girlhood room had been. The two windows were set into alcoves, which gave the room an old-fashioned, romantic look, and the mature trees surrounding the Hebrew Home for the Aged afforded a lovely view. My bedroom window had looked straight into the neighbors' bathroom.

There was one other thing about Tiffany's room that made it interesting. Next to one of the window alcoves, partly concealed by a wall, was a steep flight of stairs that led up to a midget-sized door. The door was fastened with one of those simple latches that you push down with your thumb, and from what I could see, there was no lock.

Attics fascinate me, maybe because I've never had one.

Unlike basements, which to me suggest damp walls, washing machines, and bugs, attics promise antique trunks filled with love poems and garment bags containing ball gowns. And, in this case, the possibility of family photo albums.

First, though, the bedroom itself.

Standing, I gave my legs a try. Not bad as long as I was within grabbing distance of some support, which in this cramped little room was no problem. Once it seemed certain that I wasn't going to fall on my face, I started searching.

Though the crowd downstairs wouldn't have their ears pitched for sounds from upstairs, I eased dresser drawers open very quietly, and inspected their contents almost soundlessly. Tiffany's school papers took up one of them, and considering her bad-girl act, she'd been a surprisingly good student. Other drawers contained old clothes, and a high-school jacket. Nowhere did I come across any family photo albums. Too bad, because it wasn't likely I'd get to search any of the other bedrooms.

Before mounting the steps to the attic I pressed my ear to the bedroom door. Voices reached me from downstairs, but nothing from the second floor. After double-checking the lock, I made my way up the short flight of stairs.

My legs were okay by then, and the stairs gave me no problems. The midget door wasn't so much short as it was narrow. At five feet four I had no trouble getting under it, but with a few more pounds on my hips getting through it might have been a problem.

The attic was smaller than I'd imagined, and the sharply slanted ceiling made the space even tighter. The entire space was lit by two small, dirty windows, one on the far side of the stairway I'd just climbed, and a second one at the other end of the space, beside another door. An exposed light bulb dangled from the ceiling near the attic's center, but my eyes adjusted to the dim light and I didn't use it.

The McKinneys were orderly people. A quick inspection revealed suitcases lined neatly under the eaves, and boxes of Christmas decorations labeled and stacked. "Linens" had been written on one carton, and "Salvation Army" on another. In the tallest part of the space garment bags hung from a pole suspended from the ceiling.

None of this was what I was after. I headed, instead, for the two smallish bookshelves at the far end of the attic. One was just beside the door, and the other perpendicular to it. Squatting on my heels, I glanced through the one beside the door first. The top shelf held *Readers Digest* condensed novels, and the other two shelves were filled with paperback murder mysteries. It looked as if every Agatha Christie ever written was there.

I was scanning the titles, momentarily diverted and wondering which of them I hadn't read, when a noise on the other side of the door startled me.

Someone was in the room just below. Another bedroom, probably. A drawer closed, a door slammed, and once again there was silence.

This was no time for me to linger over *The Body In The Library* and *Funerals Are Fatal*. Still crouching, I turned to the other set of shelves. It seemed to hold nothing but school books and a couple of computer software instruction manuals.

Someone was going to miss me soon. Straightening my knees, I quickly looked over the top shelf.

Sometimes you get lucky. There they were. Three imitation leather photo albums, two of them old enough to have cracked along their seams. Tucking all three under my arm, I tiptoed back to the other door and down the steps into Tiffany's room.

A few minutes later I was back downstairs, my now bulging tote hooked over my shoulder. The crowd was just as thick and I hadn't been missed. Intending to retrieve my coat, I went out onto the screened porch. It had been thrown across a metal chair with some others, and as I tugged it free I became aware of voices, not from inside the house but from the other direction. Turning toward the sound, I saw Pookey Dunn and Neil Howard standing outside, shielded from the light rain by only the overhang from a garage roof.

The house was awfully crowded, sure, but I found something conspiratorial in the way the two men had distanced themselves from everyone else, and in the way their heads were bent together.

I hadn't realized I was staring at them until Pookey noticed me. The look he returned was so chilly that I immediately turned away.

As I slipped my coat on, a bus pulled over to the stop on the corner, discharged two passengers, and pulled away. I had no idea where that bus went, but if it didn't go where I wanted to go, it would bring me to another bus or a subway that would.

I made my way into the living room, hugged Kitty and told her I was going to get a bus, hugged Patricia McKinney, hugged Colin McKinney—he was swaying so by then that he almost brought both of us down—and headed for the door.

"You're leaving?" Courtney asked. "So are we. As long as you're heading downtown, we'll drop you."

I almost hugged her too.

The back seat of Justin's Toyota was a bad joke, but it was still better than a bus.

"That wasn't nearly as grim as it might have been," Justin said as he pulled onto the Henry Hudson.

"It's not over yet," Courtney said. "The interment is tomorrow, and the cemetery's way up in Westchester."

"Great."

"And I don't know what to do about this."

She opened her hand. In it was a key.

"Uncle Colin and Aunt Patricia want me to go by Tiffany's apartment and see if there's anything I want. There probably isn't, but I promised."

As Justin slowed to pass through the toll booth at the Manhattan Bridge, he glanced across the seat at his fiancée.

"So what's the problem?"

"Tiffany lived in Woodbury. That's way out on Long Island. Maybe on Sunday . . ."

"Have you forgotten? We have the Blankenships on Sunday," said Justin. "They're up in Connecticut and the party's for us. We have to be there."

"Oh. Well, maybe I can get to Tiffany's one day next week. Otherwise I'll skip it. Nobody would know."

By then the police had been through Tiffany's apartment and so, probably, had her parents. My ego isn't so strong that I thought my search would turn up anything new but you never can tell.

"I live near Woodbury. If you'd like, I'll take a look at Tiffany's things for you. Not that I can be sure what you might want, but . . ."

It sounded lame to me and if Courtney hadn't been getting married in two weeks it might have sounded lame to her, too. Brides tend to get addled.

"Of course you can be sure," she said eagerly. "You know my taste exactly. I didn't like her clothes, but maybe she had a bread maker. I didn't put that on my registry list, you know."

Courtney the budding baker thrust the key eagerly at me, then began rummaging through her handbag. "Her address is somewhere in here. She lived in a condo development called Woodbury Village. Here it is. Eighty Fallingleaf Circle."

As I said, sometimes you get lucky.

13

AND SOMETIMES YOU'RE NOT SO LUCKY.

"... and do you remember that marlin? Down off Belize?"

"I remember! That sucker must have weighed eighty pounds."

"Whoa!"

"Yeah! Took the four of us all morning to reel him in!"

This was history Sam and Rosaleen were talking, but it wasn't my history. I couldn't tell a marlin from a tuna, and to tell you the truth, the only time I'm likely to care is when I see the words on a menu. Did they notice I didn't have a lot to say? Billy may have—once or twice I caught him looking at me—but since he was responsible for the occasional "Whoa," I wasn't sure.

My contribution to the conversation that was jumping like a fish on a line from one side of the dinner table to the other amounted to a couple of "No kiddings" and "Wows." Almost everything else had come from Sam and Rosaleen, and it was all fish. My homemade authentic New

England clam chowder seemed to have gone over well but I couldn't be positive. Rosaleen's recent adventure with a barracuda off Key West had so enthralled Sam and Billy that the soup had disappeared from the bowls without mention.

Yes, I'm whining, but this was sort of a big deal to me. Given a simple recipe and plenty of time, I'm an okay cook, but I'm not a confident one and probably never will be. For lack of another scapegoat, I'll blame it on my upbringing. Why not? That's what most of us blame our problems on.

At Chez Indermill in suburban New Jersey, circa 1960's, Saturday night company got roast chicken with a pop-up *done* button when the weather was cool, and hamburgers on the grill otherwise. When there was no company around, we subsisted on such delicacies as fried porkchops, macaroni and cheese, frozen French fries, spaghetti with sauce straight out of a jar, and that Friday night favorite, fish sticks.

After years of this, and after treating my ex-husband to some of the same, I struck out on my own not too long after the Age of Aquarius arrived. Saturday night company got a tofu bake during those heady times, or perhaps soyburgers. Brown rice was *de rigueur*.

When the eighties happened, the rules changed again. French cooking, then light Provençal cooking, and nouvelle cuisine. First-press olive oil. Portabella mushrooms. Mesclun, for God's sake! The first time I was offered Mesclun I thought a hallucinogen was about to appear on my plate.

I'm afraid that entire decade passed me by, food preparation-wise. For me, Manhattan in the eighties was a place to make a living, and dance, and fall in love. Cooking had nothing to do with my life. Anyway, I'd already learned to cook twice: the fish stick way, and the tofu way.

I've strayed from the subject of our dinner with Rosaleen, but maybe now you understand why I was peeved about the silence surrounding the clam chowder. Shucking clams is not something I do for the pure joy of it.

The roast beef was next. I'd controlled my tendency to overcook, and had pulled it from the oven at a point where

I half expected the poor thing to bellow in pain when Sam pierced it with the carving knife.

Rosaleen looked at the crimson flesh the way a vampire looks at a virgin's throat. "Just the way I like it, but remind me to give you my own recipe before I go, Bonnie. You won't believe how tender a roast can be."

"Looks perfect to me," Sam said as blood gushed from the raw wound.

"Awesome," Billy offered.

Rosaleen reached for my wineglass. "It must have been ESP that told me to bring this Côte d'Rhone. That Merlot you got is a good all-around wine, Bonnie, but nothing goes better with a roast than a Côte d'Rhone."

"Right," Billy agreed.

Right? Billy's glass of wine was a special concession on his part. He generally won't touch the stuff, and as far as I know can't tell Burgundy from grape juice.

I'd washed the good crystal glasses for this dinner, and the blood red wine was reflected in the gleaming facets. At the same time, blood was seeping into the potatoes I'd arranged so artfully beside the roast. It was at the moment that Rosaleen handed my glass back to me that I experienced what amounted to an epiphany. I couldn't marry Sam. It wasn't going to work. I'd been fooling myself that things would be fine, that all that was necessary was a little compromise, but no amount of compromise could make me eat raw flesh or, for that matter, make me drink a drop of Côte d'Rhone. I set my glass down on the table.

On top of my epiphany came a string of lectures delivered by voices that only I could hear.

You'd be crazy as a loon to give him up, my mother said, and a couple of my Manhattan woman friends gave me stern lectures. *How many men like Sam do you think are flexing their muscles out there in this big starry universe?* they asked. *For one like that I'd move to Long Island in a shot!* My father, a practical man, added, *It's not as if you have a career going for yourself.*

It wasn't those voices, though, that finally talked me into jabbing my fork into the slab of bloody flesh Sam slid onto my plate. *You'll probably never find anyone better*, the voice of my own fear said. *So you don't like rare beef? Try eating catfood up in Washington Heights when you can't afford Chinese carryout anymore.*

I forced myself to ignore the voice that spoke next, the one that said, *You're staying with this man for security. You're turning into a wimp.*

I smiled, at Sam first, then at Rosaleen, and then at Billy. "I'm glad you like it but save room for dessert. Hot apple pie with ice cream."

"Whoa!"

"Homemade?" Rosaleen asked.

"Of course," responded the Happy Homemaker, though it's hard to imagine the level my anxiety might have reached if I'd actually tried rolling out my own pie crust.

Half an hour later I let Rosaleen convince me she should do the cleaning up. Wanting—needing—a few minutes alone, I locked myself in the upstairs bathroom with one of the three photo albums I'd taken from the McKinney's attic.

I'd gone through all three of the albums on the train earlier that day. Only this one contained photos of Kitty Dunn.

She hadn't changed much over the years. As a teenager she'd been pretty and slender in a long yellow prom dress, a carnation pinned to the bodice. Her date had worn a white tux. A later photo showed Kitty sprawled on a beach towel. A still later picture—on the back someone had written the words "Kitty and Joe, Orlando, June 11, 1963"—showed her standing beside another young man, this one no taller than Kitty, and lean. She was wearing a light blue suit and a blue pillbox hat with a short white veil, and carrying a bouquet of white flowers. The dark-haired young man squinted at the camera. Maybe it was only the effect of the sun in his eyes, or the too-tight fit of his blue suit, but he looked uncomfortable.

This was clearly a wedding picture. It was equally clear that the man Kitty had married in 1963 was not Herbert Dunn. Joe's last name had been Davis, which I discovered from a photo a little further along in the album. It was a baby picture, actually. A brown-haired infant in pink. The words on the back of the photo were, "Maryann Christina Davis, May 1964."

There were no other pictures of Joe Davis in the album, but Maryann appeared another couple of times. One photo showed her at about four years old helping a chubby toddler open a Christmas present. "Maryann and Pookey. Christmas 1968."

So Kitty had been a Mrs. Davis before she'd been Mrs. Dunn. How nice that she hadn't even had to buy new monogrammed towels. But so what? Some of the women I know have changed their last names so often they can hardly keep them straight.

I tried putting as disgusting a turn as possible on what might have happened. Maybe Joe Davis had gone to jail for a crime so heinous that having been married to him, however briefly, branded Kitty for life as a . . . what? A fool? Or maybe Kitty had been his accomplice in his life of crime, and she'd done jail time, too.

Another possibility was that she'd dumped poor Joe for up-and-coming Herbert while Joe was wasting away from some dreadful disease.

The more feasible scenarios I imagined weren't nearly so dramatic. Like countless other couples who end up in divorce court, Kitty and Joe could have been too young, too unsettled, maybe too broke.

This early marriage probably wasn't something Kitty wanted publicized, but would she have killed to keep it quiet? That hardly seemed likely.

A knock on the bathroom door interrupted my train of thought.

"You in there, Bonnie? I've got to . . ."

"Just a second, Rosaleen."

I slunk out of the bathroom and past Rosaleen a moment later, the photo album concealed in a folded towel. After hiding it with the other two at the back of my closet, I hunched over the phone in the bedroom and called Tony LaMarca. He didn't seem terribly interested when I told him about Kitty's prior marriage, but he did promise to run a check on Joseph Davis who had married Kitty—perhaps Katherine—McKinney in Orlando, Florida in 1963.

"How did you find this out, anyway?" he asked.

"During the wake I went into Tiffany's old bedroom. There were some stairs, and . . ."

"And you have the albums now?" Tony asked when I finished describing my excursion into the attic. "At Sam's house?"

"Yes." I was so proud of my resourcefulness that I didn't notice how Tony's voice was rising.

"You removed personal property from the home of the deceased's parents! That's not what I asked you to do, Bonnie. All you're supposed to do is keep your eyes open. You're not supposed to turn into a thief!"

"But look what I found out."

"What you found out probably doesn't amount to anything. My question is, How do you plan to return those albums to the McKinneys without them finding out you took them?"

"I'll think of some way." I already had, but if I'd described it to Tony right then, he might have gone berserk.

"You better. And from now on, no creeping around. Just keep your eyes open."

The fishing boat that left from Montauk at dawn took us about four miles offshore and then trolled back and forth through waves so high that they regularly lapped across the deck. The day had started out overcast and breezy, and by late afternoon the wind coming off the water felt as if it just might blow that boat over. "Keep looking at the horizon," the ever-helpful Rosaleen said whenever I clutched my stomach.

Back on shore at the end of a long, long day, Billy got to have his picture taken with a three-foot sea bass, and Rosaleen and Sam had done themselves proud with a bluefish, flounder, and porgies. As for me, there had been some nibbles on my line, and once something monstrous that had almost yanked the reel out of my hands, but in the end I'd stepped off that boat empty-handed. Fishing must be an attitude thing.

During the ride back home a heavy rain was falling, and the radio weatherman announced that parts of Long Island had lost electric power. He gave us his word, however, that all this would end after midnight and we would wake to a bright sunny day.

How would we spend that next day? Golf? Good idea! Rosaleen had been polishing her game. Or how about touring the wineries on Long Island's North Fork? Great idea! Rosaleen had been researching them. She already had some good ones picked out. Or maybe an amusement park? Whoa!

That night we ate one of those creatures they'd dragged out of its briny home earlier that day. Sam, and Billy, who was spending more time at home than he usually did, cleaned the fish and Rosaleen cooked it. The dining room rang with "Whoas!"

I cleaned up after dinner, grateful as always when Rosaleen is around, for the few minutes alone. The next day had finally been planned. Billy, who couldn't drink legally anyway, had begged off, but Rosaleen, Sam, and I were going to make up a picnic lunch and tour the wineries.

Woodbury, where Tiffany had lived, is about five miles from Huntington, and on an ordinary weekend I could easily have found time to get there. With Rosaleen around, however, every daylight moment was occupied.

I flipped the dishwasher on and wandered into the living room. Sam was in the recliner and Rosaleen on the sofa. Moses, the traitor, was purring in her lap. They were watching a game show, congratulating themselves when they beat the contestants to the right answers, groaning both at the contestants' defeats and their own. At the very moment that an accountant from Pittsburgh guessed the capital of Malaysia just after Rosaleen shouted it out—"Kuala Lumpur"—one of the voices that had been babbling in my ear spoke up again.

Look at that! She even likes those TV shows that work like a sleeping pill on you. If you want to hold on to him, you'd better sit down right now. . . .

"I have to run down to Woodbury for a little while," I said, ignoring the voice.

Sam glanced at me. "Now? It's pouring."

"And listen to that wind!" Rosaleen put in.

Funny how that wind hadn't stopped us from spending the day pitching around on a boat.

"Yes," I said. "I've got to pick up something from Tiffany McKinney's apartment."

"That poor girl who was killed? Sam told me about her," Rosaleen said, and then in the next breath—"You're not going to believe this!—he asked me if I wanted to go into New York City this visit. Not this visit and not ever, I told him."

"You want company?" Sam asked, surprising me.

"No. I won't be long."

As I eased the Chrysler out of the garage, I wondered what would happen if I just stepped out of the picture. Rosaleen wasn't a pretty woman, and Sam liked pretty. Most men do. But Sam liked comfortable, too. If for Sam the choice came down to pretty, or comfortable, which would he choose? I couldn't guess. I was more alluring in my Calvin's, but women like Rosaleen, in their L.L. Bean Bushwhackers, can knock you off the trail if you don't watch out. And if you're ambivalent about whether the trail is the right one for you, you're dead.

Though Woodbury and Huntington seem to flow unbounded into each other, Woodbury was almost foreign territory to me. I'd been to a monster shopping center there several times, but hadn't explored anything else. Sam's wife had kept some local street maps in the glove compartment and they helped, but the rain, and a wind so strong that it buffeted the Chrysler, made the going slower than it ordinarily would have been. The Chrysler's windshield wipers worked hard, but visibility became so poor at one point that I pulled off the road and waited out a fierce downpour.

It was after eight P.M. when I got to Woodbury Village which, from what I saw, wasn't terribly village-like. The development consisted of a labyrinth of two-story brick-and-frame attached townhouses. They all looked alike, and the several curving streets that cut through them looked alike too. The waterfalls of rain cascading over the car windows made it all but impossible for me to make out the numbers posted on townhouse doors, and I drove slowly, opening the side window every minute or so to peer out. While I searched, street lights around the development dimmed several times, and when I finally pulled into a parking spot in front of 80 Fallingleaf Circle, I took a small flashlight from the glove compartment and stuck it into my tote bag.

Tiffany hadn't been as security conscious as I am—the burglars in Woodbury Village probably aren't as adept as those in Washington Heights—and I had opened the one lock and was in the townhouse's tiny foyer in seconds. After relocking the door, I flipped on a light switch. A lamp in the small living room and a ceiling fixture over a flight of stairs both came to life.

My first business was to get rid of the McKinney family photo albums, and some built-in shelves in the living room were ideal for that purpose. As Tiffany had mentioned, she read romances. I made space for the albums on a high shelf between two fat titles with embossed covers. Who could say that the albums hadn't been there all the while?

With no idea of what I was looking for, but assuming I'd know it when I saw it, I began searching. Apart from the living room, the condo's bottom floor consisted of a kitchen with an attached laundry room, a small dining room and a half-bathroom. Tiffany's taste in furniture, like her taste in clothing, tended toward flashy colors and shiny fabrics, but nowhere did I see anything that struck me as suspicious.

Thunder rumbled as I climbed the stairs to the second story. The light over the staircase dimmed, and then brightened inordinately. Having been through enough Long Island storms to know that flaring lights often precede a power failure, I moved quickly into an open door and ran my fingers along the wall. I no sooner found a light switch, however, than the lights that were already on dimmed again, and then went out entirely. I flipped the switch up and down but there was no response. Woodbury Village had lost electric power.

Faint light from outside still made its way through the condo's windows, but there wasn't enough to search by.

Sliding my hand into my tote, I dug out the flashlight. It was about the size of a fat pen, and emitted a pinpoint of bright light.

From what I could see, the entire second floor was carpeted in royal-blue shag. In addition to a bathroom, there were two other rooms. Tiffany had used the larger of these as her bedroom. The furniture in this room—a bed and night table, chest of drawers, and dressing table—was white and shone brightly when my light flickered over it. The bed itself was a thing of wonder. Who would have thought you could buy a four-poster bed in glossy white lacquer with black and gold spheres topping the posts?

The smaller of the two rooms had been outfitted as a bare-bones office, with a two-drawer desk, a chair on casters, and a computer on a cart. I glanced around for a printer but didn't see one. In any event, without electricity the computer was useless.

A small white phone and answering machine were atop the desk. Sliding into the chair, I opened the machine. No tape. Of course. The police had already been through the place.

Next to the phone there were a few pieces of mail Tiffany had received. Thumbing through them, I found mostly circulars and bills, but one heavy bond envelope proved interesting. Inside it was a letter, typed on the letterhead of a well-known New York City builder and dated a few days before Tiffany had been killed.

"Dear Ms. McKinney:

My partners and I enjoyed meeting you during your recent visit to our office.

This letter will confirm the employment offer we have made you. We believe that your experience in and knowledge of the building industry would make you a valuable part of our organization, and also feel that you would enjoy working with our group of dedicated professionals.

If you have any questions about the position, please

*don't hesitate to call me. We all hope that we soon
will be working with you.''*

The letter was signed by a man identified on the letterhead as a vice president.

People job-hunt all the time, and this letter proved nothing. It did suggest things, however. If Tiffany had been
planning to leak something that would cause Dunn Construction trouble, it made sense that she would be covering
herself, and her finances, by getting out.

I put the letter back where it had been, and then opened
the top desk drawer. Pencils, paper clips. Nothing special
there, except for a half-empty box of cheap envelopes. One
cheap envelope looks pretty much like another one. Still, I
would have bet several hours pay that one of these same
envelopes, with its "hot" contents, had ended up in the
back of Kitty Dunn's library book.

Closing the drawer, I opened the one under it, no easy
job as it was heavy with computer printouts. I aimed the
flashlight at them and saw columns of numbers alternating
with descriptions of construction materials. Examining
these more carefully, I recognized the project management
software Tiffany had used on the job. It appeared as if she'd
printed out the entire database. Nothing odd about that.
She'd mentioned that she often worked at home. I pushed
the drawer shut.

As I rose, there was another crack of lightning. The
blinds were closed over the one window in the room, but
the rain was crashing against it so fiercely it sounded as if
the glass might break. It occurred to me that this was pretty
creepy—darkness, wind, rain. All that was lacking for a
real haunted-house-type scene was a ghost. Then I smiled
at the ridiculous idea. Who ever heard of a haunted condominium?

After double-checking to be sure that the desk was as I'd
found it, I peeked into the room's one small closet. An
upright vacuum cleaner took up most of the floor, and the
rest of the space was jammed with clothing.

Leaving the office, I followed the pinpoint of light into
the bathroom, where the blue shag carpeting gave way to

hot pink. The oversized bathroom cabinet held about what I'd expected: jars of makeup, tubes of makeup, wands of makeup. Tiffany could have done a makeover on the Statue of Liberty's face, or made up the entire cast of the biggest musical on Broadway and had plenty left over to do a substantial job on herself.

I was on my way out of the bathroom when the sound of breaking glass stopped me dead. Thinking, at first, that the window above the desk had broken, I aimed the light into the office. The blinds weren't moving.

Suddenly there was a strange scraping noise from downstairs, followed seconds later by the unmistakable sound of a lock turning.

I had switched off my flashlight even before the front door opened and wind gusted up the stairwell. My mind was working clearly. Anyone who belonged in Tiffany's condominium would have had a key. Thieves read obituary notices. A thief, thinking the place was deserted, had broken in.

There was no good hiding place in the bathroom, and none in the office unless I wanted to fight my way past the vacuum cleaner. I trotted on my toes toward the bedroom. As I reached it, the front door closed.

I started for the bedroom closet but stopped midway. A thief would search a closet. The trace of light coming through the room's curtains revealed that Tiffany's double bed was near a corner, but that a space had been left between the bed and the wall, probably to facilitate bedmaking. I tiptoed to the bed's far side and crouched down, preparing to wedge my body between the bed and the wall, when a bright light flickered across the bedroom door. The thief was on the stairway, shining a flashlight around the upper floor. The light's reflection grew more intense, and I heard heavy footsteps on the stairs. This thief was a big man, and he was going to search the upper floor first, where I was hidden.

Heart racing, I dropped onto the carpet. The clearance between the floor and the bed frame was too small for my hips but I was able to slide my feet, which were at the foot of the bed and most likely to be seen, under the dust ruffle.

Lifting the dust ruffle near my face, I could see a strip of carpet on the other side of the bed. It helped my claustrophobia but did nothing for my sense of security.

The thief went to the smaller room first, just as I had. A desk drawer opened and closed, and then a second drawer opened. A longer period passed before it slammed shut.

Moments later the light shone on the carpet on the other side of the bed. I held my breath as the beam grew stronger and even inched under the dust ruffle.

The thief moved quickly and not very quietly, opening and shutting dresser drawers, opening the closet door and almost immediately closing it. Crossing the room, he stopped next to the bed and aimed his light toward the night table.

My heart was pounding so loudly, I feared he could hear it. I took in shallow breaths, and my lungs burned for lack of air. This was hell. Nothing could be worse, but then things suddenly were worse.

The thief sat down on the bed and aimed his light away from the floor. The bed springs shifted. If there had been enough air in my lungs I might have screamed. He was going to take a nap, maybe even spend the night, while I went quietly crazy on the floor.

There was an almost inaudible groan—"Uh"—and then he said, very softly, "This is it for me, Buddy. I'm out of it."

He rose, causing the springs to shift again. As he moved away from the bed, the beam of his flashlight fell across his shoes. They were tan construction boots with bright red laces tipped with tassels.

Neil Howard.

His light cut a path across the blue rug as he left the bedroom. Seconds later I heard his heavy footsteps descending the stairs. Filling my lungs with air, I inched upwards toward freedom as soon as the condo's front door opened and closed.

I pulled myself upright with the aid of a bedpost and hurried to the window. Through the rain-streaked glass I could see a dark pickup truck moving out of a parking spot.

The headlights didn't come on until the truck had rounded a corner.

Neil was no ordinary thief. He'd been after something specific. Since I hadn't searched the bedroom, there was no way to tell if he'd taken anything from there, but the office was another matter. Flipping my flashlight back on, I hurried down the hall.

At first glance the little office seemed unchanged. The mail next to the phone appeared undisturbed, as did the desk's top drawer. I yanked hard on the lower drawer's handle. This time it opened so easily that I almost lost my balance. The drawer was now empty. Neil had taken the stack of computer printouts.

Why? The obvious reason was that these printouts contained information he didn't want discovered.

I shined my light on the computer stand. The computer was still there, still unusable.

I tried to think through what was going on between Neil Howard and Tiffany. She had been attracted to him, but then, after doing her "homework," had developed misgivings. And now Neil had stolen a copy of a database which listed supplies—purchased for construction projects. On some of these projects he would have had a degree of control over supplies, and at the time of Tiffany's death, at least some of those supplies—the firewalls supposedly purchased for a project in the South Bronx, a marble mantel for the Ambassador Hotel—hadn't made it to the projects they were meant for.

If my gut feeling was right, I now understood Tiffany's misgivings about Neil. She had discovered that he was stealing from Dunn Construction.

Tiffany's computers, both at work and at home, were hooked into the Dunn network. Since she'd made no secret of her password, "Sextoy," Neil could have accessed her database from any Dunn computer. He might have realized that Tiffany knew he was stealing. Having spent time around Tiffany, I wouldn't have been surprised to learn that she'd dropped a few hints. As she'd said, "Why not tell it like it is?"

So Neil had stolen the incriminating printouts. That wouldn't have solved his problem completely, though. The database was still on the network.

Did Neil even have the ability to delete or change Tiffany's database once he got to a working computer? That access had been limited, and it seemed unlikely that it would have been given to an assistant foreman. If my reasoning was correct, Neil might have been able to read as much as he wanted about the projects he was working on, but he couldn't diddle with the database.

Why bother stealing the printout when anyone with access to Tiffany's database could find the real thing by flipping a switch and typing in the password ''Sextoy''?

Because Neil's ''Buddy'' *did* have the kind of access that would allow him to diddle. As for ''Buddy's'' identity, who else but Pookey, Neil's co-conspirator?

I made my way hurriedly down the stairs, flicking off my flashlight on the way. My feet crunched over broken glass as I crossed the little entranceway. I pulled the door open. Figuring it was pointless to relock it, I simply pulled it shut as I pushed the screen door out and stepped into the damp air.

A shadow moved at the corner of my vision.

Something . . . No, someone! A man was crouched near the wall of the house. He leaped toward me and I yelped with surprise and fear, but before I could run, someone else was there, behind me, twisting my arm and pinning it between my shoulder blades.

A blinding bright light was shining in my face. The first man had stepped in front of me and was shoving something toward my face. A police shield.

''Nassau County Police,'' he said. ''We had a report of a break-in.''

No, I didn't end up spending the night in the slammer, nor did I call Tony, or even drop his name. If things had gotten to the point where I was being manhandled into the back of the police car, I might have, but they never did. Fortunately I was able to show the patrolmen the key to Tiffany's condo, and give them a good reason for my being there. I was also able to give them both the Dunns' and the McKinneys' telephone numbers, and after that all it took for me to gain my freedom was a couple of phone calls, which I graciously permitted the police to make from inside the condo.

As for the thief, I told the policemen that he had never gotten any further into the house than the foyer. My flashlight beaming down the stairs had frightened him away before I'd gotten a look at him, I said.

I had a couple of reasons for lying. For one, the printouts Neil had taken were of no value to anyone unless they knew what to look for and were interested in looking for it. To voice my blurry suspicion of theft inside Dunn Construction to two Long Island policemen and expect anything to be done about it was ridiculous.

On top of that, I kept thinking about how kind Neil had been to poor Mr. McKinney at the memorial service. I know that didn't prove anything—psychopaths can put on a good act—but though I had no difficulty thinking of Neil as a thief, I certainly wasn't ready to think of him as Tiffany's murderer.

14

AFTER SAM AND I HAD TAKEN ROSALEEN to LaGuardia, after we had seen her plane lift off the ground as we drove from the airport, Sam said, "That was a full week-end."

"Sure was."

"I know you enjoy Rosaleen's visits," he continued, "and Billy's crazy about her—I think she reminds him of his mother—but having her around for more than a few hours wears me out. I feel like I have to be so damned enthusiastic about everything. Do you know what I mean?"

My heart went into a happy little tap dance that contin-ued later into the night when Sam and I made love. I fell asleep contented and thinking that all my doubts about our relationship were over. As for that epiphany I'd experi-enced a few nights before, ho hum.

After seeing Sam and Billy off the next morning, I went down to the basement. Stacked in an out-of-the-way spot under the stairs were some boxes containing personal things of Eileen's. I'd never had the nerve or the desire to search through the boxes, and the only one I opened that morning was labeled "Books." Eileen had been a big fan of romance novels.

I chose three. On the florid turquoise cover of one, a pirate with an eye patch came to the rescue of a woman tied to the mast of a ship. Another one was set on a ranch, and the third took place in the snowy north, back in the days when woolly mammoths chased women into the arms of bare-chested hulks in fur boots.

I'm a list maker, and the more chaotic things get, the more lists I tend to make. For a change, my personal life felt serene, but the combined stresses of Courtney's wedding and Tiffany's murder were getting to me. During the train ride into the city I made myself a "To do" list. It was a jumble but so was the state of my mind.

1. Check Tiffany's purchasing database. If information appears to be missing, check Neil Howard's access to computer.
2. Call Tony re Kitty Dunn's first marriage. Has he learned anything?
3. Call Courtney. Found no bread maker at Tiffany's, but tell her about picture albums that family might want.
4. Call Amanda about gifts for bridesmaids and ushers!!
5. Firm up rehearsal dinner with Pookey and caterer.
6. Call Zoe's re status of dresses.
7. Try to find Robert Annessi. I still think he was in the alley. If I'm right, did he kill Tiffany? If I'm right but he didn't kill her, why is he lying?

I booted up the computer that had been Tiffany's, and bright white characters flickered across the blue monitor in front of me. When things stopped moving at the C:\ prompt, I typed in Tiffany's password: "Sextoy."

A menu with three choices appeared on the screen. The first choice was a word processing program. Next was an accounting spreadsheet, and after that the project management software. I moved the cursor down to the last item, and pressed the Enter key.

A new menu which listed Dunn construction projects, and which also gave the user the option of starting a new project, appeared on the screen. I was only familiar with two of the projects listed: the city-funded housing in the South Bronx, and the Ambassador Hotel.

Highlighting the Ambassador project, I again tapped the Enter key. The next menu on the screen gave me a choice of creating entries, editing them, or searching for them. I typed in the word "mantel." Seconds later, a flashing message on the screen read *Not found*. I tried "fireplace" next, and finally "marble."

Not found, the message on the screen flashed.

There was a slim chance that the mantel was still there but under a different description. "Marble Fireplace Mantel" seemed to cover all the bases, but to be certain I began moving the cursor down the page. A few minutes later, I reached the last entry without finding anything that might be a marble mantel, and faced the hard reality: the database had been altered. Someone with complete access to the database had removed the entry.

Violet stared at me as if I were babbling in a foreign tongue.

"The thing is, I'm putting Courtney's wedding information on the computer, and I wouldn't want everyone to be able to access it. Not that any of it is confidential, but it is personal, and I certainly wouldn't want anyone to tamper with anything. That would be awful. Do you understand?"

I twisted my face into what I hoped was a guileless expression.

"Some of the foremen have access to the database for their projects," Violet said, "but only a few people here in the office can actually make changes or delete documents."

Feeling bold, I asked who those few people were.

"Well, there's Mr. Dunn, and Pookey, and Mr. Dunn's secretary, and me," she added. "We're the only ones. Oh, and I guess the technician could do whatever he wanted, but he wouldn't care about Courtney's wedding information. He's a college student. He only comes in a few hours a week unless something goes wrong and we call him."

Grateful for the knowledge, I smiled at Violet and handed her a little white shopping bag.

"I understand you read romances. These are a few of my favorites. I hope you haven't read them yet."

For a moment she regarded the shopping bag suspiciously. Was this a cruel joke? Was it actually filled with more unaddressed invitations? Curiosity ultimately got the best of her.

"Well, let's see." She reached into the bag and immediately handed me the one with the pirate on the cover for which I'd had high hopes. "I've read this, but . . ."

The ranch romance was new to her, as was the woolly mammoth.

"These look good. Thanks." Her eyes rested on the half-dressed specimen in the fur boots. "I'll start this during lunch."

"I'm going to be here for a while," I said. "Why don't we go out for lunch?"

Hunching her shoulders defensively, Violet said, "I brought a sandwich from home. If my work's caught up, I like to . . ."

She had glanced back at the book.

"That's perfect," I quickly said. "We can go to that new minipark on Lexington Avenue. It's beautiful. There's a fountain, and I hear there's a piano player sometimes, or a jazz combo. . . ."

The woman wasn't interested in fountains or music, but finally, reluctantly, she gave in. Not trusting her, I made her agree to a specific time.

"It's already a few minutes after noon. Let's go at twelve-thirty."

This detecting business can be downright distasteful, I thought a few minutes later as I sat down in front of the computer again. Here I was bribing this woman with books I'd never read, and then all but forcing her to leave them behind and go out for lunch.

I tapped the space bar, causing the piglet screen saver to disappear. Exiting the Ambassador project, I accessed the one for the Bronx development.

How would firewalls be listed? Simply as firewalls, or was there some other way of referring—?

Have you ever noticed how, when you get that weird sensation that someone is watching you, it often turns out to be true? I was already starting to look over my shoulder when Herbert Dunn cleared his throat.

"Good morning, Bonnie."

He was at the cubicle's entrance, and though he was looking at me, he surely had noticed the project management database on the screen.

"Hello," I said. "Pookey told me I could use this cubicle and computer for the next couple of weeks."

Herbert nodded. "He mentioned that. I'd like to have a few words with you. In my office," he added.

Herbert Dunn had not struck me as a man who wasted time chatting idly with wedding consultants, but my case was unique. Not many wedding consultants have seen as much of the father of the bride as I had seen of Herbert. The few words he wanted to say to me were probably, *If you want to get paid for this job, don't tell anyone what you saw.* I hadn't told anyone and most likely wouldn't. Not now, anyway. In a while, when the episode took on the soft rosy patina of history, I might entertain friends with it, but for the moment I felt too involved with the Dunns to breathe a word.

Herbert, however, didn't know that. He stayed there until I got up, so I had no choice but to leave the computer as it was, with the Bronx project database glowing on the monitor.

"I understand you haven't always worked as a wedding consultant. Amanda told my wife that you've had several administrative office jobs."

"Yes," I responded, though "several" was seriously understating the case.

Herbert followed me to his office door. "Take a seat inside, Bonnie," he said. "I just need to have a few words with my secretary."

Leaving him bent over the blond temp, I went into his office. It was furnished in a style I think of as *manly*—dark wood, brass trim, oversized. When I sat back in one of the visitor's chairs in front of Herbert's desk, my feet barely touched the floor.

A moment later Herbert walked in, sank into the big leather chair on the far side of his desk, looked at me for a second, almost expectantly, and then proceeded to stare down at his hands, seemingly as enthralled by them as he'd been in the limo after Tiffany's funeral service. His fingers were knitted together tightly, and I noticed that his knuckles were pale against his tan. Though his office was cool, there was a sheen of sweat across Herbert's brow.

This had all the makings of a hideously embarrassing scene. I felt like blurting out, *I won't say anything,* and running from the room. Why hadn't he just left things alone?

The noonday sun shone brightly through the window behind him. Taking my eyes off Herbert's hands, I glanced out the window. Herbert's view was of Madison Avenue. The back of Zoe's Bridal Salon wasn't visible.

Herbert cleared his throat again, drawing my attention.

"Sometimes we see things we're not meant to see. And—" Unlinking his fingers, he spread his hand wide. "—occasionally we may draw the wrong conclusions about those things."

Oh, brother. I hadn't expected him to take this route. Was he going to start telling me he'd been performing CPR on Stacey, or maybe that their bodies had been entwined in order to fight off frostbite?

Though I was not the one who should have been uncomfortable, I squirmed in my chair. "You don't have to worry about my saying anything. I won't."

"Perhaps not. Not consciously. However, you have a connection with a gossip columnist who has already treated my family . . . shabbily."

Until he brought it up, the notion of "leaking" Herbert's affair to Elsie hadn't occurred to me. Trying to take the high road in a situation that really didn't have one, I assured Herbert that Elsie Scott was merely a casual acquaintance, and added, loftily, "I'm not interested in feeding information to her."

"I'm glad to hear that. It would be a tragedy if the public got the wrong idea."

A tragedy for whom? Not for the public. For the public it would be a hoot.

Glancing back down, Herbert began shifting through some papers on his desk. I got the idea that that meant we were finished, and started to rise.

"I should get back to work."

"One more thing, Bonnie."

I sat back down.

"Tiffany wasn't only a beloved niece. She was also a valuable part of this organization."

For the first time since we'd entered his office, he looked me in the eye.

"I realize that," I said.

"In business," he continued, "there is always a need for people who are intelligent and, perhaps as important, discreet. You obviously possess both qualities in abundance."

Until then my entire interaction with this man had consisted of one brief meeting at which I took notes, one short, silent ride in a limo, and one glimpse of him doing the thing that was causing him this trouble now. He didn't have the first clue about my intelligence or my discretion.

"Would you be interested in taking over Tiffany's position? I realize, of course, that your experience may not mesh exactly, but you obviously learn quickly. As far as salary, I would be willing to go as high as . . ."

Howard Dunn was offering me a bribe. I've been offered jobs for any number of reasons, but never because someone was afraid of me. What with my taking the high road and all that, I would have said no immediately, but one thing caused me to hesitate. The salary he offered me was, in a word, staggering.

A moment later I did just that—staggered out of his office. I hadn't accepted the job, but . . . Wow! Herbert Dunn had gone on to say all the right words to me, words such as "future" and "opportunity," but the best words of all had been those about money. I could be financially independent. I'd be able—

"Are you ready to go to lunch?"

Strange, the things that can occur to you out of nowhere. Or at least the things that can occur to me. I'd never seen Violet anywhere other than behind her desk. Now, seeing her standing beside the cubicle I'd been using, in her baggy brown cardigan and worn scuffed flats, with one side of her dark green skirt hanging longer than the other, I was struck by just how eccentric she looked.

Unable to stop myself, I glanced around the office. Herbert's temporary secretary had been staring at us, but when she realized I'd noticed, she looked away. Pookey Dunn had seen us too, from the door of his office. I caught his eye but he immediately stepped back into his office.

I was having lunch with the office oddball. That's what it came down to. Twenty minutes earlier I wouldn't have cared what any of them thought about me, but suddenly I did. I'd just been offered a chance to become one of them. Not just a typing, filing, one of them, but a very well-paid one. Almost an executive.

Almost an executive. That idea brought me a few feet closer to earth. I've never been fully convinced that being a bona fide executive is a desirable state of affairs. All things considered, being *almost* an executive, who had reached that state of grace by way of a bribe, sounded pretty icky.

"Sure," I said to Violet. "Just let me log out of the computer."

"You don't have to do that," Violet said. "The network's just been taken down for maintenance."

Violet walked alongside me, staring down, her lunch dangling from her hand in a brown paper bag.

"Did you take the job?" she asked.

"What job?"

"Tiffany's job. Mr. Dunn offered it to you, didn't he? When I saw you go in his office, I knew."

She didn't know the half of it. There was no reason for me to lie, but at the same time the truth came a little hard.

"We discussed it," I said as we turned down Lexington Avenue. "Nothing was settled."

The minipark, which nestled against a new highrise, had most likely been the result of an agreement between the builder and the New York City Zoning Board. The builder gets a tax break, and the city gets a public area. Everybody wins. This public space was particularly appealing. Ornamental maple trees, though a long way from mature, already shaded much of it, and in the fountain at one side of the space, water cascaded over a smooth sweep of black granite.

An all-woman quartet, comprised of a cellist, two violinists, and a woman at a portable keyboard, was playing from a low stage near the fountain. The piece was Vivaldi's *Four Seasons*, and though I didn't know which season the musicians were in the midst of, the music was light and joyful enough to make me think of nymphs and shepherds dancing across flowery meadows.

The small round tables in the park were already filled with people eating their lunches or taking a break from shopping, so Violet and I had to settle for the stone ledge that separated the park from the sidewalk. The ledge was high enough to give me a lot of trouble, and it took a couple of tries before I managed to hoist myself onto it.

Violet pulled herself up with no trouble at all, and then used her arms to put some distance between us so that we could spread out our lunches.

"You're in better shape than I'm in," I said.

She was opening her brown bag. "I run four miles every morning, with wrist weights."

"That's impressive. Have you run marathons?"

"Oh, no." She peeled plastic wrap from her tuna sandwich, and then pried open the container of skim milk she'd brought and pushed a transparent straw into it. "I don't like to have lots of people around me. I like to run alone. It gives me time to reflect."

Upon what? I wondered, but I didn't want to know badly enough to ask.

I'd gotten my favorite street lunch—a falafel sandwich and a diet soft drink—from a sidewalk vendor. As I popped the cap on the soda, Violet glanced at the aluminum can. "That's not very healthy. If you read the label, you'll see that it's all chemicals."

It must have been the normal setting—lunch, sunshine on my neck, Vivaldi, an elderly man on a bench in front of us delicately moving one forearm as if conducting the musicians—that made me think, for a moment, that I was in a normal situation. I smiled at my companion. "Then I won't read the label. Ignorance is bliss."

"Not where your body is concerned. Your body is a temple."

Tiffany hadn't been kidding. This one was a real space cadet.

"Some bodies are, and some aren't," I said, still trying to inject some humor into this conversation.

Dead serious, Violet handed me a napkin. "You must at least wipe off the top of the çan."

I usually do and I would have then, but some rebellious streak caused me to wad the napkin up and tuck it into my pocket. Lifting the soda, I drank deeply, unprotected from the city's filth.

Violet picked up her container of milk and sucked on the straw. The liquid that flowed through it looked thin as water, but I'm sure it was germ-free and packed with vitamins.

Taking my pita sandwich in my hands, I raised it toward my mouth. "This is certainly healthy enough."

"Maybe," Violet responded, "but those vendors never look clean to me. And their carts! Ugh!"

Over the past decade I'd eaten not only falafel but every imaginable variety of mystery meat from sidewalk vendors, and I was still there to talk about it. If there was one thing I *wasn't* there for, it was to discuss my diet. I bit into the sandwich. Nasty it might be, but it sure tasted good.

The string quartet finished the Vivaldi piece. When Violet saw that everyone else in the crowd had begun clapping, she put down her milk and followed suit. The crowd quieted and one of the violinists began tuning her instrument.

"It's a very good job," Violet said.

Surprised by the comment, I glanced over at the musicians.

"I mean Tiffany's job."

I thought we'd finished with this subject during the walk from the office. Shrugging, I repeated my earlier statement.

"Nothing was settled. I'm not sure I'm interested."

"I'd take it. Not that Mr. Dunn would offer it to me. I am qualified, though," Violet assured me. "Whenever Tiffany went on vacation I filled in for her."

"Does Mr. Dunn know that you're interested?" I asked.

Violet stared off into the distance. "Probably not. He never seems to notice me."

"Maybe you should talk to him."

"I hate to push myself on someone who doesn't want me."

"It can't hurt to speak up," I said. "Otherwise, he may never realize you're interested."

The quartet began playing again. The piece wasn't familiar to me, but it was to the elderly man in front of us. He began conducting in earnest, waving first one arm and then both of them as if he were on a podium in front of the Philharmonic. Violet was staring at his back as if puzzled by such a display. It was as good a time as any to bring up the subject of Neil Howard.

"I understand that Neil Howard had asked Tiffany out. He probably feels awful now."

"Why should he?"

Why? I was talking to an alien. "Because he must have liked Tiffany. Been interested in her," I added, not sure Violet understood what I meant.

She shook her head vehemently, a display of emotion that surprised me.

"Not like that! They joked around when he came in the office, but I'm sure he didn't like her . . . that way." Her expression turned sulky. "If he did ask Tiffany out, I'm sure it was just for you-know-what. You can't blame men for acting like that sometimes."

Or women, either, though I doubted Violet would agree. "But if he wasn't attracted to her, why didn't he try to get *you-know-what* from someone who did appeal to him?" I asked. "Neil's a good-looking guy, you know."

Violet seemed to ponder that for a few moments before the vacant look returned to her face. She had finished the last of her sandwich, and the apple she'd also brought from home. After wrapping the core carefully in plastic wrap, she took a small packet from the brown paper bag and pried it open. It was one of those smelly little wipe things that leave your fingers feeling as if they've been dipped in varnish remover.

"I don't mean that Neil didn't like Tiffany as a friend," she said as she scrubbed at her hands. "I liked Tiffany, too. At least sometimes. She should have been more careful about the way she acted, though."

"We're all different," I said philosophically. "There are many ways to lead a life."

I suspect that Violet didn't agree, but rather than telling me that, she became philosophical too.

"Anyway," she said, using her arms to lower herself from the wall, "it doesn't matter now. Tiffany's dead."

"That's right."

"And Neil's gone."

My drop off the ledge wasn't as efficient as Violet's. My feet hit the ground so hard the shock ran all the way up my legs.

"Gone? Gone where?"

My fall had caused me to sound even more startled than I was about Neil's disappearance.

"He quit," Violet said. "He called Mr. Dunn this morning and resigned. He didn't even give two weeks notice or even pick up his paycheck. He said I should put it in the mail."

"How odd."

"Neil's father recently died and left him some money. He's going to build a house on a piece of property he bought in New Jersey. He paid cash," she added. "Seventeen thousand five."

I asked Violet how she had discovered all this, and learned that Herbert Dunn had switched Neil's call to her so that she could take down his forwarding address.

"So Neil's living in New Jersey now," I said conversationally as we walked back to the office. "Tiffany mentioned that you live there. I'm from Jersey myself. My parents still live near New Brunswick. Where exactly is Neil's property?"

"Near Silver Lake. He said he'd be staying with his grandmother on and off while he works on his house. I've got both addresses in my Rolodex."

And the second Violet left that Rolodex unattended I'd have them, too.

15

VIOLET NOT ONLY DIDN'T WASTE TIME combing her hair or applying makeup in the office ladies' room mirror, but she was one of those women with an iron tub for a bladder.

While waiting for her to pay a visit to the ladies' room, I would have had plenty of time to do a thorough search of the Bronx project database had I been able to get access to it. Unfortunately, though, I was now completely locked out of all the Dunn project databases. Every time I tried to get into one of them, a big bright message flashed across the monitor:

ACCESS DENIED. SEE NETWORK TECHNICIAN.

Someone had decided that I had no business looking through the ongoing project databases and had shut me out of them. What was left for me was a blank where I could create my own database for Courtney's wedding.

As if I intended to do that.

With the computer closed off to me, I found myself with

enough time to launch a barrage of phone calls: to Amanda, to Jeffrey Phipps the caterer, to the Flower Power lady, to Zoe, and to every other wedding-type person imaginable.

But the most interesting phone call I made by far that afternoon was to Tony at the precinct.

Since the cubicle offered very little privacy, I spoke softly and was as guarded as possible when I got him on the line.

"I was wondering if you'd been able to find out anything about the first husband?"

"Huh?"

"You know. The thing we discussed the other night."

"The thing? What thing?"

I scooted my chair forward, bent my head, and crunched the phone into my shoulder. "Stop it, Tony!" I said as forcefully as I could in a whisper. "I got you the damned lead. You can at least satisfy my curiosity."

"You're a natural snoop, Bonnie. Why don't you join the force?"

"Because I wouldn't like riding around in a squad car all day eating Dunkin' Doughnuts."

"Those Dunkin' Doughnuts can grow on you," he said.

"That's what I'm afraid of. Now, what about the first husband?"

"Oh, yes. Husband number one. Joe Clayton Davis. I'll tell you what I found out, Bonnie, but first, you've got to promise me something."

"All right."

"When you took those photo albums, that ticked me off. You've got to promise that in the future, all you're going to do is keep your eyes and ears open and report back to me what you hear or see, because . . ."

Tony had just given me an opening. *In the future*, he'd said. Well, Saturday night had been in the past, which made it, if you want to be technical, *pre ultimatum*. If I was going to tell him about my visit to Tiffany's condo, and about Neil Howard's break-in, this was the time to do it.

". . . because," Tony repeated, "if you are involved in anything else that I don't like, you will never get one more morsel of information out of me. Understood?"

"Understood."

The next thing I picked up through the receiver was the sound of papers being shuffled.

"Okay," Tony said a second later. "I'll satisfy your curiosity. It's quite a story."

"Was he a criminal?"

"Not hardly. Kitty Dunn's first husband, Joe Clayton Davis, was an Air Force enlisted man. Three tours of duty. Spent most of the last two in Viet Nam. Went over for the second time in July 1965. On January 14, 1966, the plane he was in was shot down over the Gulf of Tonkin. He and the pilot survived and reached land, but the pilot was seriously injured. Apparently Davis saved the guy's life. They were captured by a squad of Vietcong soldiers and imprisoned for four months, and then released as part of a prisoner exchange. Davis received a Purple Heart. After that he returned to Florida, where he had a wife—that's Kitty Dunn now—and a child, Maryann . . ."

It was, as Tony had said, quite a story, but I had started jotting dates on a desk calendar and was only half listening as he talked about the couple's divorce and mentioned that Kitty had gotten custody of the child, and that her second husband, Howard Dunn, had later adopted Maryann.

"Davis apparently fell apart for a few years—heavy drug use—but he straightened out and married for a second time in 1976, and now has a Kentucky Fried Chicken franchise in Orlando, as well as—"

"Tony! I know something Kitty would want to keep quiet."

I was startled, suddenly, by a shadow falling across the desk. Looking over my shoulder, I saw Pookey Dunn retreating from the cubicle's entrance.

"Sorry," Pookey mouthed. "I'll catch you later."

I waited until his office door closed and then, to be certain, peered around the edge of the cubicle. Violet was still at her desk, Herbert Dunn's door was shut, and Herbert's secretary was on a whispered phone call that probably had nothing to do with Dunn Construction business.

I cupped my hand around the phone's mouthpiece. "Kitty was having an affair with Herbert Dunn while her husband was fighting in Vietnam. Since Maryann was born in May, 1964, and Pookey is two years younger than Maryann almost to the day, that means that he was conceived in . . . September 1965.''

"How do you figure that?"

"Pookey was born in May 1966."

"You're not making sense, Bonnie."

"Pregnancies last nine months," I said, exasperated.

"Tell me about it! But you're still not making sense. First of all, it's possible Davis got leave and came home the September before Pookey was born. It happens."

"You haven't seen Pookey," I whispered. "He's definitely Herbert Dunn's son."

"Second," Tony continued, "assuming you're right, this is not a national secret. Family members and friends who were around at the time would know, and anybody who can count months and years backwards on their hands could figure it out."

There Tony was correct. This information wasn't a secret. Anyone who knew what to look for could find it. I was right too, though. The information was thirty years old, and it wasn't something that anyone might simply come across. Only a person out for revenge would bother digging it up at all.

After Tony and I hung up I sat doodling with dates on the calendar for a few moments longer. Tiffany had known that this juicy tidbit was there in her family's photo albums, but from the way she'd talked I wasn't sure she planned to reveal it.

I could imagine what Elsie would make of the story: *Dear Readers: Flashback to the* 60's! *Elsie knows about a Fifth Avenue society matron who, thirty years ago, was pregnant with another man's child while her husband was in a Vietcong prison camp. While hubby was earning a Purple Heart, she was breaking his true-blue American heart. Stay tuned for more.*

This was a part of Kitty Dunn's past that would cause her far more embarrassment than her having been a waitress. And this information, combined with the up-to-date gossip about Herbert and Stacey, might just be enough of a one-two punch to knock Kitty off the society pages for a long time.

Would Kitty, frightened about what her niece might reveal next, have followed Tiffany to the back of Zoe's salon? Might she have said, *Let's wander back to the storage room and see if there's anything special on the rack.* And when her niece's back was turned, could she have grabbed Tiffany by the hair and swung her head into the wall?

No. I couldn't imagine this premeditated scenario. From what I had seen of Kitty, even if she had it in her to kill her niece, she was too cool, too in control of herself, to do it in such a messy, risky manner.

But what if the circumstances were slightly different? What if the murder wasn't premeditated? What if Tiffany confronted her aunt in the back of the salon and dropped a sly hint about Kitty's first marriage and Pookey's birthdate? Or maybe not such a sly hint. What if Tiffany was as up front and in-your-face confrontational as she'd been with the van driver earlier that day? She could have pushed Kitty over the edge.

Temporary insanity. Those few moments when fury takes over, when the unconscious controls the conscious. When normally cool, controlled people can forget all about mess and risk. That was the one way I could imagine Kitty as a murderer.

It was well after four o'clock when Violet finally marched past my cubicle, her handbag tucked under her arm. I watched her until she had turned the corner at the end of the hall, and then rushed to her desk.

Her Rolodex was one of those giant wheel affairs, and it was stuffed with cards, many of them yellowing and dog-eared. Most likely she'd inherited the bulk of it from a long line of predecessors. The H section wasn't nearly as bad as some of the others. God help me if Neil's last name had started with a B, I thought while thumbing through the cards. Harvey . . . Hemmings . . . Howard. There were three of them. Alan, Isaac, and finally, Neil. An old Queens address had been scratched out, and two New Jersey addresses penciled under it in the same neat hand that had addressed almost three hundred wedding invitations. There was a listing on Lake Drive, Riverton, New Jersey, and one care of Betsy Howard, 36 Vernon Street, in the same city, and under each address was a phone number.

I quickly jotted the information on a scrap of paper, pocketed the paper, and then covered my tracks by spinning the Rolodex. I was leaving the cubicle when my eye was caught by an envelope in Violet's Out box, addressed to Neil at the Lake Drive address. Picking it up, I held it to the light. Inside was what looked like a check. I scooped the envelope out of the box and pocketed it, too.

Just in time.

"Oh, Bonnie. I'm glad you haven't gone. My wife wanted me to double check with you about the rehearsal dinner next Friday. The caterer's arriving at five P.M.?"

I was having a hard time thinking of Pookey as a lieutenant-of-industry, much less a master thief. A red splatter on his yellow necktie hinted that his lunch had involved tomato sauce, and his breath hinted that the sauce had been garlic laden.

"That's right, Pookey. His name is Jeffrey Phipps. He'll be bringing two servers, a bartender, and a kitchen person with him. You'll need to have a check ready. Jeffrey won't even unpack his things until he gets it, or so he says."

I repeated the amount that Jeffrey had told me, and when Pookey had assured me that the check would be waiting, I went on to explain other details. The caterer would supply, in addition to the food and coffee, the ice and the linens. China and silver were to be supplied by Pookey and his wife. Centerpieces for the dining tables were being delivered by the florist who was doing the wedding and reception.

The wedding party was being picked up at the church after the rehearsal by rented limousines. Those limousines would transport them to Pookey's apartment and would, at the end of the evening, return them to their homes. At the dinner, gifts would be given to the attendants by Courtney and Justin. For the bridesmaids there would be pearl earrings, and for the ushers, cuff links. I would pick these up at the jewelry store and bring them to the dinner.

Pookey gave me his full attention. "Very impressive," he said when I'd finished.

I tried to make my thank you sound a bit weary, as if getting all of this together had been a problem. The reality was that the Dunns' fat bankroll was making my job easy. In that respect Herbert had been right: money is a great expediter.

"Dad tells me he offered you Tiffany's position," Pookey said. "That's what I wanted to talk to you about earlier. I hope you'll consider it. You'd be great. You have a terrific mind for detail."

Pookey had positioned himself so that I was trapped between Violet's desk and the fax machine beside it. Trapped isn't the right word, I suppose. There was an escape route about a foot wide between the desk and Pookey's bulging middle. I could have said, Excuse me, and squeezed through, but it might have meant touching him, a prospect I found unappealing.

Not wanting to pursue the subject of the job offer with Pookey while I felt so ambivalent about it, I shifted the subject back to the rehearsal dinner.

"You've ordered the wine?" I asked.

"Yes. We'll start with a Riesling, and with the main course we'll serve a Cabernet Sauvignon that *The Times* wine columnist gave a glowing review last week. I also ordered a half-case of Sauterne to go with dessert. Sweet, but not cloying . . ."

Good grief! Wine experts were sprouting all over the place. First Rosaleen and now Pooky. I tried to look alert, interested. There was a possibility that I might end up working closely with this guy. My eyes had locked on the red tomato sauce splotch on his tie. It was dead center, a greasy little faux tie tac. Forcing my gaze away from it, I glanced out the window at the side of Violet's desk, at the driveway behind Zoe's, and then at that empty building.

"Excuse me," I said, cutting Pookey off midsentence as he was going on—I'm not making this up!—about a wine phenomenon known as the Noble Rot. As I pushed past him, something—I suspect it was the palm of his hand—rubbed into my hip, and even seemed to hold me there beside him a moment longer than was necessary. Then I was free.

"Sorry," I said over my shoulder. "If I don't get to the bridal salon right away . . ."

As far as I was aware, my business at Zoe's was finished. Pookey didn't know that, though. As I hurried from the office he was standing where I'd left him, mouth slightly open but no doubt comfortable with the explanation for my rapid departure, and pleased with the quick feel he'd gotten.

I pressed my nose into the window at a spot where white-wash hadn't covered the glass, and used my hand to block the sun's glare from my eyes. Inside the building someone lifted a box from a corner and then threw it aside. It hit the floor hard. *Thunk.*

The person moved to the center of the room. I made out a man, probably the same man I'd seen unlocking the building's front door when I'd looked through the window near Violet's desk. Now he started moving toward the back of the building. Afraid he might disappear for hours, or forever, I pounded on the glass.

"Nobody home!"

His voice was harsh. I knocked again, not so hard this time.

"Can't you hear? I said, nobody—"

"This is important," I called through the glass.

A second later the street door flew open.

"Whadda ya, deaf?"

This man was older, thinner, and lighter-skinned than the man I'd seen in the alley the day Tiffany was murdered, and rather than work clothes, he wore a dark gray suit made of a shiny synthetic fabric. He had a full head of gray hair a shade or two lighter than the suit, which had been greased back over his ears and, on top, coaxed into a pompadour that swooped across his forehead.

I've been renting an apartment in New York City for a long time. I would have bet my lease that this was a land-lord.

"Actually, I was looking for the porter," I said. "He was here a week ago. Dark haired . . ."

I lifted my hand a few inches higher than my head.

"Ramirez. He's the only one that's been here, and he's gone."

The man must have seen a question forming on my lips. "Gone like in 'disappeared,' " he barked. "Like in 'gone to Puerto Rico.' Like in 'gone for good.' Gone like in 'good riddance.' The thievin' bastard."

He was blocking most of the door with his body. Feigning desperation, I peered around him into the building. I couldn't see much, but what I could make out looked a mess, the floor trash-strewn, the walls pocked with nails and crumbling plaster.

"He can't be gone. I gave him some money as a deposit. He told me there was going to be a vacant apartment. With a working fireplace," I added, because an Upper East Side apartment with a working fireplace did sound awfully nice.

Drawing back, the man regarded me as if he were looking at a lunatic. "There's not gonna be no empty apartment, and there's not gonna be no fireplace. You threw your money away. And don't be looking at me to get it back! I got enough trouble as it is. That sucker robbed me blind. A lot worse than he robbed you."

"What do you mean?"

"Exactly what I said. I trusted him to look out for my piece of vacant property here. Next thing I know, he's stripped the place. My copper pipes and wires: gone. My mahogany wall paneling: gone. My antique bathroom fixtures: gone. Even the goddamned oak floorboards: gone. And my porter? Like I said, he's gone too. Probably called out 'Hasta la vista, sucker!' as his plane back to San Juan passed over the building."

The Long Island Railroad rumbled along, bringing me closer to Huntington. It hadn't been a bad day. I'd been offered a ridiculously generous bribe, I'd learned something about Kitty Dunn that, if made public, would have been a real embarrassment and, on top of all that, I'd done the job I was being paid for and gotten much of Courtney's wedding under control.

Most important was what I'd discovered from talking to

the owner of the vacant building. I now had an idea why the saintly Robert J. Annessi had denied pulling his van into the alley the day Tiffany was murdered. Annessi had been there doing the devil's business, helping "liberate" a building of its copper pipes and antique bathroom fixtures. Saint Bob was a thief.

I was on the phone with Amanda late that evening. We'd just finished going over menus and timetables, and were about to say goodbye, when Tony arrived home. I remember the change in Amanda's voice, how confused she sounded when she said, "Tony wants to speak to you before you hang up."

Her next words were spoken so softly I could hardly hear them. "Bonnie. What's going on? Tony's gone to get a beer, but he looks furious."

"I don't know."

A moment later Tony took the phone from his wife. "I need some privacy," I heard him tell her. A door slammed.

"Bonnie."

"Yes."

"You must think I'm really stupid, Bonnie," he said. "A brain-dead moron? Is that what you think?"

"What's . . . ?"

"I am the officer in charge of the investigation into Tiffany McKinney's murder. Anything that comes in concerning Miss McKinney eventually comes across my desk. Even if it happens in another precinct. Even if it happens in another county. And I eventually get around to reading everything that comes across my desk."

My hand on the receiver had grown clammy. A part of me wanted to babble excuses but I was too undone to think of any.

"A report from Nassau County that I got around to reading late today mentioned that on Saturday night a forty-year-old female caucasian by the name of Bonnie Jean Indermill was questioned in a B and E at the condominium of one Tiffany McKinney, deceased. This Bonnie Jean Indermill had been observed moving around the premises in

the dark with the aid of a flashlight. The responding officers—''

"I wasn't the one who broke in, Tony," I said hurriedly.
"I had permission to be there, and a key. And I was able
to put the photo albums where the family is sure to find
them."

That last bit had been added with the hope that it would
have a soothing effect. It had about the same effect as a
squirt gun on a five-alarm fire.

"I don't care about your key and your permission! If
you were being up-front with me you would have told me
about this when we talked this afternoon. You were hoping
I wouldn't find out, weren't you?"

Tony's tirade embarrassed and shamed me to the point
where, if it had subsided for only a moment, if he'd given
me time to pull myself together, I expect I would have
spilled my guts and told him that the real burglar was Neil
Howard. But Tony didn't stop. He went on, his words
scalding me through the phone line.

"Your only business with the Dunns is the wedding business. Understand? You do not search, analyze, or ask questions. You are not an investigator, and if you try to
investigate, I will find out about it and I will charge you
with something that will stick long enough to get you at
least one night in a cell on Rikers Island as a guest of the
City of New York. Got it?"

"Got it."

"From now on, Donnie, you stick to the flowers and
dresses and the rest of the girly stuff. Maybe you ought to
have a kid, like Amanda. That would keep you out of trouble."

You know, if he hadn't added that last bit, about the girly
stuff and the kid, I might have listened to him.

16

It took me two days to catch up with Robert J. Annessi.

Annessi lived on City Island, which is at the eastern end of the Bronx. When I called information, though, there was no number listed under his name. City Island isn't huge, and it was possible that I could find a house with a Cutter's Plumbing van in front of it by driving up and down the island's streets, but what if Annessi didn't drive the van home at night? What if he used his own car to go back and forth? A ten-year-old Honda would be harder to spot than a big white van with a company logo on its side. I didn't even know the Honda's color.

The best course, I decided, was to try to get to Annessi toward the end of his workday, near the plumbing supply company. Maybe I could creep up on him while he was unloading the van. If this didn't work, then I'd follow him home.

A car is not always a good thing to have in Manhattan,

but since I might be doing some tailing, I'd driven the Chrysler in to town. The phone book listed Cutter's Plumbing at an East Fifth Street address, which put it in the East Village.

Manhattan's East Village is a mixed bag of a neighborhood. A realtor with an apartment to rent down there might tell an out-of-town client that it was a "mixed-use neighborhood with a diverse population," but the realtor would never get away with telling that to a New York City client. The locals know.

At its westernmost edge, the East Village borders Greenwich Village proper. Broadway divides the neighborhoods, and at first glance there may not appear to be much difference between the two. A second glance, however, takes care of that illusion. The East Village is infinitely funkier than its more famous neighbor.

Strolling along *west* of Broadway on a sunny afternoon, you rub shoulders with Gap-clothed NYU students and stylish young moms pushing babies in strollers. Go *east* of Broadway, however, and you're in a world of black leather, sharing the sidewalk with skinny kids with shaved heads, multiple nose rings, and tattoos, and middle-aged hippies reeking of marijuana—pickled in marijuana—who, if asked, will tell you that they are artists or poets only moments away from fame.

That's the trendy part of the neighborhood. With each block you travel east, the kids become more waiflike and the hippies more strung-out until, by the time you've gone the four blocks to Avenue A, where the area called Alphabet City begins, it's a stretch to pretend there's anything trendy going on unless you're a follower of drug trends. The old tenements lining the streets are as likely to house heroin and crack dealers as struggling artists, and store clerks protect themselves from their customers with sheets of bulletproof Plexiglas. As for poetry, that depends on how you feel about "Wanna get high? Lookin' to buy?"

Scattered among these tenements are perfectly respectable companies. Not the kind of companies that have to impress with midtown offices, but small manufacturers and supply houses. Like Cutter's. If you can do your business during daylight hours, and you can fortify the place suffi- ciently at night, you probably can't beat the rent in lower Manhattan.

The wide brick building that housed Cutter's faced the street with an almost unadorned façade. Only a rusted, ban- nerlike tin sign suspended over a door at the building's side identified it. The much wider garage door at the top of a driveway bore no identification at all.

I'd already driven past when I spotted Cutter's sign through the rearview mirror. Traffic was heavy, and after waiting for a cab and what seemed to be an endless stream of cars to pass, I began backing down the street. There was an empty spot at the curb almost directly in front of Cut- ter's.

A dark, late-model car blasted its horn, so I stopped to let it pass. There were four men inside, two in the front seat and two in the back, and during the time their car moved by, all of them, even the driver, stared at me. Half a block up, the driver pulled to the curb but none of the men got out. Odd. They looked too healthy to be addicts hunting for a fix and too straight to be dealers. And they hadn't stopped at Cutter's, which was the only business I'd noticed on the block. Hollywood types, maybe, scouting locations? Or real estate developers looking for the next hot neighborhood?

I continued backing up. The spot I'd seen moments be- fore, however, had been taken by another big car. There were two men in this one, both of them in the front seat. I pulled the Chrysler to the curb directly across the street from them, a few doors down from Cutter's. After looking around, I pressed the mechanism that locks all the car's windows and doors.

To my right, beyond the sidewalk, was a row of shabby tenements. The one nearest me wasn't as run down as the others. On its steps sat a trio of old men drinking Corona beer out of bottles, while a dark-skinned woman, who was trying to sweep around them, grumbled in Spanish. A small child clung to the frame of the tenement's open door.

There was nothing to do but wait and watch. The way Cutter's was laid out, there was no knowing whether Bob

Annessi was inside or miles away. During the next few minutes a customer in a pickup truck pulled in to Cutter's driveway and blew his horn. When the big door was opened, he drove inside. Shortly after that a bigger truck pulled up and remained in the driveway while three men loaded a huge carton into it.

When that truck had driven away, one of the men who had parked across the street from me got out of the car. At Cutter's entrance he said something to a workman, and then followed him inside. A moment later he emerged from the shop and returned to the car. It appeared that he and his companion were waiting for some special piece of equipment.

The sun was shining brightly into the mirror mounted outside the Chrysler's window. It can be adjusted from inside the car, but by then I was feeling more comfortable about where I was. Lowering the window, I adjusted the mirror, looking back through it as I did. Funny, but when I'd driven through the intersection a half-block back, a clot of young men had been standing around in front of a corner bodega. Now the intersection was deserted. And what was with all these big cars full of men? Two more of them had pulled up behind me. And . . . how strange. A phone company van had pulled through the intersection and was blocking it.

Closing the window, I glanced toward the tenement nearest me. The three old men were gone, and while I watched, the woman who had been sweeping grabbed the child under one arm and walked back into the tenement, shutting the door behind her. Moments later the child's dark eyes peered out at the street through a first-floor window. Then, abruptly, a blind was lowered over the window.

There was action at Cutter's now. The big garage door opened long enough to allow the pickup truck to leave, and then slammed shut. The smaller door at the other side of the building opened almost immediately after that and a stream of workers hurried out.

Annessi! He was wearing a khaki shirt and pants this time, and a loop earring, but I recognized him right away.

He walked rapidly up the block. Where could he be going but to his car?

I reached for the keys hanging from the ignition, so excited that the tapping sound coming from somewhere on my right hardly dented my consciousness. As I turned the key, the tapping grew louder. Metal against glass. I was afraid to take my eyes off Annessi, afraid I'd lose him. I glanced quickly across the Chrysler's wide front seat.

The piece of metal tapping against my car window was a police shield, and holding it up to the window was a big black man wearing dark wraparound sunglasses and a white T-shirt. When he knew he had my attention, he signaled that I should lower the window. I did. About three inches.

"NYPD Undercover Narcotics Squad," he said quietly. "I'd like to see some identification please."

Was he serious? You bet he was. No sooner had he gotten those words out than the phone company van that had been at the end of the block pulled ahead of me. The van's back doors swung open and a small army of men spilled from it and into the street. At the same time this was happening, the two men from the car across from me and the four men from the car that had parked up the street jumped from their vehicles and trotted toward me. One of them waved his hand, gesturing to the others. His green New York Jets windbreaker flew open, revealing a holstered gun.

My fingers shook as I dug my driver's license from my wallet and the Chrysler's registration from the glove compartment and passed them through the window. The cop examined both of them quickly, looking at me hard, and then back at my license photo.

"This automobile is registered to a Samuel Finkelstein. What is your business in it?"

I held my left hand toward him. "I'm his fiancée. We live together."

He scarcely glanced at the ring. "And what is your business on this street?"

"I was heading home from Greenwich Village when I started feeling weak and dizzy. I decided to pull over for a few minutes."

My voice quavered, which may or may not have helped

my story. The cop pushed my license back through the window. "Get out of here now, and in the future stay away from places like this."

I turned the keys in the ignition, released the emergency break, and did exactly what the man said.

I passed Robert Annessi as he was unlocking a gray Honda with a big, rusting dent in its fender. When I reached the corner, I glanced back. Annessi had gotten into the Honda, but instead of pulling out he had turned in his seat to watch the police action. I considered waiting him out but decided against it. After my second run-in with the police in five days, the thought of Huntington was suddenly very comforting.

As I've said, Billy wasn't much of a reader. For some reason, though, the article in the morning paper caught his attention. He read aloud.

> *"Drug sweep in East Village nets heroin and co- caine cache.*
> *"Yesterday afternoon members of an NYPD nar- cotics task force raided a tenement on East Fifth Street which was a known drug location. In addition to 400 pounds of heroin and cocaine, the police found a cache of automatic firearms. Three people discovered in the apartment were taken into custody and are be- ing held pending indictment. Residents and business- men in the area, who were warned in advance about the impending police action, praised the police ef- fort."*

"That sounds like something cool to do," Billy said when he'd finished reading.

"What?" Sam asked.

"Be a cop. Like Tony. Like, you know what I mean? Only I'd want to go into something cool, like, you know, narcotics. Like you stake out a tenement, and like maybe you bug it, and . . ."

Between hearing the article itself read aloud, and endur- ing those continual "like you knows," my nerves were stretched so taut that I could hardly swallow my coffee. Never mind that Billy was the least likely police officer imaginable.

Likely or not, Sam saw an opening here. Billy so seldom evinced signs of ambition that Sam tended to jump on any opportunity to steer his son toward that Valhalla, a paycheck from a source other than Finkelstein Boys Moving Company.

"Police work's not bad," Sam said. "Good benefits, and after twenty years you can retire with a big pension. Why don't you find out about taking the test?"

His father's enthusiasm immediately dampened Billy's. "Yeah. One of these days I'll get over to the police station in Huntington and pick up an application."

"If you need to use a car, I'm sure Bonnie can do without the Chrysler for a few hours."

"No way," said Billy. "If anybody sees me show up at the police station in that thing, they'll like, you know, throw my application in the trash can."

Noticing the puzzled expressions on both our faces, Billy raised his hands, palms up. "That's what drug dealers drive. Big white cars. Everybody knows that."

Billy was exaggerating, and he was also leaping at any excuse to avoid picking up a job application, but as someone once said, "From the mouths of babes . . ."

I called Cutter's Plumbing Supplies as soon as Sam and Billy left for the day.

"What are your hours?" I asked the woman who answered the phone.

"What are you lookin' to buy?"

I couldn't imagine why that mattered, but rather than get into some drawn-out thing with her, I said, "A faucet."

"A faucet? You'd be better off going to Home Depot."

"And pipe," I added. "Copper pipe."

"How much?"

"How much?"

"Yeah. Like, you got a residence, an apartment building . . . ?"

"Like, about fifteen feet," I said from between gritted teeth.

"Width?"

This was insane. "What's the narrowest it comes in?"

"Half-inch, but you don't want half-inch. With half-inch, you can't, like, take a shower and flush at the same time. You should go with three-quarter. . . ."

"Fine! When's the latest I can pick it up?"

"Before we close," she said.

I would have screamed if victory hadn't been just a word or two away. "And when is that?" I asked.

"We lock the doors at four-thirty on the dot."

"Thanks."

Given rush-hour traffic, I figured that Annessi would get home no earlier than 5:15. To be safe, though, I decided to be on City Island at 5:00 the next afternoon.

There was no parking near the ornate bridge that leads onto City Island, so I crossed it and parked near the Island's main street in a spot that would allow me to wheel quickly into traffic. Because that gray Honda was going to be hard to spot, I'd positioned the Chrysler beyond a curve in the road where I could watch cars coming over from the Bronx mainland.

I was near a pier, and for a while traffic was so light that my eyes kept wandering toward the water. New York was enjoying a beautiful day. Eastchester Bay was dotted with small boats, and fishermen dangled lines into the water. On a grassy spot, two little kids played with a ball while their mother sat nearby on a blanket nursing an infant.

At a few minutes after 5:00 P.M., traffic coming onto the island picked up tremendously. From then on, all my attention went to the cars coming toward me.

I don't understand why people buy cars the color of pavement, but many of them do, and the street was thick with cars in various shades of gray. I squinted into the afternoon sun, trying to distinguish the dumpy gray Honda. Twice I thought I had it, and once had started the engine and almost forced my way into traffic before I realized I was about to follow a gray Chevy.

After watching oncoming traffic for almost an hour my optimism was fading. Annessi could very well have had bowling league tonight, or Yankees tickets. There could be dozens of reasons why someone wouldn't go directly home after work.

Minutes ticked by. I stretched to stay alert, blinking to keep my eyes focused on those cars. The woman with the baby and the two children folded her blanket and left with her brood. It was time to start dinner.

Finally the gray Honda with the rust spot on its fender came around the curve. Close behind it followed a black sedan. I started the engine but wasn't able to ease into the stream of traffic until the black car had passed.

City Island is approximately a mile and a half long, and about a half a mile wide at its broadest point. The street plan is simple. City Island Avenue, where most of the island's businesses, including its numerous seafood restaurants, are located, runs the length of the island. Branching off this avenue are the residential side streets, most of which run into dead ends at the water's edge.

I remained close to the black sedan until it turned up one of the side streets. Then, though there was no reason to think that Annessi would recognize me behind the Chrysler's wheel, I stayed a few car lengths behind the Honda. Annessi was almost past a drive-in that sold that soft-type ice cream when his left turn signal started blinking.

Oncoming traffic was light and Annessi was able to make the turn without waiting. Seconds later I followed him.

The street I turned onto was about as long as a city block, and a dozen or so houses were crowded together on either side of it. At the end of the street was a small wooden pier. I trailed Annessi to the last house on the right. Two names were printed on the mailbox mounted on a post near the street: Florio, and under that, Annessi. Florio must have been the in-laws' name.

Robert Annessi pulled into the driveway and I pulled in behind him. When he got out of the Honda, he took a step toward me. For a moment there was no sign of recognition. He may have thought that I was a stranger who had pulled in to turn around or to ask directions. After a couple of seconds, though, something clicked. I could see him draw in a deep breath. A question seemed to be forming on his lips, but then he glanced toward the house. There was a screen door about ten feet from where he was standing. A few steps and he'd be inside.

I stuck my head out the car window.

"Mr. Annessi? I have to speak to you."

He didn't move until I opened my car door. Then he quickly approached the Chrysler.

"I know who you are. What are you doing here?"

"I have to speak—"

He interrupted me. "Everything I had to say I said to the police."

"But you didn't tell them the truth," I said.

"Daddy?"

A little boy was on the other side of the screen door. Annessi and I had both glanced in that direction when a woman appeared behind the boy. Annessi held his hand up to her, a combination wave and gesture that said, Just a minute.

"This lady needs directions," he called to the woman. Leaning down, he said softly, "If you don't get out of here, I'm calling the cops. You've got no right to upset my family."

I was so sure that I was right about Annessi that I hadn't considered the alternative, but for a second or two it occurred to me that this might be a terrible mistake. If by some slim chance Annessi hadn't been in the alley, and if he called Tony . . .

Oh, that was a grim possibility. I put it out of my mind.

"Your family's going to be a lot more upset if you lose your job," I said. "What if your boss finds out you're stripping empty buildings on his time, and using his van to haul stolen property?"

Annessi rubbed his lips roughly with his fingers. "This is a pain in the ass."

Bingo! I was one hundred percent sure of myself now. "All you've got to do is tell me what you saw in the alley that afternoon."

"There's nothing to tell."

"I still want to hear it."

He glanced over the hood of the Chrysler. The woman and little boy were still in the doorway.

"Not here," Annessi said. He pointed out toward the main street. "Half a block back you passed a drive-in that sells ice cream. I'll meet you in the parking lot in ten minutes."

He straightened and started toward the house.

"If you don't show up, I'll be back." My voice was very low, but from the way Annessi frowned over his shoulder as he walked to the screen door, I knew he'd heard.

I backed out of the driveway, drove to the corner, and turned right. A couple of hundred feet further I turned into the circular drive in front of the ice cream concession and backed into a parking spot.

It was a little after six, and except for a trio of teenagers horsing around at a table under the drive-in's awning, the place was quiet. Too close to dinner for most ice cream customers, I supposed. The girl working the concession rested her chin in her hand. After giving me a bored glance, she continued flipping through a magazine on the counter.

Not long after I pulled into the parking lot, Annessi came trotting along the main road in gym shorts, a T-shirt, and sneakers. His face was flushed and when he turned down the driveway he was breathing hard.

His eyes scanned the immediate area before he climbed into the passenger seat. The second he was inside he lowered the sun visor to shield himself from the street.

"Everybody wants to know everybody's business around here." He puffed for breath as he spoke. "I told my wife I was taking up jogging. Let's get this over with fast. What do you want to know?"

I was all too happy to hurry things along.

"You were in the alley behind Zoe's Bridal Salon around the time Tiffany McKinney was killed. I don't care why you were there, but I want to know what you saw."

"Like I said, I didn't see anything. You think if I saw that girl's murderer I wouldn't tell the police? No way! I may not be perfect, but hell, I'm not going to keep quiet about a thing like that."

"So the whole time you were there you didn't see anyone go through that open gate?"

He shook his head. "No one."

"What about someone from inside the bridal shop? Did anyone come to the back door?"

If I hadn't been staring so intently at him I suspect that Annessi might have lied. As it was, he started to shake his head again, but our eyes met and what had begun as a head shake turned into a neck roll.

"Yeah," he said. "I saw . . . you know . . . that girl. Tiffany McKinney."

"In the door?"

He nodded. "I recognized her right away. The same nasty bitch—forgive me for speaking badly of the dead—who had given me such grief over that parking spot. I figured she was taking a smoking break from work."

"She didn't work there," I said. "She was a customer."

"I know that," Annessi said. "She worked for Dunn. I just thought she was getting some work done while she was in the shop."

"Why is that?"

"Because when she first came out the door she was talking into one of those little recorders. You know what I mean? People dictate into them, or use them to keep notes for themselves. Anyway, she sat down on the step and lit a cigarette. I could tell she recognized me. Blew smoke my way, ugly, like she was saying, Up yours."

"And after that, she kept talking into the recorder?"

"That, and smoking. And then . . ."

"Yes?"

"I was headed into the building—I'm almost inside the door—and I happen to look back to where she is. Well, she stands up, turns her back and bends over like maybe she's tying her shoe or something. Only that's not what she's doing. What she's doing is showing me her ass. Her skirt was hiked up so that I could see her underwear. That girl was some piece of work," he added, unnecessarily.

"She turns back around," Annessi continued, "and I can tell from her face that she's cursing me out. I—um—well,

I flipped her the bird. Seems kind of stupid now, looking back on it."

"What happened then?" I asked.

"What happened? She's pissed as all hell. Throws her dictating machine against the wall."

"*She* threw the machine?"

"Yeah. That's when I figure she's crazy, and I start ignoring her. She's nothing to me, anyway. I finished my business and got out of there. Didn't see her again."

"Did you lock the driveway gate when you left?" I asked.

"No. Figured the porter would lock up after I was gone."

Stooping slightly, Annessi peered beneath the sun visor. "I got to get going. You're not going to tell any of this to the police, huh?"

I shrugged. "I can't promise that."

"You know, all I'm trying to do is take care of me and mine," he said with a cloying smile. "Half the people in construction are on the take one way or another. Even those fancy Dunns. They're no better than anybody else. You read about those firewalls that were missing in the city project over in the Bronx?"

I nodded.

"Well, a guy I was talking to knows a guy who heard from a friend of his that they were never even ordered. Someone inside Dunn Construction just pocketed the money. Hadn't of been for that fire they would have gotten away with it."

Annessi opened the passenger door and stepped onto the pavement. Before he jogged off, though, he stuck his head through the window.

"Happens all the time."

Annessi was trying to justify his own thefts, but what he'd just said was pretty much what I'd been thinking myself.

Had it been worth the effort of tracking Annessi down? It seemed so. When I'd discussed the possibility of a missing tape with Tony, I'd wondered why the murderer hadn't simply pocketed the entire recorder. Now there was an explanation. When Tiffany, frustrated by the recorder, had thrown it against the wall, the tape had popped out onto the ground. All the murderer had to do was bend down and pick it up.

As I was sitting there thinking this over, an old red Volvo pulled in beside me. In the front seat was a couple, and in the back two children, a baby strapped into a car seat and a little girl of perhaps four. The baby was sleeping and the little girl, whose cherubic face was framed by strawberry-blond curls, seemed to be happily looking forward to her ice cream cone.

As a rule I prefer regular ice cream to the soft stuff, but I was breaking all kinds of rules already. Why not another one? I got in line behind the dad and his little girl.

The kid was so cute, so sweet. The "What ifs" are dangerous territory that I try to stay out of, but what if Tony hadn't been entirely out of line. What if I was missing . . .

The little girl took the strawberry cone her father handed her, frowned, and said, "I asked for chocolate."

"You said . . ." her father began.

"Eeh!" the kid yelled. Raising her arm as if to crack a whip, she flung the strawberry cone across the sidewalk. Dad, balancing two other cones and muttering several choice words, herded the now screaming child back to the Volvo.

My "What ifs" disappeared as quickly as they'd arrived.

"A large vanilla cone with sprinkles," I said to the girl behind the counter.

17

THE FINKELSTEIN BOYS BOOKKEEPING and various "girly" stuff, not to mention a torrential afternoon rain, kept me at home the next day. It wasn't until Saturday morning that I was able to go looking for Neil Howard.

At that point my thinking was that Tiffany had been tracking Neil's thefts and that Neil, somehow discovering that, had asked her out with the hope of being able to shut her up. Maybe he'd thought he could romance her into submission. Who can say? But before that had happened, an opportunity to shut Tiffany up permanently had presented itself and Neil, or else his "Buddy," had taken advantage of it.

Never mind that Neil seemed an unlikely murderer to me. This was the only scenario I could come up with, and I wanted to see it through. There was no reason to suppose that Neil was going to open up to a woman he'd never even spoken to, but at least his paycheck gave me a reason to pay him a visit. If nothing else I could see what $17,500 cash gets you in rural New Jersey.

If you ask me, New Jersey gets an undeserved bad rap. Okay, so I'm a Jersey girl. Maybe I'm kind of defensive about strip malls and air pollution and big hair. There are parts of New Jersey, though, that could pass for rural Pennsylvania or northern New York State. A quick glance at a map and I realized that Silver Lake, where Neil was building, was one of those areas.

After crossing the Hudson on the George Washington Bridge, I headed west on a divided highway. Traffic was light, and it wasn't long before the road was following the curves of the Susquehanna River and speeding by large tracts of forested land. As I turned north the terrain became mountainous, or in any event, hilly. Less than forty miles from Manhattan and not a smokestack in sight. So there!

Riverton is situated at the edge of the Susquehanna in a valley between a wildlife preserve and a state forest. I pressed the accelerator hard, and when the Chrysler had passed over the crest of a hill, the town lay before me. There's nothing fancy about the place. Homes tend to be modest—most of them were originally built as vacation cottages for working-class families—and shops are more likely to sell live bait than antiques.

I'd been there a number of times. When my parents, my brother, and I used to pile into the car for a Sunday excursion, the Riverton area was a popular destination. The center of town didn't appear much changed, and as I drove down the main street I recognized a general store where we bought whatever we needed to complete our picnic lunches and, at the riverfront, the park where we spread our blanket and ate.

That didn't mean I knew my way around, though, and my New Jersey state map stopped far short of a Riverton street guide. I stopped in a cafe for directions to Vernon Street and a container of coffee to go. It was about 11:30 A.M. and the place was empty. The notion of brunch didn't seem to have reached this area. There's breakfast, and then there's lunch, with nothing in between. The waitress, a pretty young woman with long auburn hair and restless blue eyes, seemed glad to have company.

"Go up to the first light and take a left," she explained as she pressed a cap on my coffee container. "Vernon Street's about four blocks. Who are you looking for?"

You'd never be asked that question in Manhattan or, for that matter, in Huntington. For a moment the cloud of paranoia I'd been operating under clicked in, but I got a grip on myself. There was no way a waitress in this out-of-the-way cafe—the nametag on her uniform read "Cathy"—could have been planted by the NYPD for the express purpose of keeping me in line.

"Betsy Howard."

"Oh? I know Betsy real well. When you get to Vernon Street, take a right. The house is gray. White shutters."

Her eyes had stopped wandering. She stared at me, plainly interested in my business with Betsy Howard. I put it down to small town curiosity, and after thanking the young woman for the directions, paid for my coffee and left without satisfying it.

There was a round holder between the Chrysler's front seats where a cardboard container of coffee fit almost, but not quite, perfectly, so I only sipped on the straightaway. When it was time to turn or brake, I always put my coffee in the holder and braced it with my hand.

The left at the first light and the right on Vernon Street gave me no trouble. My system wasn't foolproof, though. The gray wood bungalow with white shutters was set further back on its lot than the other houses on the street, and I was almost past it before the name Howard on the mailbox caught my eye. I pressed hard on the brake but forgot to hold the coffee container. By the time the car stopped, the container had toppled and hot coffee was running under the seats.

I sopped up some of the mess with a tissue, and then got out of the car with the dripping container still in my hand.

The fence around the small front lawn was white picket, and the screened front porch at the front of the bungalow was bordered by a trimmed boxwood hedge. Two wood planters, bright with purple and yellow pansies, flanked the few steps leading to the screen door. I was almost certain a storybook grandmother would answer my knock.

"Can I help you?"

The woman who had walked up behind me wasn't what I'd expected. She was about my height but heavier, and her faded blue jogging suit hugged her flesh in some crucial places the way that casing hugs a sausage. Her iron-gray hair was cut very short and her complexion was florid. In one hand she held a muddy garden hoe.

Ordinarily none of this would have bothered me. This woman, though, was the spitting image of my high school commercial arts teacher, the terrible Mrs. Utterback, a woman whose brow was permanently creased from years of glaring at her miserable students. The commercial arts, consisting of typing, steno, bookkeeping, and some nonsense called "office practice," weren't nearly as arty as I would have liked, and I wasn't nearly as good at them as Mrs. Utterback would have liked. Even now, her voice can still haunt me on bad office days. "Where is your brain, Bonnie?" she would ask, implying that it was lost forever.

"Mrs. Howard?" I asked this apparition.

She nodded.

"I'm Bonnie Indermill," I said, stepping down to the path. "An acquaintance of Neil's. Is he around? I've brought his last paycheck from Dunn Construction."

"Do you know Cathy?"

She was looking at the coffee container in my hand but I couldn't imagine what she was talking about.

"Cathy?"

"At the cafe. She and Neil are . . ."

Betsy Howard must have thought better of what she'd been about to say, because she let it drop.

"You must be a very "special" acquaintance of Neil's to come all this way," she said. "You could have put his check in the mail."

Was that a humorous tone behind her words? I couldn't decide. I considered, briefly, whether anything might be gained by pretending to have something "special" with Neil, but this woman didn't strike me as gullible.

"I had another errand out here," I said, not committing myself either way.

She rubbed the back of her hand across her forehead. "I haven't seen Neil since the day before yesterday. He must have decided to stay at his place near the lake. There's a little trailer on the property. Sometimes when he works late he sleeps there. Neil's a grown man," she added. "He can do what he wants."

She was interrupted by the loud ring of a phone from inside the house.

"Excuse me."

Dropping the hoe, she trotted up the steps and into the house. "Oh, it's you, Cathy," I heard her say through the screen door, but then her voice dropped and the rest of the short conversation was lost to me. A moment later Mrs. Howard pushed the door open and rejoined me on the walk.

"That was Cathy," she said. "You have her worried."

"She has nothing to worry about from me," I responded. "Are she and Neil going out?"

"Cathy thinks so, but apparently Neil didn't show up for their date last night." She lifted her shoulders carelessly. "I mind my own business about Neil's social life. I suspect that many women are interested in him."

And she suspected that I was one of them. Betsy Howard wasn't nearly as ferocious as I'd first feared. There was a half-formed smile on her lips, and laugh lines crinkled around her eyes.

"I'd like to see Neil. And give him his check," I added, gripping my tote protectively. "Maybe you could tell me how to find him? I know Silver Lake is on the map, but . . ."

"Of course," Betsy Howard said. "It's only a mile or so from here. Go back to the main road. . . ."

She gave me detailed directions. When she had finished, I thanked her and we said goodbye. As I pushed through the gate, though, I remembered my manners.

"Mrs. Howard? I'm sorry about your recent loss."

She had been bending to pick up the hoe. "Loss?" she asked, straightening.

"Your son. Neil's father."

Mrs. Howard frowned. "The loss must be *very* recent indeed. I spoke to both of Neil's parents last night."

I shook my head. "Sorry. I must have misunderstood."

"Yes."

Her eyes followed me as I made a U-turn and drove away. There was no reason for me to feel foolish; I'd only repeated what I'd heard from Violet. Still, I was glad when I turned the corner and was out of Betsy Howard's sight.

Her directions had been precise, and I found Lake Drive off the main highway with no trouble. It curved through a heavily forested tract where the few houses had lots of space between them. Traffic was almost nonexistent, and as I drove my mind played over the last of my conversation with Betsy Howard. Neil's parents were still alive, which meant that either Violet had lied to me about how Neil had gotten his property, or Neil had lied to Violet.

The first option was absurd. Violet might not win a Miss Mental Health competition but there was no reason why she should come up with such a pointless lie. The second option, though . . .

Neil had cooked up this inheritance story to satisfy anyone who might be curious about how he could afford to quit his job. Money inherited from a deceased father was, after all, much more acceptable than money stolen from an employer.

As I rounded a sharp turn, my eye was caught by a small red car some distance behind me. I don't know what caused me to be suspicious—maybe it was just my state of mind—but I sped up. The red car did the same, and maintained the same distance between us.

Finally, about a quarter-mile beyond a small filling station, I came to a creek spanned by a narrow concrete bridge. As Mrs. Howard had promised, a dirt road was just beyond this bridge. I again glanced in the rearview mirror. The little red car was nowhere in sight but I made the turn quickly and without giving a signal, just in case. The Chrysler lurched onto the rutted road.

I'm reasonably fond of woods, but given a choice, I prefer to experience them at a distance. Sitting in a swing on a country porch after a cookout, listening to the crickets chirp and watching the sun set over the treetops—that's my idea of enjoying the woods. As a teenager I may have spent too much time watching bogeyman-in-the-woods movies. For whatever reason, these unfamiliar woods felt almost smotheringly close and confining, and the low branches scraping across the car's sides and roof heightened the feeling. When the road abruptly widened and I saw the sky through the windshield, I startled myself by sighing out loud with relief.

I passed several building sites along the road, and the sound of a buzz saw, carried over the rustle of leaves, indicated that civilization wasn't so far away. Still, I couldn't imagine myself living in such a place.

"Private Property. No Trespassing."

The sign—hand-lettered on a wood plank—swung from a chain stretched across the road, and another wood sign— "Dead End"—was nailed to a tree. There was a turnaround at that point. Pulling into it, I got out of the car.

The chain was suspended between two sturdy iron posts, and locked with a padlock. If Betsy Howard's directions were right—and so far they had been—Neil's property began here, and his building site was a couple of hundred feet in. The chain struck me as a paranoid touch. None of the other people building in the area had felt it necessary to chain off their property.

I left the Chrysler in the turnaround—locked securely against bogeymen—and set out on foot. I was wearing a T-shirt, jeans, and sneakers, which ordinarily would have been okay for a short walk up a wooded road, but the ground was wet and it wasn't long before mud had splattered my shoes and the bottoms of my pants. As I yanked my leg free of a bramble, I found myself wondering what Tiffany would have thought of this place. One look around and she probably would have tottered off as fast as her high heels would carry her.

A minute later I reached the clearing where Neil was building, and admitted to myself that the man had done pretty well with his money, or better put, Dunn Construction's money. The little creek I'd driven over before turning onto the dirt road meandered along one side of the property, and at the other side, a downhill slope afforded a nice view of the lake below.

Near this slope, the foundation for a house had been marked off, but construction hadn't started. On the far side of the marked-off foundation, stacks of building materials were shielded by a plastic canopy. Parked alongside the materials was the trailer Betsy Howard had mentioned, its once-beige paint pocked with rust. This trailer was so tiny that faced with living in it, I could have been persuaded to pick up a hammer and start building that house myself.

There was one other semipermanent structure on the property—a metal storage-shed sort of like the one in Sam's backyard. This shed, though, was at least the size of a generous two-car garage. Neil's truck would have fit easily inside, I realized, or perhaps he'd set up a woodworking shop for himself. Or maybe he was hiding his most valuable stolen goodies in there.

Neil's truck was nowhere in sight, but before I assumed he was gone and started exploring, I called his name:

"Neil?"

As I'd expected, there was no answer. I started up a muddy path toward the trailer, and as I got closer called out again. Again there was no answer.

I was surprised to find the trailer door standing partly open. It wouldn't have provided much protection from the elements anyway, the top half being a tattered screen, but from the look of the puddle of water on the table just inside, the door hadn't been shut at all during the previous afternoon's storm.

I knocked hard once on the frame, and then pulled the door wide. A glass pane which could have easily been flipped up to cover the top portion of the window swung on its hinges beneath the screen. Someone's carelessness—who else but Neil could be responsible?—had allowed the wind and rain to play havoc with some blueprints on the minuscule dinette table just inside the door. A denim jacket hanging on a chair next to the table was soaked.

Stepping inside, I looked around at the few things Neil had in the trailer—some changes of underwear and jeans stuffed into a drawer, a few dirty dishes crammed into a sink. On top of the two-burner stove was a cast-iron frying pan coated with decades of congealed grease. The smell of sour towels, and worse, greeted me in what passed for a bathroom at the trailer's rear.

A dog-eared phone book sat under a filthy telephone, and the blinking red light on an answering machine indicated that Neil had messages waiting. I wouldn't have minded listening to the messages, but I didn't quite have the nerve to do it.

There was no sign of the item I was most interested in finding—the computer printout Neil had taken from Tiffany's desk—but it was the kind of thing that could easily have been destroyed.

Searching the trailer took only a minute or two. On my way out, my feet squished over the carpet near the door and my arm brushed against the soaking jacket. At the door, I turned back and looked over the small space.

My mother has a theory that all men are, at heart, slobs, and that the pristine female influence is all that saves them from squalor. Neil's housekeeping style certainly added weight to her argument. Why, though, wouldn't he want to keep dry? Dirty is one thing but wet is quite another.

As I pushed through the door, my eyes were focused straight ahead toward the storage shed. I didn't see the girl until she was right beside me.

"Remember me?"

To jump out of one's skin is impossible, but I sure know what the phrase means. For a few seconds I felt as if only my grip on the door frame kept me and my skin in the same place.

"Cathy," she continued, oblivious to the fact that she'd almost given me heart failure. "From the cafe. You stopped in. . . ."

I took a deep breath. "Yes, I know."

"I dropped by to see how Neil's doing with his house. He doesn't seem to be around, though, unless he's in the shed or"—her blue-eyed gaze darted to the trailer's door, then back to me—"inside there."

She may have learned my name when she called Betsy

Howard, but there was no reason not to go along with her charade.

"My name's Bonnie," I said, "and no, Neil's not in the trailer. I haven't seen him."

"Oh. And I don't see his truck around. Maybe . . ."

I fell into step beside her and we walked slowly toward the big shed. My heart had stopped racing, but Cathy's sudden appearance had intensified the uneasy feeling I'd had since looking around the trailer.

"Do you drive a red car?" I asked.

"Yes. Oh, you must have seen me. I wasn't following you," she added hastily. "I wanted to see Neil about something else."

Such as his no-show the evening before.

"Neil's grandmother said you and Neil were supposed to go out last night," I remarked.

Cathy seemed to droop like a flower too long without water. "He was supposed to meet me at a restaurant out on the river after my last class. I only waitress in the morning. Afternoons I'm in the pre-nursing program at the community college."

"What time did your class end?" I asked.

"Five-thirty. I got to the restaurant about six. When Neil didn't show up I called here but there was no answer. I waited at the restaurant until almost seven before I left. Then, when you showed up earlier today . . . well, I noticed your beautiful engagement ring, and I know Neil dated a lot of girls in the city. . . ."

An overactive imagination can sure get you a lot of misery. Cathy's eyes were glistening with tears.

"I hardly know Neil."

I told Cathy the same story I'd told Mrs. Howard—that I was there to deliver a check—and then asked if Neil wasn't usually pretty dependable.

Cathy rubbed her fist over her eyes as she nodded. "He always has been. We haven't gone out very often, but he never stood me up before."

She still looked ready to burst into tears. We were only a few feet from the big aluminum shed by then, and as much to take her mind off her trouble as to satisfy my own curiosity, I asked Cathy what was in it.

"I don't know. Sometimes Neil pulls his truck inside to work on it, and he keeps some machinery that's worth money . . ."

I dug a tissue from my tote and handed it to her. Then, leaving her to collect herself, I circled the shed. It was big and windowless, the only entrance being a double-width garage-type door that opened from the top. When I reached this door, I tugged on a handle near its bottom. The door held. Just under the handle there was a keyhole.

"Where would Neil keep the key?"

Cathy sniffed into the tissue. "He keeps all his keys with him, in his jacket pocket."

"A denim jacket?"

She nodded, and I returned to the trailer feeling worse with every step about what was going on. If Neil had killed Tiffany because she knew he was stealing from the company, and if he'd then been swamped by guilt . . .

Suicide. That's what I was thinking as I rummaged through the pockets of the clammy denim jacket. Sure enough, there was a ring of keys big enough for a prison warden. I hurried back to the shed, my heart racing once again. Wanting to be rid of all responsibility, I thrust the keys at Cathy. She wasn't thinking along the lines I was and took them willingly. After a moment, she selected two.

"One of these, I think."

She crouched by the side of the door. The first key turned easily in the lock. "This one," she said, and began raising the door.

The searing odor of gasoline poured from inside the shed, stunning us both. Cathy fell back on her hands, but the door's pulley system had been engaged and it continued rising. The hood of a dark blue truck was now visible under it. I was afraid to see what might be in the front seat, but even if I hadn't been, the smell would have driven me away. Turning my head, I grabbed Cathy's arm and pulled her away. When she had recovered her footing, we both ran to the far side of the trailer.

"I have to call the police," I said, pulling the screen door open.

"Do you think Neil . . . ?"

She didn't finish her sentence. Maybe she couldn't. I dialed 911. "I think there's been a suicide," I told the operator. "Carbon monoxide poisoning."

18

I WAS BOTH RIGHT AND WRONG.

Neil Howard had died of carbon monoxide poisoning at least twenty-four hours before his body was discovered, but it wasn't suicide. The police were calling his death a "suspicious incident," and *possibly* an accident. The tabloid press however, excited by what may have been one of fate's more grotesque tricks, had already deemed it a "freak accident," and one especially hysterical Monday headline had suggested divine intervention visited upon the man who surely had killed Tiffany McKinney. Not that there was one iota of proof that Neil Howard had committed the murder, but headlines sell.

On the rear of Neil's truck there had been a winch, run by a small gasoline generator that was powered off the truck's engine. Neil had been in the process of unloading a heavy item from the bed of his truck when, for some reason, he'd misjudged its trajectory. The item had struck him on the head, either before or after bouncing off the wall of the shed, knocking him unconscious, but it was the carbon monoxide spewing out of the truck engine that ultimately killed him. As for the shed's closed, locked door, an odd thing had happened. Neil had left the lock engaged, which was no problem as long as the door was raised. For some reason, however, the door had dropped with enough force to click the lock into place.

Oh, yes. The soggy blueprints in Neil's trailer revealed that he'd planned to have a fireplace in his new house, and what a whopper it was to have been. The item he had been unloading from his truck was the huge marble mantel that the Ambassador Hotel so badly needed, and an extensive search of Neil's property had turned up numerous other items which were missing from Dunn's inventory.

Here, uncut, is the *Inside Elsie* column that appeared in Monday's paper:

Death Haunts The Ambassador Hotel

No, dear readers, the latest death connected with the Ambassador didn't occur at the hotel itself. It happened in a New Jersey hamlet miles from the Upper East Side. **Neil Howard**, a former employee of **Dunn Construction**, who last worked for that company at its Ambassador Hotel construction site, died in what some authorities are calling a freak accident. Accident? Perhaps. It has been suggested, though, that Divine Intervention played a role. Police suspect that in addition to stealing thousands of dollars worth of supplies from Dunn, Neil Howard may have murdered darling young *Tiffany McKinney*, whom your reporter met—you'll never guess!—in front of the Ambassador Hotel.

Your reporter, who ordinarily is not given to flights of fancy, can't help feeling that the long-rumored Curse of the Ambassador is still trifling with human mortality.

Over the next several weeks you'll learn more about the victims of the Ambassador's curse. From diplomats to rock stars to construction workers, no one is

safe. We must ask ourselves: Who will be next? One
of the Dunns? The wedding reception for lovely young
Courtney Dunn and her betrothed, **Justin Harwood
III**, is being held next Saturday evening in the Ambassador's ballroom. Courtney and Justin: let's hope
you've done nothing to anger Providence.

Ta ta till next time. Elsie.

Monday evening Sam and I had dinner with Tony and
Amanda at their house. Amanda, having gotten her doctor's
okay, was back on her feet and cooking, down-home style,
like nobody's business. Fried chicken, mashed potatoes and
gravy, green beans, cornbread. With every bite, my triglyc-
erides inched up a few points.

Amanda had cooked all this comfort food to take her
mind off the hysterical phone calls she'd received from
Kitty and Courtney in the wake of Elsie's column. Or so
she said. Frankly, I thought the pecan pie she'd made for
dessert almost justified Elsie's nonsense.

After dinner, Sam, Tony, and I sat in the back yard while
Amanda loaded the dishwasher. It was her idea that I
should relax after my recent ordeal, and though the "girly"
thing would have been to insist on helping her, I wanted
to talk to Tony.

Tony and I were back on good terms. After learning all
the facts, he'd made an understandable fuss because I
hadn't kept him informed from the start. Once that was out
of his system, though, he'd apologized for yelling at me,
and had even mumbled something about my "good work."

"I still don't get it," I said. "Neil Howard had worked
around machinery for a long time. If his garage door had
a tendency to slide by itself, you'd think he'd have propped
something under it while his truck engine was running."

Tony nodded. "It was a stupid thing to do."

"People do stupid things," Sam put in.

Sam was nice enough not to mention that he thought my
hunting down Robert Annessi, and then Neil Howard, were
a couple of those stupid things, but after the talk we'd had
the night before I was very aware of how he felt.

He was sitting beside me, his big hand linked with mine,

staring across the LaMarcas' lawn as if contemplating the effect of sunset on the rose garden that Tony lovingly tends. Looking at Sam's profile, I experienced a surge of affection for him. Sometimes I forgot how much he genuinely cared for me.

I turned back to Tony. "But the fact that the garage door was locked—"

He cut me off. "If it closed hard enough, it would have locked automatically. Anyway, it's not my case. The local cops can worry about it. They have their own theories."

It was a certainty that the mantelpiece, swaying at the end of the steel rope, had gone off course, striking Neil. It was also a certainty that a big dent in the aluminum wall over the spot where Neil's body was discovered had been created when the huge slab of marble banged into the aluminum.

So much for certainty. Now for theory. Perhaps the blow to the wall had created a tremor in the aluminum shed which caused the door to drop. The tracks the door moved up and down in were well oiled, and police investigators had been able to make the door fall by pounding on the shed's walls. They hadn't, however, been able to make it fall with sufficient force to lock.

The theory I preferred was simpler in one way, but more complicated in another. There had been a second person— "Buddy"—helping to unload the mantel. This person had deliberately caused the heavy slab to swing out of control. When Neil was knocked unconscious, but not killed, this person had decided to let carbon monoxide finish the job. He slammed the shed door and left.

As I said, simple. The complicated part was finding this person. He, or she, had left no fingerprints, and any footprints or tire tracks that might have been there had been washed away by the rain.

After learning that Neil had been stealing from Dunn Construction, the New Jersey police questioned the people Neil had worked with at Dunn, ostensibly as routine procedure. Pookey hadn't been asked to provide an alibi, but according to Tony, he'd volunteered the information that, if necessary, he could account for almost every minute of his time for the past few days.

The blinking answering machine in Neil's trailer had proven a dead end, too. Cathy's message was the last one on the machine. There had been two other calls before hers, but in both cases the caller had hung up without leaving a message.

Tony preferred my "Buddy" theory too, but as he kept telling me, a death in New Jersey wasn't his problem, and neither was corporate theft. And if they weren't his problems, they definitely weren't mine. He had apologized for yelling, sure, but his sentiments hadn't changed. And now Sam was echoing those sentiments: *Keep out of it.*

At that point I did think it was over for me. With the wedding less than a week away, I had girly stuff to attend to. Amanda was going to see to that.

Five P.M. Friday. The countdown had begun.

My "to do" list for the rehearsal and the dinner afterwards wasn't too onerous, mainly because not one thing had been left to chance. All of Amanda's troops had received their marching orders. I thought nothing could go wrong.

It's always humbling to recall those many times in my life when I've thought nothing could go wrong, only to have everything go totally to hell around me. This time, though, things were bolted down solid.

Three limousines were at the curb, their uniformed drivers ready to whisk the wedding party to Pookey's Sutton Place duplex.

The first few notes of Wagner's *Lohengrin* resounded from inside St. Bonaventure's. Moving close to the entrance, I peered into the dimly lit church. It's an imposing building, with a timbered vaulted ceiling over the nave. The afternoon sun shone through massive stained glass windows, casting beams of light across the wood pews.

There's an old superstition that it's bad luck for a bride to rehearse, and Courtney, who had decided not to tempt fate, was observing from a pew. When the organist reached the segment of music sung in adolescent circles as "Here

Comes the Bride, Big Fat and Wide," Herbert Dunn, and Amanda, who was standing in for the bride, began moving slowly forward. Step-touch, step-touch.

"You'll take your father's arm," Amanda said to Courtney, "but don't hang on it."

Herbert rubbed his arm in mock protest and said, "What a grip!"

Ahead of the father and daughter stand-in were the other pairs: maid of honor Maryann and usher Pookey, and then Stacey, Taylor, and Alex with their escorts. Every one of them, except for Maryann, who wore her usual let's-get-this-over-with expression, was grinning self-consciously. Kitty studied the procession from a pew at the front of the church while Justin and his best man, standing near the altar rail, smiled sheepishly and the minister looked on approvingly.

When Amanda looked back to say something else to Courtney, I caught her eye and waved. It was time for her humble foot soldier to head into battle.

Before leaving for Pookey's apartment, I double-checked with the limo drivers. Yes, they all had the address, and if any of them thought there was something ridiculous about hiring limos to transport people less than a mile in a city thick with cabs, none of them showed it.

Everything's going like clockwork, I said to myself as I flagged a cab. During the short ride to Sutton Place I looked over the six-course menu Amanda had come up with. The meal would start with a citrus fruit cup with mint leaves, followed by pumpkin soup, and then a salad of endive and watercress. The main course was boeuf Bourguignon with new potatoes with dill, and fresh green beans. For dessert there was something called Floating Island, and after that, bittersweet chocolate morsels and coffee.

Jeffrey Phipps had found it acceptable, and so did I.

I was on the verge of throwing a major tantrum, complete with jumping up and down and screaming, right there in front of Pookey and Maddie Dunn's building.

"It is not as if you weren't told," Jeffrey Phipps snapped. "I made it quite clear that nothing would be unpacked until that check was in my hand."

Phipps's black van was parked at the curb. Two attractive but languorous young men slouched against its fenders, and a middle-aged Hispanic woman was in the front seat, her head nodding to the beat of Latin American music blaring from the radio.

Jeffrey stood, hands on hips, blocking his van's rear doors. Maybe he was afraid I might try to unpack the damned thing and prepare dinner myself.

From under the building's awning two doormen and Pookey's housekeeper, who was wearing a starchy black-and-white uniform, watched the proceedings without so much as a hint of alarm. The housekeeper, when asked about a check, had responded, "No. Mr. Dunn didn't leave one with me." "No," she had said again when asked whether Maddie Dunn was at home. "Mrs. Dunn went to see her personal trainer."

Given some leisure time to speculate, I might have come up with some fun reasons for this one-on-one fitness phenomenon, but faced with the caterer's insurrection I was in no mood to meander into X-rated territory.

A dozen ideas ran through my mind, all of them nutty. Run to the nearest grocery store, buy food, and prepare dinner myself. For fifteen people? Absurd. What about something casual? Pizza. Chinese carryout. For this crowd? Crazy.

My purple tote hanging on my arm was heavier than usual. In it were the gifts for the wedding party: four pairs of pearl earrings and four pairs of silver cuff links shaped like champagne buckets, all of them wrapped exquisitely in iridescent white paper and tied with lace ribbons. The pearl earrings and the champagne-bucket links were worth a bundle. Would Jeffrey be willing to hold them as ransom?

"I have some jewelry—"

He didn't let me finish. He must have thought I was about to offer him my Timex wristwatch and my gold-plated earrings.

"Jewelry? Don't be ridiculous! I want a check, or better yet, cash."

"All right," I quickly said. "A check."

Digging through my tote, I pulled out my checkbook and wrote out a fat check. When I handed it to Jeffrey, he scrutinized it as if examining a counterfeit hundred-dollar bill.

"You're paying?"

"Mr. Dunn will reimburse me as soon as he gets here," I said. And if he didn't, his father would if he knew what was good for him.

Jeffrey looked at the check again, and then abruptly handed it back to me. "I'll wait for Mr. Dunn's check. At least I know he's got the money somewhere. You just be sure to get it to me as soon as he arrives."

He turned to the young men leaning against the van. "Let's get this stuff inside. We're running terribly late."

I'll never be certain why Jeffrey changed his mind. I'd like to think that my trust in Pookey Dunn's reliability made him feel guilty, but that's probably not the case. He was probably afraid that my personal check would bounce.

It would have.

Maddie Dunn moved buoyantly—hair floating, full-skirted pale green dress flowing, limbs gliding as if unfettered by poundage—not surprising when you consider that she weighed in like a butterfly. When conversing and wishing to make a point, she had a habit, a vanity, of tossing her head so that her dark curls brushed over her jaw, and then flipping them back impatiently with her hand, as if annoyed by their impertinence. Her accent, as I mentioned earlier, was thick as buttermilk, her high-pitched voice lilting upwards at the end of every sentence.

It's just as well that she totally ignored me, because too much exposure to the accent, the hair-flipping, and those Lilliputian biceps could easily have brought out my anarchist streak.

She and Amanda had bent their heads over the place cards on the dining table. After setting down the little gift boxes in the correct places, they backed away from the table and looked it over.

The cloth was lace-trimmed Irish linen, ironed smooth as a sheet of glass. The silver service and crystal glassware picked up the light from the small chandelier over the table, which would be dimmed once the two pairs of silver candlesticks were lit. The centerpiece, salmon-colored roses floating in a crystal dish, added to the table's almost intimidating elegance.

Amanda and Maddie exchanged self-satisfied smiles.

"You are a wonder," Maddie said. "You must give me your card. I insist."

As if Amanda was about to put up a fight. Reaching into a pocket in her silk maternity smock, she withdrew one of those little cards she had agonized over only weeks before and handed it to Maddie. The other woman responded by clapping her hands delightedly and sending my friend a kiss through the air between them.

"Isn't she gorgeous?" Amanda said when Maddie had fluttered away.

Maddie's vertebrae, visible through the back of her dress, looked like the spine down the center of an open pea pod.

"She'd never make it through a famine."

"She'll never have to," my friend responded. "Don't you love this apartment? I mentioned to you that Maddie has a decorating business, didn't I?"

"You sure did, and—"

I'd been itching to get in a few digs about the balloon valances and the riot of wallpaper patterns, but before I could—

"Pssst!"

Jeffrey was at my side, his mouth to my ear.

"So where's my check?"

What a partnership this was! Amanda got air kisses; I got hisses in my ear. I put as much hostility as possible in my return whisper—"In a minute"—and headed into the living room.

Wine and laughter flowed. I think that getting through the rehearsal had produced a feeling of relief. *My God! We've done it!* the members of the wedding party seemed to be thinking, even though it wasn't done yet.

Courtney and Justin, the center of attention, held hands and acted like a couple in love, while their hostess, Maddie, sang praises of their honeymoon destination, Bermuda.

"Those dahlin' pink houses and those adorable li'l scooters?" Herbert and Kitty, though both socializing like mad, had stationed themselves at opposite sides of the group, while the best man had attached himself to Stacey. Stacey didn't appear to mind this, and if Herbert had a problem with it, he wasn't going to announce it there.

Pookey, who was playing bartender, appeared to be enjoying himself, his guests, and most of all the hors d'oeuvres. Jeffrey's young men had changed from their jeans into white shirts, black pants, and bow ties. No longer languorous, they carried their trays of appetizers—sesame chicken fingers, mushrooms stuffed with ham, and miniature quiches—with pantherlike grace. The women picked daintily, the men more heartily, and no tray got past Pookey intact. I'm hardly a member of the diet police but if this guy didn't watch it, one of these days his featherweight wife was going to have herself a real tubby hubby.

I was supposed to be unobtrusive. That was one of Amanda's orders, and in this group it wasn't difficult. With my black slacks and white shirt—again my outfit had been dictated by Amanda—I blended in with the waiters and kitchen help. Crossing the room, I sidled up to Pookey and no one, Pookey included, was the wiser.

"Excuse me," I said softly.

With one hand he was reaching for a quiche, and with the other signaling something to his wife. If he heard me, he ignored me. Within seconds, he had swung his large body the other way and joined a conversation taking place between Maryann and Justin's handsome, widowed father.

Feeling foolishly out of place, I watched Maddie nibble at a mushroom and touch her lips to her wineglass. She knew I wanted to speak to her husband. I could tell by the way she fixed me with an almost contemptuous gaze. And then, as she turned to say something to Kitty, she lifted her nose into the air. Not by much. Just a millimeter or so. But it was enough.

Storm the Bastille!

I grabbed Pookey's arm as he was about to shove the quiche into his mouth. His hand faltered enough so that he ended up with a nice yellow smear under his nose.

"Yes?" he asked, wiping away the spot with a cocktail napkin.

"I need the check for the caterer."

I could have been bumming a handout on the street from the way he looked at me.

"Remember? We talked about this. . . ."

"Oh, yes. That. My office is upstairs. Second door on the left. My checkbooks should be in the top drawer of my desk. If you'll bring me the one I use for business . . ."

He turned away from me.

Business expense? Right. Funny business. Fuming, I left the living room and climbed the stairs to the second floor. Not only hadn't Pookey written the check in advance, but now he was treating me like his personal servant. How rude, I thought, flinging open the door to Pookey's lair.

Like the rest of the house, the room had been decorated to within an inch of its life. The color scheme of the carpeting, wallpaper, and curtains was right off a rep tie— gray with diagonal maroon and black stripes—and the furniture was black leather with big chrome studs set into its seams. The knobs on the desk drawers were giant chrome studs, if you can picture such a thing.

Sliding into the humongous chair behind the desk, I opened the top drawer. Sure enough, there were Pookey's checkbooks, one covered in black leather, and the other in maroon. His initials—PKD—were embossed in gold on both of them.

He's not only rude and tacky, I thought, glancing through the maroon-covered ledger. He's stupid. I could steal a check, or get his account number. . . .

Wrong book. There was an eye-popping mortgage payment, and a check written out to the electric company. These had to be personal expenses, though with the way Pookey separated personal from business, maybe not. To be certain I thumbed back a few pages. The stubs showed checks made out to department stores and gourmet grocers, doctors and pharmacies. All personal.

I was about to close the ledger, when my eye was caught by an entry from a month earlier. All that was written in the description column was the word "Cash." If the check had been for $15,000 or $20,000, I might have wondered at the large amount of cash Pookey had carried out of the bank, but wouldn't have given the transaction further thought—but the check Pookey had cashed had been for exactly $17,500.

That's a whole lot of money, even for someone with wealthy parents to fall back on. And speaking of wealthy parents, this check had been written two days after Amanda and I met the Dunns.

I don't have that much on hand, Kitty had said over the telephone. *I can loan you a thousand or so. . . .*

Pookey had covered this $17,500 check with a deposit made one day before writing it. The deposit was identified as having come from a brokerage account, which meant that he had sold securities of some kind.

There are a lot of reasons why Pookey might have wanted exactly $17,500 in cash, in a hurry, and even if it turned out that he had been Neil Howard's benefactor, there could be a simple explanation. Neil could have done $17,500 worth of work here in Pookey's apartment, or at his beach house.

I put the checkbook back in the drawer, wondering as I did why, if Pookey had been involved in something illegal with Neil—if in fact he was "Buddy," as I suspected—he would allow me access to this bit of evidence. Pookey didn't strike me as any genius, but would he be *that* careless?

When I got back to the living room with the second checkbook, Pookey had joined the circle of people around Courtney and Justin. I tried an unobtrusive "Excuse me" first, and he reacted by brushing his hand past his ear as if a pesky gnat had buzzed him. Once again I resorted to the tug on the sleeve. Once again I got that cool "Yes?"

I thrust the checkbook and pen at him, and repeated the amount.

"Um." When he had written out the check, he handed the book and pen back to me. "Remember to record that."

"Yes, sir," I responded smartly, but he'd turned his back again. Walking from the living room, I reconsidered the question of carelessness.

When Pookey had seen me at the office, my role had been that of a thinking person. In a limited way, he'd respected that role. Here, though, in my black slacks and white shirt, I was part of the faceless, voiceless "help," brought in for the afternoon to serve. Sure Pookey recognized me, but in his overdecorated domain the help, and particularly the temporary help, only served. My role had changed, and thinking wasn't part of my job description.

19

THE LONG ISLAND EXPRESSWAY. TEN-thirty A.M. on the Big Day. The radio weatherman was telling us that the day was going to be "unseasonably cool, with a fifty percent chance of light rain."

"It's good luck if it rains on the bride, I think," Amanda said. "It may be bad luck, though. I'm starting to get my good luck things and my bad luck things confused."

"That's always been one of my problems," I said.

During the moments when Amanda wasn't obsessing about how the wedding would turn out, or issuing orders and double-checking instructions, or making me synchronize my watch with hers, my mind kept drifting back to that $17,500 check. Those moments were few, though.

Amanda's Filofax was in her lap and her new cellular phone in her hand. She was Field Marshal Montgomery getting ready to storm across Normandy. I was not only her foot soldier and her chauffeur, but also her worried friend.

She had been hiccupping, delicately but audibly, for several minutes. With every little "hic," my hands on the steering wheel grew more tense.

"Are you sure you're going to be all right?"

She rummaged in her handbag for a package of crackers. "It's only morning sickness. And anxiety."

We were approaching a series of banked curves. I knew them well and when traffic was light, as it was that morning, I sometimes roared through these curves like a teenager turned loose in Daddy's car. Guess there's some Bubba in me, too. Not that morning, though. The day promised plenty of excitement without the added thrill of worsening Amanda's stomach problems. I needed her as much as she needed me. Pressing the brake, I took the curves at a sedate forty-five miles an hour.

"You want to go through the drill again?" I asked.

Amanda laid the phone on the console between us and opened her Filofax. "Okay. At eleven o'clock I meet the girls at Bendel's beauty salon for makeup and hair. A designer from Flower Power will be there to do their hair ornaments. When they're finished, we go to the Dunns' apartment and the girls get dressed. The photographer should get there . . ."

Amanda's schedule included most of the hand-holding and the things that called for a delicate touch. While she was making certain that the girls all looked like angels, I would be grubbing around the Ambassador Hotel making certain that there was toilet paper in the restrooms and that the last of the plaster dust had been swept from the floor. While Amanda was making sure that the candid photos of the girls preparing for the wedding ceremony were never less than flattering, I'd make sure that Flower Power didn't try to festoon the Ambassador's ballroom with wilted vines.

". . . and you're responsible for making sure the caterer has everything he needs." Amanda glanced my way. "I'm glad you two get along well, because Jeffrey can be difficult."

I almost set Amanda straight on my relationship with Jeffrey but she hiccupped again, louder, so I kept my mouth shut. She was tearing open another package of crackers when the cellular phone rang.

"Would you answer that?" she asked.

Picking up the phone, I pressed the talk button and said in my best secretary voice, "Ms. LaMarca's office."

"I'm going to die!" the familiar voice howled into my ear. "It's a disaster!"

"What's wrong, Courtney?"

After several seconds of sobs so heart-wrenching I began to fear that Justin had done another about-face, she blubbered, "It's my gown. Where's Amanda? I've got to talk to her RIGHT NOW! This is the most horrible thing that has ever happened to me!"

Amanda was chewing crackers but had tilted her head, curious. I was reasonably certain that nothing very horrible had ever happened to Courtney, and that whatever horribleness was going on with her gown wouldn't amount to much, so I glanced at Amanda and shook my head as if dismissing the incident. Keeping my voice calm, I asked Courtney what the problem was.

"When I had my last fitting, my gown was perfect. Now it's gigantic and under the light the seed pearls glow purple! I picked it up last night but I didn't look at it until just now. It's horrible! Huge and purple! Zoe's has ruined my life."

"What is it?" Amanda said. She reached to take the phone, but abruptly changed her mind and clamped her hand over her mouth. "You better pull over," she mumbled from between her fingers. "I may be sick. What does Courtney want?"

I gritted my teeth. "Nothing important."

The Chrysler was moving much too quickly when it hit the road's shoulder, and for the next few seconds I was afraid that Amanda and I would be the subjects of a grisly photo in the next day's tabloids. When the car finally skidded to a rock-spraying stop, Amanda was out of it in a flash.

"Listen," I said quickly into the telephone. "Leave the gown with your doorman and meet Amanda at Bendel's like you planned. I'll deal with the dress problem."

"It's not just a problem! It's a tragedy. I'm going to tell Daddy to sue—"

My best friend and boss was leaning against a concrete wall retching. A huge oil truck, whose driver was probably living on amphetamines after thirty-six sleepless hours, roared by near enough that the Chrysler pitched in its wake. This was no time to discuss lawsuits.

"Just do what I'm telling you, Courtney," I shouted. "I'll make Zoe find your gown, and if she can't, I'll get you one that fits and doesn't glow purple!"

After hanging up on the sobbing bride-to-be, I scooted out the passenger-side door intending to help Amanda. Instead, she helped me. Hurrying toward her, I stepped on a large, wobbly stone. My ankle turned and I might have ended up on the ground if Amanda hadn't caught my elbow. I limped back to the car with Amanda behind me.

"My stomach's so much better," she said brightly. "I've got a good feeling about today. Don't you, Bonnie?"

The sidewalk outside Zoe's Bridal Salon, 11:30 A.M.

The gown in its plastic wrapper weighed a ton, my ankle was throbbing, the first drops of rain were dotting the shoulder of my dress, and Zoe's guard didn't want to open the door. In answer to my first buzz he'd pointed at the hours printed in discreet gold leaf on the door: Saturday: 12:00, Except By Special Appointment.

The shop's lights were on and through the window I could see people moving around inside. There was quite a crowd, which meant that one or more bridal parties were there. I leaned on the buzzer, so insistent that the guard relented and cracked the door an inch.

"Do you have an appointment?"

"No, but—"

He pointed, once again, at the gold lettering. In response, I pointed to the Chrysler, which was parked at a meter.

"This is an emergency and if you don't let me in, I'm going to drive my car through the window."

That was not the right approach. The guard huffed angrily, and if Zoe hadn't recognized me at that moment, there might have been quite a scene. Opening the door wider, Zoe looked at the bundle hanging over my arm.

"Is there a problem, Ms. Indermill? We have two groups here at the moment."

Her voice was very low. Mine was not. "You gave Courtney Dunn the wrong dress. It's huge and the seed pearls glow purple."

I was taking Courtney's word for this. The kid was no rocket scientist, but she surely knew huge and purple when she saw them.

Zoe's eyebrows rose to meet her hairline. "That's impossible."

I hefted the dress into her arms and before she could object, unzipped the garment bag far enough to reveal a cluster of seed pearls on the gown's bodice. Sure enough, even under the grayish daylight—purple! It was a pale iridescent purple, not nearly as bright as Courtney's hysteria had led me to expect, but purple is purple.

Zoe blinked. "Oh my. Oh my," she said, and then clasped her hand to her forehead. "That's the princess's dress."

Wearing an expression not too different from a theatrical mask of tragedy, Zoe ushered me into the shop and urged me, in whispers, to have a seat, a mint, anything I wanted, while she straightened out the problem.

The shop bustled with bridal entourages, and every second or so someone let out a delighted giggle or a dismayed groan. It was a giddy, exuberant scene, but between what had happened to Tiffany in the back of this shop, and the tension I was under right now, I couldn't enjoy it.

Plopping onto the now-familiar pink settee, I examined my foot. My sneaker squeezed like a corset, and over the rim of my low-cut sock where my ankle bones used to be, nothing appeared but swollen flesh. I flexed the joint. It didn't feel too bad and it still supported me, but this was going to be a long day and I had a lot to do.

Wouldn't it be ironic if Courtney's wedding, which had survived the taint of two murders and several mentions in *Inside Elsie*, was thrown into chaos by something as insignificant as my stepping on a wobbling stone?

A wobbling stone . . .

I may not be much of a mom type, but when it comes to nurturing ideas, I tend to be quite fertile. Sometimes, though, it takes a while before ideas that have rooted actually sprout anything that makes sense. Leaning back into the settee, I closed my eyes, and slowly cultivated my newest idea.

Robert Annessi had said, ". . . that girl . . . Tiffany McKinney . . . stands up, turns her back and bends over like she's tying her shoe. Only that's not what she's doing. What she's doing is showing me her ass. Her skirt was hiked up so that I could see her underwear. That girl was some piece of work."

Yes. Tiffany McKinney had been some piece of work. But this behavior would have been gross even for her. She was an office worker, after all, and not a porn film actress. Why would she do something so lewd?

Because her cassette had run out, and she needed a flat surface so that she could open her recording machine and turn the tape to the other side. The step provided that surface.

Zoe reappeared, leaned over me, and whispered, "Thank God the princess hasn't been in yet to pick up her gown."

"Which means that Courtney's gown is here?"

"Of course," she muttered, glancing around nervously. "One of my consultants is looking upstairs in the fitting area."

"Her gown's lost?" My voice had risen to a level just short of a shriek, causing several heads to turn our way. I started to get up, too agitated to stay still.

Zoe was making quick downward gestures as though to press me back onto the settee. "It's merely misplaced," she said, conscious of the audience that we were attracting. "We should have it for you momentarily."

Dodging her hands, I got to my feet.

"I lost an expensive earring in the alley the first time I was here. Is the back door open?"

She shook her head. "No, but the alarm's off. All you have to do is push the bar. . . ."

"When I return, Courtney's gown *must* be here. If it isn't, you had better find a substitute that is spotless and will fit her perfectly. And it better be a damned nice one," I added in clipped tones as I limped toward the back of the shop.

Drops of rain slithered past the collar of my dress and down my back when I angled my head and peered into the narrow space between the step and the wall. Nothing was visible except some loose chunks of concrete. Crouching, I worked my fingers into the space and tugged on the concrete step. It rocked slightly, and there was a faint sound as small objects that had been trapped behind it clinked to the ground.

Since it was Saturday and Courtney Dunn's wedding day, it seemed unlikely anyone would be in Dunn's offices. Still, conscious that I could be seen from there, I glanced across the street. A single light burned on the third floor. It appeared to be coming from the open area where the cubicles were located, but I didn't see movement or anything else to indicate that someone was up there.

Leaning back, I put all my weight into moving the step. It may have been unseasonably cool but the effort caused beads of sweat to break out across my chest. It also caused a seam at the back of one of my shoulders to rip. The step slid a couple of inches before my hands gave way and I collapsed hard on my elbow. Ignoring the pain, I peered into the widened space.

If I hadn't been acutely aware of my surroundings, not to mention in pain, I would have shouted with the thrill of discovery.

On the ground behind the step, in a crevice too small for my hand to fit into, lay a cassette from a hand-held tape recorder.

I had to get my hand into the crevice, but the way my elbow felt, I wouldn't be able to muster the upper-body strength to move the step far enough. Lowering myself to the ground at the step's side, I used my feet—bad ankle and all—to shove the concrete block. Seconds later I was in a full-blown sweat, but the little cassette, seemingly undamaged, was safe in my hand.

A manufacturer's label, its print so small that I could

hardly read it, indicated that this tape held sixty minutes of dictation, thirty minutes on each side. The tape was completely wound out on side A. If Tiffany had been dictating on this side, she had reached its end before removing the tape from the machine.

Sitting there on the ground, with my skirt hiked up and my legs splayed out in front of me, I tried to reconstruct what might have happened in the alley in the moments before Tiffany was killed.

Robert Annessi hadn't seen anyone approach Tiffany, which meant that she had finished dictating on side A of the tape, and had removed the tape from the Dictaphone before her killer walked into the alley. As she'd tried to reinsert the tape, however, it had slipped behind the step. Furious, mouthing curses, she'd turned and thrown the recorder into the weeds.

When Tiffany's murderer had approached her, he—Neil Howard? Pookey Dunn?—hadn't been aware she'd been using the recorder at all. There was a chance, though, that she'd seen the killer before finishing side A of the tape. Maybe he'd been across the street in front of Dunn Construction's offices, or maybe he'd been parking his car. And just possibly Tiffany had mentioned him. "There's Pookey," I could imagine her saying, drawing out the *ooo*.

Standing, I dusted off my backside with my hand—who would have thought that navy rayon would show so much dirt?—and wiped the sweat off my forehead with my sleeve. As I lowered my arm, I saw that my elbow, scraped raw, was sticking through a tear in my sleeve. The very image of an elegant wedding consultant, I headed back into the store to see about the other missing item.

Courtney's gown, seed pearls glowing ivory under the lights, was on a rack near the shop's front door. Zoe was all smiles as she zipped the garment bag around it, and her smile stayed in place even as she took in my torn sleeve and the nasty scrape on my elbow. Hurrying from the store, I turned to say goodbye. Zoe's eyes appeared to be glued to the seat of my dress. Resisting the impulse to check out what was going on back there, I raised my arm to flag a cab. This was one of those times when a reality check can only slow you down.

It was after two o'clock when I got to the Dunns' apartment and dropped the gown into Amanda's relieved arms. After receiving appreciative hugs from Courtney and her mother, and numerous air kisses from Maddie, I got a new set of orders from Amanda.

"I'm not going to be able to check on the church," she said in a rush of words as she steered me toward the elevator. "You're going to have to make sure that everything is set up the way we want it. As soon as you've done that, go to the hotel. I'll call the caterer from here to tell him you'll be a little late. And Bonnie . . ."

"Yes?"

"You look a mess. What happened?"

"There was a problem at Zoe's."

The elevator door opened and I stepped inside. Turning toward Amanda, I saw that she was gaping at me. She must have thought I'd gotten into some rough stuff at Manhattan's most chichi bridal salon.

"Did you bring another outfit?"

"Just shoes," I said, and the thought of the pointy-toed high heels waiting for me in the Chrysler made me feel like writhing in pain.

Taking my wrist with one hand, Amanda pressed an envelope into my palm with the other.

"Kitty asked me to give you this. It's her thank-you for finding Courtney's gown. She said it would be nice if you looked more . . . appropriate. Once you've checked the church and opened the hotel, why don't you run into Ann Taylor—Maddie said there's one right around the corner from the hotel—and pick up something. In a neutral color," she added unnecessarily.

When the elevator door had separated us, I looked into the envelope. It contained three one hundred-dollar bills.

While the elevator made its way down, a string of objections ran through my head—The nerve! Treating me like a charity case. As if I didn't know enough to pull myself together.—but by the time it had reached the ground floor

I was thinking along different lines. With this much money and three-quarters of an hour's time, I could get myself something appropriate indeed.

I tried calling Tony from the lobby of the Dunns' co-op building. He was out, and so I left a message: "Important we speak. Amanda can reach me."

20

The Ambassador Hotel, 5:30 p.m.

"Am I too early?"

Violet looked even more eccentric than usual. Her flower print dress, with its Peter Pan collar and puffy sleeves, looked like something an eight-year-old would wear to a birthday party. The waist tied in back with a sash, and the hem fell to an unflattering length, too long for a fashion statement and not long enough for elegance, beneath her knees. It was just the right length, however, to emphasize her muscular calves.

"No, Violet. You're the first, but the other guests should be here soon." I nodded toward a table near the ballroom door. "There's a seating chart."

She was carrying a beige raincoat over her arm. I suggested she check it, and then find her table and go into the ballroom, a suggestion that caused her to hunch her shoulders and look incredibly put upon.

"I don't want to be the first."

"Well, there's a bar inside. . . ."

She shook her head. "I don't drink. I'll wait out here for a while."

The Ambassador's lobby furniture—groups of uphol-stered chairs around marble-topped tables—was now in place. Violet gave her raincoat to one of the coat-check's two attendants and then found herself a chair largely hidden by a flower arrangement. Once she sat down, she shrank from my view, and disappeared from my mind as well.

Walking in my stocking feet to the lobby entrance, I checked over the entire scene once again. The change at the Ambassador was astounding. It had taken God-knows-how-much construction overtime, the services of an indus-trial cleaning crew, and a hothouse full of flowers, but the hotel's ground floor looked terrific.

Outside, the ugly scaffolding had been replaced by a wide maroon awning. The gray sky had given way to a late-afternoon burst of sunshine, and in the awning's shadow two tall trim men with enough gold braid on their uniforms to pass as Prussian army officers stood at near-attention, ready to direct guests to the ballroom and dis-courage would-be gate crashers.

Inside, garlands of blue hyacinths and pink pansies, in-terwoven with white sprigs of baby's breath and fern leaves, were draped between the chandeliers. Every con-ceivable raised surface held bouquets in gleaming crystal vases. Over the steps leading to the ballroom, a trellis had been erected, and garlands had been woven through its white wood slats.

I looked terrific, too, at least by East Side chic standards. My new dress and jacket were so near the color of pave-ment that jaywalking would have been asking for big trou-ble.

"You look very nice," Amanda said as she rushed into the lobby. "The bridal party won't be here for . . ."

It seemed that when the sun had peeked through the gray sky, the bridal party had decided to stop for some im-promptu photos in Central Park. It would be about twenty minutes before they got to the hotel.

The microcassette was in the pocket of my new jacket.

I patted it, making certain, for about the fiftieth time, that it was safe.

"Have you spoken to Tony?"

"No time," Amanda said. "Anyway, I forgot my phone. It's at the Dunns' apartment." She glanced at my feet. "Put on your shoes. The guests will start arriving any second."

I wriggled my toes in the newly installed carpet. My ankle felt and looked better but my dress shoes would be the test. Retrieving them from the Ann Taylor shopping bag that I'd stashed on the floor in the coat-check room, I proceeded to make myself respectable. Then, with an almost inaudible groan—that shoe did pinch—I followed Amanda into the ballroom.

If the lobby looked terrific, the ballroom was spectacular. The flower garlands and bouquets helped what I'd thought of as a gloomy space, but so had a good cleaning and the late afternoon sun. It shone through immaculate windows onto newly finished floors and woodwork, and sparkled off pristine white china that had been laid on the many tables circling the room. The old mantel over the fireplace hadn't been replaced, but it had been polished until the crack almost disappeared in the marble's gleam.

On a platform at the far end of the room, a six-piece band and two vocalists, all dressed so elegantly that they might have been members of the wedding party, tuned their instruments and voices. The buoyant sound of a trumpet running up and down the scales caused me to turn to Amanda and smile. She was smiling too.

As we stood there beside the double doors admiring what we'd accomplished, wedding guests began streaming into the hotel, bringing with them the hum of voices that lets you know the party is starting.

I patted the tape in my pocket again, but my thought— I wish this was in Tony's hands—was fleeting, obliterated by Amanda's whisper: "Show time!"

The Ambassador ballroom, 9:15 P.M. The vocalists wailed "The Twist" in harmony with the tenor sax. The hum of voices had become a roar.

The salmon and the Cornish game hens were history, and

the obligatory ceremonial marriage dances were done with. The music was hot and getting hotter, and the ballroom rocked with society types. Bridesmaids swiveled and dipped, sometimes awkward in their ankle-length gowns, and ushers, their ties and collar buttons loosened, lurched wildly. Even the usually dour Maryann was out there twisting like crazy with the best man. She reeled with the music, her hair hanging in damp tendrils and her eyes shut as if she were in a trance.

If there were stars on the dance floor, Pookey and Maddie Dunn were among them. Maybe they'd taken lessons. They sure surprised me, but then people often do. Kitty Dunn was a good dancer, too. Looking not at all motherly, she was taking a rollicking turn with Justin's handsome father. Herbert Dunn wasn't in her class by a long shot. His arms pumped madly as he tried to keep pace with a tall red-faced woman who was wheeling all over the place.

Courtney and Justin were sitting this one out at the head table. They'd been the center of attention for many hours now—smiled upon and cried over, photographed and toasted—and at this point were probably looking forward to the evening's end.

I certainly was. Forbidden by Amanda to even think of sitting down, I just wanted to go home and collapse. There was still the wedding cake to cut, though, and even when that was finished and the band had played the obligatory encores of "Shout," Amanda and I wouldn't be done.

"Not until the last guest . . ." she began when I started making noises about leaving.

"Got it!" I snapped. "But I'm going to take a break."

My irritability was compounded by the fact that there was only one working phone in the hotel and it was continually being used by guests. Earlier that evening I'd gone to a pay phone on the street to call Tony, but he'd still been unavailable. I left the ballroom intending to try again.

The woman working at the coat-check was leaning on the counter looking thoroughly bored. As I passed her, I noticed Maryann Dunn's battered, stuffed briefcase perched at the front of one of the wire shelves over the racks of raincoats. Had Maryann managed to get in some reading while waiting at the back of the church, or maybe dictate a memo or two during the impromptu photo session? I could picture her hiding out in a limo, mumbling into the black Dictaphone that was always ready for action in her briefcase.

Hum. I paused midstep. That little machine in Maryann's briefcase might not be exactly like the one Tiffany had used, but it was the same size, and the same size cassette would fit into it.

Right now Maryann was on the dance floor, possibly a wee bit interested in something other than her billable hours. She couldn't possibly plan to do any dictation in the next half hour or so.

I approached the coat-check, hand in my pocket as if searching for something, and said to the attendant, "I seem to have lost my claim check. Could I trouble you for . . . ?"

Profoundly bored, she stifled a yawn. "No problem. Which is yours?"

I pointed to the battered briefcase, which the woman obligingly hoisted onto the counter. As an afterthought, I glanced behind the counter to the place where my Ann Taylor bag had been earlier. That, I was surprised to see, was no longer there.

"I have a shopping bag, too. It was on the floor there in the corner."

After seeing for herself that there was no shopping bag in the corner, the woman wedged herself between two racks of coats. In a moment she was back, empty-handed and shaking her head. "Maybe the other girl gave it to someone. She's on break right now."

"Great security," I said.

"We were told this was an elegant event. We're not supposed to give anybody a hard time."

"La Bamba!" the vocalists' voices rang out. "Da dumdum da da da dum-dum . . ." the horns bawled. When a handful of women, perhaps hesitant about trying their luck with the Latin beat, streamed into the lobby and made their way toward the restroom, I shielded the briefcase with my body. Where could I possibly listen to the tape?

To use the recorder I had to be alone, which eliminated the hotel's entire first floor. I also had to be able to see, and the only other floor with lights that I knew I could deal with without electrocuting myself was the eighth. Members of the bridal party had been up there earlier, but surely none of them would leave the ballroom before the cake was cut.

Once the moment of activity in the lobby was over, I grabbed the briefcase and headed into the elevator. It had been shined up, but that didn't mean it had been renovated. When I pushed the button for the eighth floor and the doors slammed together, shutting me inside, I sure didn't like the feeling I got.

It was a moment before the elevator started moving, and to assure myself that if it didn't move at all I'd be able to attract some attention, I glanced through the small, eye-level window in the door. Yes, there was life in the lobby. The coat-check woman, a guard—

I suddenly became aware of someone, of the shadowy contours of a face behind the arbor leading into the ballroom. By the time I turned my head to focus, though, the elevator car was rising and all I saw were the flowers woven into the white lattice. Fearing what I might see but more afraid of what I might not know, I leaned nearer the window and tried to look down. It was too late. The elevator had entered the closed shaft. Nothing was visible but the floors that ticked slowly past, almost as dark as the shaft itself.

The rooms set aside for the bridal attendants were at the west end of the eighth floor. The double doors leading to that wing were open, and lights shone down the hallway.

Exiting the elevator, I turned left and pushed through a door leading to the east wing. That hall was dim, lit only by red exit signs in the middle and at the end, but I didn't need much light to get where I wanted to go. Familiarity may breed contempt, but it can also breed comfort. In the infamous room 813 I knew where to find the dressing table and I knew how to light the lamp on it. I also knew that Howard Dunn wouldn't be visiting the connecting love nest for a while. There are limits, even for tycoons.

The floor appeared deserted but I walked quietly, and opened the door to room 813 without making a sound. Once inside, I shut and locked the door behind me.

One of the windows had been left open and a cool breeze moved the curtains. I made my way to the table and touched the lamp's brass base, causing a circle of light to fall across the rich wood surface. Sitting down then, I opened the briefcase. Maryann's recorder was right where it always was, on top of a mass of papers, anchored by a leather strap.

I pried the device free and inserted the cassette with little trouble. Figuring out which buttons rewound and fast-forwarded the tape was more difficult, but after a few false starts I managed that, too.

This was not the time to listen to all thirty minutes of side A, start to finish. If Tiffany had recognized the person who would within minutes murder her, and had said his name, it would be on the last few seconds of the tape.

I wound the tape until only a few more turns of the uptake spindle would conclude it, and then pressed the Play button. The words that followed were so faint I could hardly tell that a woman was speaking them. The volume control had little effect, and even when I turned it to the highest level, all that was audible was the faintest hint of Tiffany's voice:

". . . up there in the window . . ."

I turned the recorder in my hand, searching for another volume control, and spotted the problem. A microscopic graphic near a tiny lever indicated that the recorder was set for earphones.

I pushed the lever to the alternate setting. Tiffany's voice blasted from the recorder.

". . . she looks like a loon, waving like that. Good. She's disappeared."

My heart thudded as if it were breaking free of my chest. Huddling the machine in my lap to muffle the sound, I groped for the volume control.

I was so intent on finding it that the door to the hall was wide open before I realized it was moving.

"Shit," the voice on the tape blared. "She's coming

outside. Looks like she's going to wait for the light and cross—'' The machine clicked, and Tiffany's voice stopped abruptly.

The room was deathly quiet. Violet hesitated for a moment in the rectangle of dim light from the hallway, and then moved into the room, closing the door behind her. Taking a few steps toward where I sat, she extended her hand, almost as if she were going to offer me something. Instead, she waved a key in front of my eyes before dropping it onto the dressing table.

"I have a master key too."

She spoke in such a flat, unagitated tone that despite what I'd just heard I experienced a stab of hope. Had she overheard enough of the tape to understand what Tiffany had been saying? Even if she had, did she realize that I understood the significance of Tiffany's last words?

"Weren't you enjoying the reception?" I asked lightly.

Violet shook her head. "I don't care for parties. Too many people. I saw you, you know."

"Pardon me?"

"From the office window. I often work on weekends, when nobody's there to bother me. I saw you in the alley, pushing that step."

Too nervous to react quickly, I wasn't prepared when Violet's hand swooped down over mine and grabbed the recorder. She struggled with the little device, and the tape flipped out onto the bed.

"I was never sure whether there was a tape or not," she said, staring at it. "I knew Tiffany had been dictating when I waved to her from my cubicle, but I didn't see a tape recorder when I got down there. When the police talked to people in the office, they didn't mention a tape. Neither did the newspapers, so I thought there was nothing to worry about. But then, when I saw you today, I thought you might have found one. I looked in your shopping bag but it wasn't there."

Violet's face betrayed no emotion. Trying to follow her lead, I responded simply, "Oh."

"I thought Tiffany was at least half decent, but you should have heard her that afternoon in the alley. All I wanted to do was thank her for some books she'd left on my desk. She was in a nasty mood, though. She started teasing me, telling me that Neil Howard had asked her for a date. I didn't believe her, but when I told her that, she said she'd bring me a picture of the two of them together. Then she said that I was turning red, and she laughed at me. Even when she started to go back inside the building, she kept laughing at me."

"And so you followed her and grabbed her hair. . . ."

"Tiffany made me do it. It was her own fault."

With Violet standing between me and the door there was no getting out of the room. She seemed calm, however, almost to the point of catatonia. If I could just keep her talking, maybe I'd get a chance to run for it.

"And what about Neil's death?" I asked. "Did you have anything to do with that?"

A trembling in my voice showed my fear, but Violet didn't notice. Obviously, though, Neil was hard for her to talk about. She clutched her hands and started pacing back and forth between the bed and the closet door.

"That was an accident," she said. "Anyway, it's partly your fault."

"My fault?"

Violet's eyes fluttered past mine and seemed to focus on something in the distance. "You're the one who put those ideas in my head."

Bad ankle or not, I had to get away from this lunatic. And if I could, I wanted to get away with that tape in my hand. She was near the closet when I made my move. Bracing myself, I lunged and snatched the tape from the bed.

I'd taken Violet by surprise, but the surprise didn't last long enough for me to get out of the room. As I tried to clamber over the corner of the bed she grabbed my wrist and pulled so violently that I ended up on my feet facing her as if we were about to dance.

"I thought you were half decent, too, but you're making me . . ."

She tried to reach the tape in my other hand, and in the struggle my bad ankle cracked into the dressing table's leg. Unable to support myself, I toppled forward, breaking Violet's grip on my hand. The windowsill stopped me, but not by much. My waist rested across it while my free hand clutched desperately for a handhold. The view was terrifying. For a hundred or more feet there was nothing, and then there was hard pavement. Even if the new awning was strong enough to break my fall, it was to the left of the window. I couldn't hope to land on it.

Violet's weight was against my back, crushing my breath from me. She may have wanted me to go out that window, but she wanted that tape first. She got a grip on the sleeve of my jacket and began pulling my hand nearer.

I can't say that during this struggle my life passed before my eyes, but the horrors of being the subject of an *Inside Elsie* column did. *The Curse of the Ambassador strikes again, with the death . . .*

The thought of that—the ultimate indignity—got me moving again. Taking aim as much as was possible, I flicked my wrist to the left and let the tape drop. Violet's weight lifted as she followed its trajectory. I took advantage of that to slip from beneath her and crawl backwards past the dressing table and the foot of the bed. Violet remained at the window, staring down. I don't think she was aware of anything except the tape, until I flung open the door to the hall.

I heard a grunt of surprise—"Uh"—but didn't look back.

At my best I wasn't the runner Violet was, but fear is an amazing motivator. I pushed through the double doors at the end of the hall a good fifteen feet ahead of her, and running like an Olympic contender. The elevator was still on the eighth floor, and opened the instant I pounded on the call button. I leaped inside and could have kissed the doors when they slammed shut in Violet's face so violently that the entire car shook.

As the creaky old contraption drew close to the ground floor, the band was playing "Shout."

"I don't understand this," Sam had said. "You're letting the feelings of this kid—she's twenty years younger than you are—influence you. Don't you think that Courtney's going to come down to earth eventually? People do, you know. That's what happens when they grow up."

He was right of course, but there has to be a spark, something sizzling, perhaps out of sight, but not out of mind.

We're still seeing each other. *Dating*. It feels strange to me, but Sam still hopes that things will work out. And maybe they will. Five months ago wasn't the time for me to say that security and contentment are enough. Five months from now, who knows?

But this is not the time for me to meander over the many paths my life might take. This is Amanda's time, and I want her to enjoy it. She has put the crib quilt aside and is loosening the ribbon from one of the last unopened presents. The wrapping paper is glitzy enough to make me curious about what's inside, but I can't sit here watching. The cake is waiting, the coffee should be ready, and, as I told you, my knees are starting to cramp.

The women probably will be leaving before long. That's just as well. I want to get an early start tomorrow. I've got to call those temp agencies. Earlier this week a couple of them mentioned jobs that sound promising. By tomorrow night I want to have some idea about what's in store for me next.

EPILOGUE

I GAVE MY ENGAGEMENT RING BACK TO Sam not too long after Courtney Dunn's wedding.

The end—though neither of us has called it that yet—came not with an explosion of tempers, not with shouted accusations and slammed doors, but with a couple of sighs and a few tears.

It started with a postcard Amanda received from Courtney. "Bermuda blissful! Water amazing! Fantastic! Wonderfully wildly happy!"

Those superlatives really got to me. With Sam, there wasn't going to be anything blissful or amazing or fantastic, anything wonderfully wild. There was going to be security, and a level of contentment, and that was all. Realizing that, facing it squarely, I was saddened. I realized I couldn't go through with the wedding, at least not then, at that time. I want security and contentment, yes, but I want the emotional highs too, and I'm not yet willing to forget how good they feel.

That's not the case with Pookey Dunn. Pookey admitted that he was the source of Neil's $17,500 cash, but insisted that the money was due Neil for work he did on Pookey's beach house.

Maybe that's true. Maybe when Neil mentioned his "Buddy," he was talking about himself, the way I sometimes say to myself, "Get a grip, Bonnie." And maybe Neil somehow managed to change Tiffany's database himself. And maybe pigs can fly.

Until evidence proves otherwise, I'll continue to believe that Pookey was Neil's Buddy, and that their friendship probably involved variations on the following scheme: Pookey, as purchasing director, would enter a purchase on the company's books—let's say for $35,000, though I suspect that the amounts were generally smaller. Pookey would then cash a company check for that amount, and put the money into a dummy company which he had set up. Neil, working in a supervisory capacity on various projects, was responsible for covering up the fact that the supply or piece of equipment or whatever, was never installed, and as reward for his hard work, received a portion of the stolen money.

If this is true, though, Pookey covered his tracks well. Five months have passed since the incidents at the center of this story took place, and the only possible dummy company that has turned up is Maddie Dunn's decorating concern, M&P Interiors. Apparently M&P is very well funded, but from what I've heard, the investigation initially instigated by Herbert Dunn came to a standstill when Herbert realized just how deeply his son might be involved. I was gratified to hear, however, that Pookey is no longer the company's purchasing director. His title is now Director of Business Development, which probably puts him some distance from the company's cash box.

I learned these things from Amanda, who has remained friendly with Kitty Dunn and Courtney. For obvious reasons the Dunns aren't terribly fond of me. As you've probably guessed, I didn't take the job with Dunn Construction.

head, which caused her ultimately to confront Neil at his building site. The first was that maybe Neil really had been attracted to Tiffany, and the second, that you never get anywhere if you don't speak up.

"I called him at his place a few times and asked if I could visit, but he always said he was too busy," her statement to the police reads. " 'Maybe some other time,' he said."

A record of phone calls made from the house Violet shared with her mother confirmed that a number of calls had been made to Neil's trailer. Violet admitted that when Neil's machine answered, she hung up without leaving messages. "When he stopped answering his phone at all, I had to go see him," her statement continues. "I'd already found where Neil was building by studying a county map."

When she got to Neil's building site, he evidently refused to satisfy her curiosity about Tiffany, or anything else Violet might have been there for. Neil told her that he didn't have time to talk. Apparently that's when she took my advice about speaking up. She told Neil she'd always liked him. Neil's response was, "Sorry, but no way."

Refusing to give up easily, Violet followed him into his shed and offered to help him finish unloading a slab of marble from his truck. Rather than being appreciative, though, he became rude, and finally, vulgar. As the mantel had swayed on the winch, he'd said, "Get out of here, Violet. Go away. You're fuckin' disturbing me."

Hurt and angered, she'd pushed the mantel into Neil's head, knocking him to the ground. Then, upset by what she felt Neil had made her do, she ran from the garage, slamming the door behind her. In her statement, she claims she didn't realize that the truck engine was running. I don't believe her. Violet seems to have a thing about finishing what she starts.

The case hasn't yet come to trial, but it is expected that Violet's lawyer will claim temporary insanity. However, since she was sane enough to wipe her fingerprints off everything she'd touched at both murder sites, that defense may not hold. Whether or not it does, though, Violet will be out of circulation for a very long time.

21

THE POLICE ARRIVED AT THE AMBASSA-
dor not long after the last encore of
"Shout." Courtney and Justin and several other members of the bridal party got
to share the elevator with some of New
York's finest.

Violet was found sitting on the bed in
the infamous room 813, and went with
the police so submissively that she might
have been drugged. The tape I'd dropped
out the window was recovered from the
top of the hotel's new awning.

Tony told me that Violet displayed no guilt when dis-
cussing how she'd bashed Tiffany McKinney's head into
the wall of Zoe's salon, and then smothered what remained
of her life with the plastic garment bag. It was Tiffany's
own fault, she insisted. Tiffany shouldn't have laughed at
her.

Neil Howard's death appeared to bother Violet more, but
not so much that she was tortured by guilt. It was partly
my fault, she explained to the police. I put two ideas in her